*Second Cut*

LAURENT BOULANGER is the author of the critically acclaimed novel *The Girl From France*, winner of the 2014 Paris Book Festival Awards, and *Better Dead Than Never*, 2014 eLit Bronze Winner for Best Multicultural Fiction and CWAA Ned Kelly Award Finalist for Best New Fiction. *First Kill* won a Tom Howard Mystery contest Honorable Mention for Best Crime Fiction.

SECOND CUT

# SECOND CUT

## Laurent Boulanger

**SNIPER BOOKS**

Sniper Books
Sniper Books is an imprint of Lake Ozark Press



Typeset in Garamond

Cover design © 2018 Lake Ozark Press

FOR
Michael Verde

# CHAPTER ONE

The frail body of a young girl lay in a pool of mud alongside Albert Park Lake, next to one of the few remaining elm trees.

Over a thousand elms and pre-settlement native gums had been removed to make room for the Grand Prix track three summers ago, not without causing a wave of protests from greenies, conservation groups and concerned local residents. The removal of those trees had caused the loss of wildlife habitat and the disappearance of bird life in the area. In addition more than one-hundred-and-fifty homes had been damaged during construction work, which required dynamic compaction of the unstable landfall foundations.

Late December is always hot in Melbourne, and even at 6.24 a.m., it's hard to stay in bed because of the bright daylight and the twenty-seven-degree temperature. But on Wednesday the 17th, I didn't get the chance to enjoy a long cool shower to get the day under way. The call had come through half an hour earlier, giving me just enough time to slip on a business skirt and a white blouse, and slick my auburn hair back with extra-hold mousse. I grabbed a can of Dr Pepper from the fridge on my way out of my second-floor apartment on Chapel Street.

The crime scene looked as if it had already been contaminated by on-lookers. As I'd anticipated, Channel Seven and Channel Ten news crews had set up camp not less than twenty meters from the little girl in a blue floral dress and

1

white school socks, just off Lakeside Drive. The cream-coloured Carlton Cress building was visible opposite the lake when I glanced around. Back to the scene, I noticed one ambulance, blue and red lights beaming, and two marked police cars sealing off part of the area. Not enough to keep curious minds away. Three unmarked cars were parked near the scene, one a grey Lexus which I recognised but couldn't immediately place.

A sickness rose from my stomach. I knew I wouldn't be able to finish the can of Dr Pepper I held in my hand. There's nothing quite like the murder of a child to stuff up your morning.

'Here we go,' I said to my partner, Senior Sergeant Frank Moore, 'the same circus all over again.'

Frank Moore was head of the Crime Scene Division at the Centre. He joined the Forensic Branch in 1975, straight out of the Royal Melbourne Institute of Technology (RMIT) with a Bachelor in Criminal Justice Administration. He was one head taller than me and maintained a neatly brushed dark moustache on a gaunt face. His thin, brown hair was receding, revealing a large bald spot at the top of his cranium. His green eyes sat too far apart from one another, and he wore a white shirt too small and too old for my taste. His mannerism was that of someone nervous, the type of person who couldn't stay still for one minute without clicking the back of a pen or flicking another cigarette. When we first began working together, he got on my nerves, but his genuine concern for my well-being during my two-week induction program at the Victorian Forensic Science Centre (VFSC) forced me to see him in a different light. Frank wasn't a bad person, just lonely and misunderstood like most people I knew in this line of work.

Only recently, I'd found out Frank had had a crush on me for years. When he announced his infatuation in the comfort of my own living room, I was unsure how to react. Finally when I told him there'd be no chance of a relationship between the two of us in this lifetime, it left a bitter taste in his mouth. But after I nearly got killed during a recent homicide, we became good friends again. The passing of time and the regularity of personal and professional crises between colleagues were always good yardsticks to measure the depth

2

of a friendship.

I was the first civilian to conduct both the duties of crime-scene examiner and investigator. And as recently as six months ago I was also licensed to carry a .380 semi-automatic, one of those guns designed to eject one cartridge and chamber a new one without manual intervention of the shooter after each shot is fired. Frank bought me the Mustang Plus .380 stainless frame, featuring a blue slide and adjustable sight, as a present after I nearly got myself killed in a murder investigation the previous Easter. I wasn't really into guns, but since Frank gave me the piece, I found myself sleeping with it and carrying it everywhere I went. After being involved in homicides for over five years, I knew there were some really sick people out there, and the older I became, the more I lost faith in my fellow man.

We parked near a group of police, ambulance and various forensic experts, I felt a pain at the back of my skull. The scenery reminded me of a child we found in a water drain a few years back. Everybody looked, but no one knew what to do. Was the girl still alive? Was she dead? Whose child was she? And who would have the burden of announcing to the parents that their dearly-loved daughter would no longer be coming home? It took months before I managed a full-night's sleep. I'd not been myself since then. In spite of all my training, I couldn't understand how a human being could do such a thing to another, especially a child. I remembered when I was a young girl, when I didn't know there was such a thing as really bad people out there, when I placed my trust in whomever was willing to listen or be interested in me, the child found in the drain could have been me. It could have been anyone's child. I realised how most people lived in a delusional world where they thought having a home in the suburbs meant security. But the reality was that no one was safe, not even in the confines of a family home.

For a while, I truly believed I was going to give up this job forever. But my sense of justice always got the better of me, and I reasoned that if I refused to solve child murders with passion and integrity, maybe no one else would bother putting in the effort.

But that was years ago.

We stepped out of the white Ford Falcon with government plates, and clipped our IDs to our breast pockets. Frank's was blue, indicating he was a member of the Victoria Police. Mine was light green, with a computer strip allowing access to various restricted places, such as the Police complex on St Kilda Road and the Victorian Institute of Forensic Medicine (VIFM) in South Melbourne, which incorporated the city mortuary.

As I paced alongside Frank, him carrying a Physical Evidence Recovery Kit (PERK) - the necessary scissors, scalpels, brushes, tweezers and packages needed to recover evidence at a crime scene - I knew this time things would be different. I gripped my briefcase filled with photographic and video-recording equipment.

'I don't want to do this investigation,' I whispered, almost to myself.

Frank didn't turn around. 'We'll talk about later, Kristina.'

It was really Kristina Oliveira Dos Melina, but I'd dropped the middle names of my Brazilian ancestors when I moved from my parent's home. And the DR stood for a PhD in Criminal Justice which I earned while I was still wet behind the ears. Although I didn't like using the DR in front of my name, it served its purpose. It gave me the confidence I needed when others thought I was nothing more than a good-looking chick with a gun.

'There's not going to be a later,' I went on. 'We've already talked about this a thousand times before. I refuse to get involved in child-murder investigations, that was the deal.'

'Tell Goosh, not me.'

'Oh, yeah, good one. You know what the sonofabitch thinks of me '

Frank's mouth shifted to a cocky, conceited smile. I hated the way he could be my best friend one minute and a distant colleague the next.

Goosh, the Deputy Commissioner of Police, had initially opposed the idea of having a civilian conducting a sworn officer's duty, but after being pressured from all sides, he gave in. A short, fat man with an arrogance to match his puffy face, Goosh had temporarily succeeded in suspending my contract for a few weeks the previous year. But he knew now that I wasn't the type of person to give in easily, and only extreme cunningness and deception would get me out of my job, which I believed he was capable of. He even went as far as writing a personal letter to the Victorian Director of Public Prosecution, detailing that my capacity as a civilian crime-scene investigator would water-down the State's ability to make out a satisfactory case. Without a shred of evidence, he tried to demonstrate the prosecutor's usage of unsworn members to investigate serious homicides as a move the defence would relish. I knew his argument was weak since the force was already using civilians for fingerprinting work. Little by little, sworn officers were being pulled off fingerprinting, and public servants trained instead. Fingerprinting was only the beginning of an overhauling blue-print which placed more police officers on the streets and allowed civilians to conduct forensic analysis. The model had been a success in several U.S. states, and, as a result, the Minister for Police and Emergencies in Victoria had pushed for reforms in the Senate, where she obtained the necessary votes to implement the program.

Nothing ever came out of Goosh's letter to the Victorian Director of Public Prosecution.

I knew if I refused to conduct a child-murder investigation, Goosh would insist on having my file reviewed and argue my incompetence in my present position. Since he hadn't succeeded in getting rid of me to date, this was a chance I was willing to take.

I took control of the crime scene, as per my job description. As a crime scene examiner, I was concerned with physical evidence, including cataloguing the area by means of photography, video-recording, note-taking, and collecting evidence for further analysis and court presentation. But my primary duty was to contain the crime scene and get rid of unwanted visitors without delay.

My eighteen-month stint at the FBI in Quantico had taught me well. In fact, I was the only investigator in Australia who had undergone such vigorous training, giving me the ability to contract out my services for a fee which provided me with a financial lifestyle with little to complain about.

Everyone around the body of the young girl turned eyes on me when I pushed my voice as if someone was trying to beat the crap out of me. The one thing I've learned over the years is that authority is often measured by how loud one can bark.

'I want everybody out of the area. And I mean *everybody*.'

5

Pointing at a few heads. 'You, you and you, go stand down the other side. Who got here first?'

A uniformed officer stepped forward.

'I did, Dr Melina.'

Without me asking, he passed me a copy of his log book. I skimmed through the two pages, where he had diligently recorded the time of arrival at the scene, the type of area, some names of people present, weather conditions and details of the body found.

I said, 'What are all these people doing here?' Preservation of the crime scene was critical at this stage. The more people present, the greater the potential for contamination and destruction of evidence. Large numbers of people at a scene also tended to distract and hinder photography and examination.

'I was just about to clear the scene.'

'Do it now, and I want police tape all around the area. I want you to organise a group of officers to conduct a line search. Use natural boundaries whenever possible, the edge of the water down there, right up to those trees up this side. We're looking for anything that doesn't belong near a lake. And that includes rubbish, food wrappers, absolutely anything. Don't use your fingers to pick up the stuff, and yell out if something looks suspicious. And I want no one smoking, eating or drinking in the area.'

'Are we doing the line search before recording of the crime scene?' He was referring to photography and video-taping.

'Senior Sergeant Moore and I will take care of that now.' Then: 'Now, before anyone else disappears, I want a list of all the people present. Those who can't justify a reason for being here, get their names and addresses, and send them back where they came from. Others, tell them to wait a few minutes while we establish whether we need them or not. You got that?'

He nodded.

I gave him my half-emptied Dr Pepper and his log book, and moved on.

As we approached the body, the crowd began to dissipate outwardly. On-lookers had covered the area with footprints. There was a good chance they'd just destroyed the most valuable piece of evidence: fresh sets of shoe prints in mud. There'd be no chance of making casts for further analysis and comparison tests.

We began with a preliminary examination, sometimes referred to as a general survey of the crime scene. Hands in our pockets, we moved in towards the body. I was looking for latent footmarks, tyre marks, fingermarks or anything which indicated how the girl might have gotten here.

The weather had been hot in the past few days, and the mud present by the edge of the lake was due to water overflowing and not rainfall. The air was fresh and clean, but soon it would be filled with carbon monoxide from traffic moving city-bound for a hard day's work.

The palms of my hands were clammy from the heat or from being nervous, I couldn't tell.

'What do you think?' Frank asked, kneeling close to the body.

'Could be a rape-and-kill scenario.'

'She's still wearing her underwear.'

'I noticed.'

'If someone raped her, do you think they'd put her underwear back on?'

I didn't answer. He knew as well as I did that anything was possible. With the amount of forensic material made available to the general public in the form of books, videos, courses and websites, it was easy for a killer to seed false clues at a crime scene to set investigators off-course. As the years were rolling past, killers were getting more educated, gaining knowledge on every damn procedure conducted during an investigation. I had no doubt that some criminals knew more about criminal procedures than people in the force. Fact was, as our means of catching criminals was becoming highly sophisticated, involving all sorts of advanced forensic detection, and as recently as last year DNA analysis on fingerprints, criminals knew they had to do their homework if they wanted to succeed. Fortunately, the majority of petty crimes were conducted by people who never put much thought into their task. It was the serious crimes, like the one I was facing on that Wednesday morning, which could turn life into hell.

I circled the area, trying to figure out how the body got

there. Did someone drag her from a car or carry her to where she was now resting? With all the footprints left by the on-lookers, it was hard to identify any trail marks. We'd have to rely on eyewitnesses and collection of trace evidence. Since the killer had to come in contact with the girl, there would have been a transference of material, no matter how small. This could come in the form of direct transfer, that is one which is transferred directly from one person to another, or from indirect transfer, that is material collected by one person, such as grass or dirt from a backyard, and deposited into another area where such material is rare or non-existent. Still, there was a chance that much of the trace evidence we'd find would be accounted for by the media vultures and the public who had preyed around the body before we'd arrived at the scene.

'Someone had to drive her here,' I commented. 'The nearest house is half a kilometre away. I doubt the killer carried his load in a bag-pack.'

From the silver briefcase I had with me, I removed a Minolta SLR camera and checked for batteries. I loaded the SLR with colour film and began shooting the body. I made copious notes in my log book of camera settings, including film speed, shutter speed, and frame numbers. I knew any photography I would undertake from this moment might one day end up in court, and my expertise with a camera cross-examined. I used a photographic tape measure and two stainless steel markers to provide visual references concerning size and distance. This was a hell of a slow way to conduct photography, but when at a crime scene, attention to detail was imperative.

The girl's blond hair was painted with mud. There were no visible lacerations on her legs or any other parts of her body. She was still face down. I shivered at the thought of what we would find once we flipped her over. She looked between nine and twelve, but it was hard to tell at this stage without seeing her face. There was no yardstick to measure how fast some children grew, especially in a city boasting one of the world's largest ethnic diversities.

I shot five thirty-six-exposure films of the body and its surrounding area, including two black-and-white rolls.

I'd visited the area before, only because it was less than five minutes from where I lived. Albert Park was an amazing place, set only a few kilometres from the city centre. Established in 1862, Albert Park was permanently reserved as a public park in 1876. It is recognised as one of Melbourne's most popular parks and as the home of amateur sports in Victoria. It includes a golf course and more than twenty grounds for various field sports, including tennis and bowling clubs.

The addition of the Australian Grand Prix track made the park world-famous for one week a year, to the dismay of the Save Albert Park group which wanted the race closed permanently and the park restored. Save Albert Park had the support of the Australian Conservation Foundation, the peak Victorian trade union council and all three opposition parties - Australian Labor Party, Australian Democrats, and Greens. In a short time, the group had become recognised as both the strongest defender of parks and an inspiration to other groups for the defence of Melbourne's heritage, rights of citizens and democratic principles.

When I finished photographing the surrounding area, I returned to where the body lay. 'God, Frank, I really have a bad feeling about this one,' I said, kneeling down to closely examine the girl.

Frank removed his pen and log book from his bag and began scribbling details. 'You're taking this too much to heart,' he said, his eyes focusing on his task.

The impact was similar to a mild blow at the back of the head. 'What am I supposed to do? Distance myself from the fact that I'm standing here taking pictures of a dead girl at seven-thirty in the morning? Jesus, Frank, no wonder you're still single.'

He pursed his lips for a few seconds, shot darts with his eyes, and said, 'That was uncalled for. Just because you've been sleeping with this clerk guy for the past six months, it doesn't give you the right to consider yourself an expert on people's marital status.'

'Yeah, yeah, whatever. And he's not a clerk, he's a *communications officer.*'

'No, shit.' He shifted from one foot to the other. 'Frankly, he can even be Bozo the Clown, I don't give a horse's arse. Can we just get on with this? If you've got a problem with this investigation, go and complain to your superiors. I'm tired of your whining.'

I swallowed hard, feeling tears well in my eyes. No way I was going to let myself break down in front of him. Since I began going out with Phillip Wood six months ago, a guy I met while doing some investigative work for a telecommunications company, Frank had been acting the jealous guy.

But what really bothered me was how could he be so insensitive to the girl who was lying in front of us? Was I being unreasonable? Was it so wrong to feel for other people's pain?

I slipped on a pair of surgical gloves, feeling the smoothness of talc powder against my fingers, and placed one hand on the girl's thigh.

'She's still warm. Bastard must have dumped her less than ten hours ago.'

When I finally turned the body around, I was surprised at the lack of blood. I looked up to Frank and said, 'No wounds of any sort. Could be poisoning. Doesn't give us much to work with.'

'The lab will come up with some hard evidence.'

It took us two hours to photograph and video tape the entire area. Most of the on-lookers had now vanished, and the only people present were police officers and forensic experts, whom I had summoned to the crime scene. Traffic had built up on Princes Highway, and the temperature climbed five notches on the Celsius scale. My blouse was sticking to my back, making the whole process even more unbearable. I wanted to slip my jacket off, but there was no where to put it down.

Frank looked as if he'd just stepped from under a shower, his bald spot covered in perspiration beads. Two large sweat patches had formed under his arms, extending past his rib cage.

I slipped off my surgical gloves and moved to the officer whom I first spoke to when I arrived at the crime scene.

'Any witnesses?' I asked, my pen and log book ready.

'Yeah, well, sort of, the guy who found the girl. He's standing over there.' The officer pointed to a man with a white bichon frise by his side.

'Has he seen anyone?'

'Nope. I asked him if he could wait around in case you wanted to talk to him.'

'What do you think?'

'What do I think what?'

'Did he do it?'

'Hey, I wouldn't have a clue, that's you're job.'

'Just asking, that's all. No harm in asking someone else's opinion.'

I paced to the man, who seemed preoccupied with his dog sniffing something invisible in the grass. At first glance, I guessed he was in his mid-thirties, probably unemployed or in between jobs. He wore jeans and a white polo shirt with that famous penguin logo. His hair was brushed neatly to one side, but he wore a five o'clock shadow. He could have looked terrific with a regular workout, if only someone bothered telling him.

'Hi, how're you doing? I'm Dr Kristina Melina, and I'm in charge of this investigation. You don't mind if I talk to you?' I extended my hand, which he shook firmly.

'No, sure, go ahead.'

'You understand you don't have to answer any questions, and you can get a solicitor?'

'I don't need a solicitor, I only found the girl, for Christ's sake.'

'Just doing my job.' I removed a small tape recorder from my right breast pocket and pushed the recording button. 'Don't mind if I tape this? Saves me writing illegible notes at a hundred miles an hour.'

'Suit yourself,' he said, but seemed slightly uncomfortable, his hands digging inside the pockets of his jeans.

I repeated the beat about his rights, just to make sure we had it on record.

'Wanna tell us exactly what happened?'

'Sure. As I told the other police officer, I was walking my dog Lucy, as I do every morning, and have been doing for the past five years, and there she was. Nothing else to it.'

'Did you see anyone?'

'Usual morning traffic, nothing which looked out of character.'

'I'm going to be blunt here. Would you have had any reason to kill that young girl?'

He hesitated for a few seconds, absorbing the impact of my question. 'You're nuts. You think I'm going to kill someone and wait for your guys to show up, and then hang around with my dog to give you a two-minute story? What the hell's wrong with you?'

'There's no need to be offensive. It's very common for killers to be the ones who find the victim—it puts them in a situation where no one thinks they've done it.'

'Well, I haven't done shit, and that's that.' He pulled the dog's leash in anger, almost strangling the poor thing, and added, 'I've got better things to do than talk to the lot of you. No wonder this town is in the state it's in. Christ, if you did you job properly, shit like that would never happen.'

Oh, great, I thought, now we're not only responsible for finding those who kill, but the reason why they kill in the first place.

Okay, next time I wouldn't try the blunt approach. It worked well on television, but in real life it wasn't very effective.

I watched the man walk away, realising I hadn't even had time to ask him his name, but reassured myself that the officer who got to the crime scene first did gather the list of names I'd asked him to.

I walked back to where the girl had been lying. She had been whisked to the mortuary, awaiting her turn for an autopsy, which I dreaded having to attend.

'What did he have to say?' Frank asked.

'Saw nothing, did nothing.'

'That was rather quick.'

'We'll need to talk to him again. I think I've hit a nerve.'

Frank's mobile phone went off. The traffic had built-up ten-fold since we arrived at the scene, and Frank had to scream into the mouthpiece to get a word in.

'Yes...No, now? She's already at the mortuary. Now? Yeah, well, sure.'

He punched the end button.

I raised one brow, and he said, 'Goosh. Wants us at the St Kilda Road Complex in half an hour.'

I didn't bother asking why.

There was no need to.

If the Deputy Commissioner of Police said to be there in half an hour, then it wasn't a request, but an order.

We gathered our equipment and took the box of packed evidence to Frank's Ford Falcon.

He opened the boot, and I emptied the contents of my arms into the back of the car.

'I'm not going to play games here,' I said matter-of-factly.

He didn't answer.

I went on, 'I'm going to tell him straight to his face that I don't want this investigation, and if he wants to find someone else, to do it, then it's up to him.'

Frank chewed on my comment as we climbed into the car. Finally, he turned to me and said, 'I think you're making a mistake. This is not the right time to pick and choose your cases. You've been on the job for less than a year. You know this is the opportunity he's been looking for. The perfect moment where he can humiliate you in front of everyone.'

I passed one hand over my forehead, wiping off the excess perspiration. 'Don't think I haven't thought about the whole deal. I know what's at risk. I just want to sleep at night.'

'Get a desk job.'

He revved the engine and reversed the car.

God, I hated him sometimes.


The St Kilda Road Police Complex was a twenty-storey high building complex, a few hundred metres from The Domain, a large hotel in South Melbourne, which incorporated its own restaurant and cafe bar.

I hated the idea of having to spend a good deal of my time in this concrete-and-glass fortress with its own rules, office gossip and back-stabbing. Not much different from any other office environment, where people were so bored to death, half their time was wasted making up stories or putting some dirt out on a colleague.

After passing a security check-point in the small, wood-panelled foyer of the building, Frank and I took the elevator to the ninth floor, where Goosh and god-knows-who-else would be waiting for us.

The air conditioning in the building was heaven-sent. My blouse was still stuck to my back from perspiration as I realised in despair I probably stunk like some cat's leftovers. I was dying for a shower, something which I'd intended to do as soon as I finished collecting evidence at the crime scene, but now I knew it wouldn't happen for at least another hour.

I glanced at the numbers indicating floor levels above my head and said to Frank, 'If he comes up with any comment close to harassment, I'm going to file an official complaint.'

'That's going to get you somewhere,' Frank answered, wiping his forehead with the back of his sleeve. He too looked as if he could have done with a shower. There was a solemn expression on his face, but I wasn't sure if it was because he was angry at me, or because that was the way we all looked when we returned from a crime scene.

'You're going to back me up on this, aren't you?' I asked.

I turned around, waiting for an answer to my question, but all he did was shrug and look the other way.

Fine, I thought, I'll just have to handle it by myself.

When we entered the conference room, Goosh was going through some files while sipping hot brew from a mug which read, '... because I said so.'

Kind of summed up his attitude.

The mahogany table with matching chairs seated up to twelve people. Through a large bay window, we had a view of South Melbourne and beyond. There was a water fountain close to the entrance, but no one ever bothered using it. A white board with several markers stood on the other side of the room, just in case someone had to explain procedures which were not easily conveyed by the spoken word. The room was often used when detectives and other crime-scene experts gathered for briefing.

Goosh's face was puffed and reddish, as if he'd climbed the emergency stairs to the ninth floor instead of taking the elevator. His suit must have been Italian-made because of the perfect cut. Still, no amount of tailoring could disguise the fact that he looked like a stuffed sausage in whatever suit he wore. I could have sworn he'd put on another two kilos since I'd last seen him, which was less than three weeks ago. The top button on his white shirt was undone, and his red-and-black striped tie was loosened like a schoolboy who couldn't take the heat.

He ignored us for the first ten seconds, and when he did look up, he seemed neither surprised, nor interested. His heavy eyes quickly dropped back to the contents of his manilla folder.

'Any ideas, any clues, anything at all?' he suddenly hissed, not bothering with greetings or anything which looked remotely like some form of courtesy.

I looked at Frank, who indicated with a movement of his brows that I should be the one talking. Frankly, I didn't know what business it was to Goosh so early in the investigation. So far we'd established next to nothing.

'The girl was not raped as far as we could tell,' I said.

'Cause of death?'

'Uncertain at this stage. We'll have to wait for the autopsy report.'

'Mmm... You do understand that I'd like you to attend the autopsy?'

I shifted from my spot and swallowed. 'Actually, I wanted to let you know that I won't be working on this case.'

For the first time since we entered the room, he glared into my eyes. 'Why would that be?' He played nervously with a blue biro.

'This is not the type of work I feel comfortable with.' I could feel my stomach churning, waiting for him to jump out of his seat and elevate the tone of his voice to Jurassic levels.

Instead, he smiled and said, 'So what type of work are you comfortable with? You keep reminding me how you have a PhD in criminal justice. Why is this case suddenly outside your expertise?'

'It's a child murder. I don't do child murders.'

He sipped from his mug, puzzled over my statement for a few seconds and said, 'Well, then, I guess we'll have to find someone to replace you.'

I straightened in my chair, still waiting for his normal verbal diarrhoea to come down on me like every other time I complained about something.

But it never happened.

Instead, Goosh returned his attention to his manilla folder as if I'd said nothing unusual. He took it extremely well, and as a result, I couldn't help thinking that there had to be a hidden agenda.

I shifted on my chair and said, 'How long will it take to find another investigator?'

Goosh chewed his lower lip while Frank rolled his eyes to the ceiling.

*Did I say something wrong?*

'Look,' Goosh said, 'you're going to stay on the case for a few more days at the most. Let me make a couple of phone calls.'

'Can't we get this moving a little faster?' I didn't know why I was being so unreasonable when he remained polite. Maybe I wanted him to insult me because to date it's been the only type of response I'd received from him.

'Kristina...' Frank began to protest.

Goosh waved one hand in the air. 'No, no, Dr Melina is right, if she can't cope with the job she's been given, she should butt out. I've always said this isn't a job for a woman. Hell, I understand. Who wants to wake up every morning and have to deal with murderers, rapists, child pornographers and the whole lot of them? Given the choice, I'd get married and stay in the kitchen. That is *if* I was a woman."

I felt a tightness in my throat. I knew there'd be more than met the eye when he agreed to find someone else to take over the investigation.

Frank slapped his hand on his forehead, probably wondering what he was doing with two idiots like us.

I shook my head and said, 'This is not about a career change. I'm keeping this job for as long as I want. It's only about this case. I don't want to work with dead children. I don't want to work these cases, and it's not like I've never made myself clear in the past. Everyone understood the conditions of my appointment when I came on board. You're trying to push this into some kind of incompetence bullshit when that has nothing to do with it. My initial agreement was clear, and everyone knew it.'

'Oh, sure they did. I certainly did. I was looking for someone all-rounded. Someone who didn't pick and choose. Someone who wasn't afraid to get his hands dirty and get the work done.' His tone was now infested with anger. 'This is not a McDonald's where you get to choose your own meal. This is the real world, and in the real world you have to take what you're given. Murders are not committed with you in mind, Dr Melina, and the sooner you get that in your head, the easier your job will be.'

I stood from my chair as if someone had lit a firecracker in my underpants.

'I don't have to take this bureaucratic crap! To begin with, I don't even work for you. I'm not one of your employees, I'm contracted, and I don't have to listen to you.'

Goosh stood on his feet, his forefinger stabbing the air. 'You listen to me *Ms* Melina. I've had just about enough of you. I'm telling you now that I'm going to do the best I can to get you out of this contract. There will come a time and a place when I'll never have to see your face again, and when the police will be better off without you.'

I opened my mouth, but no words came out. I turned to Frank, but he was looking down at the table. Who could blame him? If I'd been him, I'd just storm out of the room and let us deal with our own problems.

'I've got work to do,' I said tartly and raced for the door.

'Come back and see us when you've calmed down,' Goosh yelled as I slammed the door behind me.

I spent the next ten minutes in a rest room allocated on the same floor as the conference room. My eyes were puffy, but I couldn't cry. I was more angry than anything else. Life had a way of turning against me sometimes, to the point where I didn't want to move on. But by the same token, I wasn't going to let that sonofabitch walk all over me, tell me what I was capable or wasn't capable of doing.

All my life I fought the odds, tried so hard to stand for what I believed in. It felt unbelievable in this day and age that women were still being treated as second best. The newspapers loved to print stories on job equality, how far we've come in the nineties, and how everything was perfect out there. But everything was far from being perfect. Men still believed themselves superior, and even though they were more careful about what they said, their actions clearly indicated what was on their minds. Women still had a damn long way to go before they'd receive the respect they deserved. I hated to sound like a whinnying feminist, which I wasn't, but so far life had dealt me men with little to offer.

I rinsed my face with cold water and took a deep breath. The cold water cut through my pores, helping me to wake up to the reality of life. Nothing ever changed, and I'd better get used to it. I fixed my shoulder-length, auburn hair with a flick of a hand in front the mirror and forced a smile. The day was just beginning and already I wanted to go back to bed.


I parked my blue Lancer in the car park of the VIFM in South Melbourne. All I had found out to date was that the murdered girl's name was Tracy Noland, and her mother had been contacted.

The VIFM is a body corporate with perpetual succession which was established by the Coroners Act 1985 in the State of Victoria. The Institute is based at the Coronial Services Centre in Melbourne, a purpose built facility in Kavanagh Street, Southbank. Its principle function is to provide timely, high quality and high value forensic medicine and related services, including teaching and research.

The VIFM is also the statutory body in charge of Forensic Pathology, Clinical Forensic Medicine, Forensic Toxicology and other forensic scientific services in the state. Over three thousand post-mortem examinations take place each year at the mortuary, the Coronial Services Centre, located in the same blue-grey building complex. Other than autopsies, the centre incorporates histology, microbiology and molecular biology laboratories, all contributing to forensic investigations. The building complex also incorporates the Coronial Services Centre and the Coroner's Court.

As I walked towards the blue-grey building, a tightness gripping my throat, I wondered how the hell I was going to digest the autopsy of an eleven-year old girl when I had a son who had turned twelve that same year. This was too close to home, and I hated myself for ending up in situations I swore I would avoid throughout my life.

As I crossed the car park and entered the VIFM through an automatic sliding glass door, memories of my last child investigation came back to mind. A few years back, while investigating the death of a young girl, I swore I would never work in child investigation. It was the hardest thing in the world to do, and although I wanted to help as many people as possible, I had my limits. I was no hero, and if the VFSC couldn't understand that, then bad luck. It wasn't a decision that I'd made lightly, but some people were better suited to one type of investigation than others, and child homicides were not something I handled with ease. Investigations of such kept me awake all night for weeks, sometimes months. It wasn't uncommon for a flashback nightmare to hit me out of nowhere, sometimes years after the event.

I presented my green photo-ID card with a metallic strip at the reception and stated my purpose.

'Dr Main is waiting for you in his office. Viewing of the body starts in fifteen minutes.' The receptionist picked up the phone and announced my arrival to Dr Main.

Dr Charles W. Main had had the unfortunate occasion to meet me after a serious breach of security last year at the VIFM when I managed to break into his office, kick a security guard in the shin, and steal documents from his filing cabinet.

Initially, Dr Main wanted me charged with trespassing and theft of confidential material, but the decision was reversed after it was explained to him that it was because of my unlawful action that an important murder investigation had been solved.

To date, I hadn't spoken to Dr Main, and as I climbed the staircase to his office, perspiration dripped down the small of my back. I had no idea how he was going to receive me since I had not organised my attendance at the autopsy and hadn't spoken to him since my little incident. Only one thing was certain. I wasn't going to investigate the death of Tracy Noland, and the sooner he found out, the better.

Dr Main's office was the same as I remembered: three-by-three metres, cramped with a green four-drawer filing cabinet at one end and an outdated 486DX computer taking up most of his desk. He was sitting there, his door halfway open.

'Come in, Dr Melina.'

As I took a seat behind his desk, his look was non-committal. He avoided eye contact for fear or embarrassment of who I was. Was he another man who was afraid of women who followed career paths so far dominated by males?

'I'm glad you could make it.' His tone contradicted his greeting.

I glanced at his salt-and-pepper hair and straight nose. He was quite handsome, and had I met him somewhere other than at this work place, I might have been interested in him in a non-professional manner. He had creases under his blue eyes, which gave him an air of wisdom, the look of someone you could trust. But I knew looks were not everything.

'To be honest with you, Dr. Main, I didn't want to be here in the first place.'

I must have gotten his attention because he locked his eyes into mine and snapped, 'No need to be offensive.'

I felt heat on my face and immediately retracted, 'I'm sorry. It wasn't a personal attack. What I wanted to say is that I don't wish to pursue an investigation in which a child has been murdered. It's just not something I'm very good at.'

'Investigations?'

'Dealing with dead children.'

He rubbed his chin with his thumb and forefinger. 'Does this mean you won't be attending the autopsy?'

'I'm currently in charge of the investigation. Until a replacement is found, which I hope will be in the next twenty-four hours, I have little choice.'

He smiled, but I puzzled as to whether it was because I was forced to do something I hated, or because he was glad I had retracted from investigating Tracy Noland's death. I still hadn't figured out if Dr Main was a friend or a foe. He probably felt the same way about me.

'Mrs Noland should be here any minute,' he said, sucking the cap of a silver fountain pen. 'She's going to identify the body before the autopsy begins. The description and clothing of her missing daughter fit the body we found. We're certain it's Tracy Noland, but the body still has to be legally identified.'

I wondered why he bothered explaining all this. I wasn't a graduate student on work experience and knew forensic procedures like the back of my hand.

'Do we know what killed her at this stage?' I asked.

'No idea.'

I stood from my chair and said, 'I guess I'd better make my way to the viewing room.'

'You do that. I'll join you in a minute.'

I left his office, feeling slightly nauseous.

# CHAPTER TWO

The viewing room was divided into separate sections in the form of two rooms. One had seating arrangements for witnesses, the other was blue-green from floor to ceiling, designed for the sole purpose of identifying the unfortunate beings who happened to end up at the mortuary. The rooms were separated by a glass partition, covered by a green curtain, which would remain shut until the body was ready to be identified.

Currently, around one percent of Victorians died every year, with one-eighth of that one percent ending up at the mortuary for one reason or another. The previous year, just over one hundred autopsies were murder victims. The autopsies performed at the Coronial Services Centre is divided into two types: medical autopsy and medical-legal autopsy, the latter also known as homicide autopsy. Tracy Noland's autopsy fell under the second category, where the procedure had been ordered by a proper legal authority, in this case the VIFM. Basically, a medical-legal autopsy is required in all homicide cases, and it was clear at this stage that the young girl's death wasn't a natural cause.

While I was seated in the front row, sandwiched between Frank and Dr Main, the entrance door to my left opened, and in walked a forty-something woman with a face of stone. I guessed this had to be the little girl's mother. She seemed upset, but her grey eyes gave no indication she'd been crying. I guessed her to be around eighty kilos and one-seventy in height. She wore a budget-type, ankle-length white summer dress with a pair of brown, leather sandals. Her brown hair fell over her forehead and was tied into a pony-tail. Her nose was short and round, and her lips chunky and painted dark red. She avoided eye contact, giving no indication that she noticed our presence in the room.

We waited patiently in embarrassing silence while someone wheeled the dead girl's body on a galvanised mobile cart from the cool room, down a maze of corridors and into the viewing room.

Finally, the assistant pathologist pulled open the green curtains to the viewing room.

Laying on the galvanised mobile cart, the young girl, whom I'd seen this morning at Albert Park, was covered in mud, but her face was still identifiable. I recognised the blue dress we found her in. She wore a toe tag, filled with an accession number and identification, which still remained to be confirmed by her mother. The girl had been reported missing the previous night, and the description Mrs Noland had given the police matched the body we'd found this morning.

Frank whispered something to her, which I didn't hear, but assumed had to do with the identity of the young girl.

'Yes, it's her'. Her tone was surprisingly deadpan.

My heart sank so low that I felt as if I was going to pass out. How in the world did I end up in a room with a bunch of strangers, staring at the white corpse of an eleven-year old girl?

The mother of the young girl seemed emotionless, but maybe she was only experiencing some form of time-delay reaction. I'd seen people who'd refused to accept the death of a loved one for days, sometimes weeks after it occurred. I'd heard of some who still wouldn't accept the cold, hard truth years after the person died.

The grieving process was a strange one, sometimes a never-ending phase where people left behind hung on to the hope that their loved one would come back one day. When someone got killed, the victims were multiple, ranging from brothers, sisters, parents, other family members and friends, all suffering from varying levels of grief.

And then there was the temporary presence of strangers like me, who could never quite distance themselves

22

emotionally from the curse which had inflicted other human beings.

When we left the viewing room, churning emotions challenged my choice of career. Why was it that I had a morbid fascination with other people's misery? I liked to believe it was compassion which drove me to the job I was doing, but as time went by, I wondered if that wasn't just an excuse to avoid facing the real reason behind my unhealthy interest. Was there a dark side to me which I refused to face? Deep down, did I enjoy the grieving pain I experienced every time someone died?

Down the hallway, which was covered in a dark blue carpet, just past the reception area, the girl's mother stood like a marble statue, while Frank and a uniformed officer were chatting. I stared at her for a few seconds, wondering what was going through her mind. I thought about my son Michael and tried to imagine how I'd react if the same thing had happened to him. He was the only person who truly mattered in my life, the only reason I managed to wake up every morning and find the strength to carry on in a world that had gone mad.

I tried to sneak out of the building, determined not to get more involved than I already was. Soon, this case will be behind me, handed over to someone else, and I would get on with life as if this whole incident had been nothing but a bad dream.

But before I made it past the reception desk and out the side door, Frank spotted me and said, 'Hold on a sec, Kristina.' Then he turned to Mrs Noland and muttered something I didn't catch.

She turned to me, her eyes cold and empty.

Obliged, I paced towards her. God damn, *why can't they just leave me alone?*

'I'm so sorry about Tracy,' I said, injecting my tone with sincerity. 'The police will do the best they can to find the person responsible.'

She forced a smile and said, 'I understand you're investigating the death of my daughter?'

I gave Frank a cold stare, but in return he shrugged as if to say *what the hell did you want me to say?*

'That is correct,' I said dryly. 'But someone else will take over the investigation. I'm only working temporarily on this case.'

'You find the killer, Dr Melina,' she commanded, obviously not registering what I'd just said. 'I'm never going to sleep again for as long as I know this person is still out there.'

There was bitterness and anger in her tone which was hard to ignore.

I swallowed hard and was about to protest when she went on, 'I know you've got a child of your own. As one mother to another, please do your best to find the killer.'

And then she let a tear roll down her face.

The first tear since she walked into the mortuary.

*Oh, God!*

I couldn't help myself.

I took her hand in mine and said, 'I will, Mrs Noland. I'll do the best I can. I promise.'


After Mrs Noland had gone, I gathered my notes and went to lunch with Frank in the VFIM's staff canteen. A few people were scattered at various tables, talking in low voices as if they were afraid to wake the dead.

I was trying to get some information on what Goosh had said after I left the St Kilda Road Police Complex this morning.

'So he said nothing else?' I asked, pulling the ring from my Diet Dr Pepper.

'All he said was that the police needed a real expert, and despite your qualifications, he didn't think you were a real expert.'

'And what did you say?'

'Nothing. What was I supposed to say?'

'You said nothing?'

'Kristina...'

I made a throaty noise and sipped from my Dr Pepper. 'Well, you can tell that sonofabitch that I've decided to stay on the case. Changed my mind.'

Frank locked his eyes into mine, his way of asking if I was serious.

I nodded.

A smiled appeared on his face, and he said, 'This is great, Kristina. I was hoping you would re-consider. Well, I'm sure Goosh will be delighted to hear that.' He placed his right hand on his mobile phone, which was laying next to his coffee cup. 'Do you want me to tell him the good news now?'

We both laughed loud enough for the other people in the room to stare at us.

'Ah, almost forgot,' Frank said between laughs. 'Some neighbour of the young girl called the station. He said he wanted to talk to someone about the murder.'

My face straightened.

'Did you get a name?'

'Not me. I wasn't the one who took the call.'

I scribbled something in my notebook about chasing up this lead.

I finished my cheese-and-salad sandwich and knew it was time to face reality.

I hate autopsies, and they're not something I would wish on anyone. In fact, as I was waiting in the homicide room for Dr Main to make an appearance, I told myself that when I'd die, I'd make sure it would be a straight-forward death. Only people who died under suspicious circumstances or old age ended up at the mortuary. I knew what they did at the mortuary with the dead. Although the autopsy consisted of straight-forward clinical procedures carried out with the greatest respect for those whose souls were floating above the room, no matter how many autopsies I attended, I couldn't help feeling nauseous about the entire procedure.

Attached to the homicide room was a viewing room, where Frank and a police photographer were sitting on high stools, ready to witness the forthcoming autopsy.

The autopsy room consisted of a blue-green concrete floor, a galvanised table with holes to allow water and fluids to drain, a small-parts dissection table with drains, a vertical mechanical scale to weigh each organ, and a tank for delivering water to the table and collecting fluids. The ceiling was white with various pipes criss-crossing like spider webs. Yellow plastic bio-hazard containers were scattered in various parts of the room.

Every pathologist has personal preferences when it comes to post-mortem instruments. Dr Main had his own collection, which included dissecting and brain knives, scissors, saws of various sizes, a skull key, forceps, scalpels and chisels, all succeeding in making me shiver just by looking at them.

A strong disinfectant smell filled my lungs, as if we were in a hospital, except that unlike a hospital, anyone lying flat in this room had nil chance of ever getting up again.

Air conditioning hummed from the ceiling, making the room cold and uninviting.

I noticed a sign which read, 'Absolutely No Smoking, No Eating, No Drinking In This Room,' and wondered how anyone could.

Without warning, a mortuary technician rolled in a galvanised mobile cart with the body of Tracy Noland. She was still wearing a little blue floral dress, but no black leather shoes and knee-length white socks she wore when we found her were gone.

Dr Main followed thirty seconds later. He took me to the change rooms adjoining the main mortuary laboratory, where we traded our clothes for blue hospital pyjamas, green surgical gowns, giant white rubber boots and white disposable plastic aprons. Without a word, we returned to the homicide room, where Frank and the photographer stared at us like children stare at monkeys at the zoo.

'How are you holding up?' Dr Main asked, glancing towards me.

I was standing in one corner of the autopsy room, next to a cork board filled with various procedural instructions, trying hard not to be a nuisance. All I wanted was the damn thing to be over and done with.

'Great. It's exactly what I look forward to every day after lunch.'

He laughed gently, and I couldn't help smiling at his reaction to my own humour. But when I looked back at the mobile cart and the dead body of the eleven-year girl, I realised there was nothing to smile about.

He saw me looking at the high window strip along one of the walls, where sunlight spilled into the chilly laboratory.

'Natural light is better when conducting an autopsy,' he said.

'You can see skin discolouration from carbon monoxide poisoning. Colours are more vibrant, more real than in artificial light.'

I nodded, unsure if this was a good or bad thing.

'Okay, Dr Melina, I'm going to be recording the autopsy to help with the report. If you have any questions, you can ask me when I'm finished.'

I nodded as he slipped on a pair of yellow surgical gloves.

Mrs Noland managed to talk me into this, and now I knew there was no turning back. This investigation was another one of those moments in life which I had to go through, gritting my teeth, hoping the end would be coming soon. But as it was, I was perfectly aware that I was at the beginning of the investigation, something which made me even more upset.

I stood straight and told myself that no matter how badly I wanted to get out of this, now that I'd made the commitment to find out how and why Tracy Noland died, I was better off taking it as well as I could. Complaining wasn't going to get me anywhere other than in a state of anger.

Dr Main began by taking photographs of the entire body clothed. When he finished, he switched on a video camera, next to the dissection table, angled in such a way that the entire autopsy would be clearly recorded.

And then, he began the examination.

'Subject is an eleven-year old girl known as Tracy Noland. She has blond hair, blue eyes, fair complexion'. He proceeded with measurements and weighing of the body. 'She's one-hundred-and-forty centimetres tall and weighs forty-seven kilograms. The front of her body, including her face, and all her clothes are covered in mud. At first glance there seems to be no visible injuries of any kind.'

Tracy Noland was then undressed. Every item of clothing was carefully bagged in large yellow envelopes marked 'PATIENTS CLOTHING' in bold green characters. Each envelope was labelled with the item number, case number, date, time, and a small description of the item in question, all ready to be sent to the relevant departments of the VFSC.

Dr Main proceeded with the examination while I stood quietly where I'd been standing since I walked into the room.

'Hands, fingernails are clean apart from mud.'

I noticed she had a hairless, clean public region, making me realise she hadn't even reached puberty yet.

Dr Main examined the entire body, noting nothing unusual. 'No wounds or bruising of any kind. The victim wasn't sexually assaulted or beaten.'

But when he looked further, he added, 'There is some bruising on the inside upper lip, although not on the outside. Suggested smothering at this stage.'

As Dr Main gathered his surgical instruments for the internal examination, I tried to figure out who could have killed the young girl. I knew it had to be someone who knew her, or someone who saw her routinely. I crossed out a chance attack since she hadn't been sexually assaulted, and the most-common reason killers grabbed little girls at random is to satisfy their sadistic sexual gratification.

Did Tracy Noland witness something she wasn't supposed to have seen? Did someone catch her in the act and decided to get rid of her just as a precaution? It was far too early to establish a modus operandi or in-depth psychological profile of the killer.

I was purposely lost in thought when Dr Main conducted the internal examination of the body. When I did pay attention to what he was doing, it was no little girl on the table, but a whole body cut open from the breastbone to the groin, her inside exposed, her vital organs lying on the dissection table.

My lunch came up to my throat for a split second.

*That's it, I can't take any more of this.*

I excused myself and left the autopsy room. Whatever Dr Main would find, I'd read it in his report.

I rushed to the women's room down the end of the corridor, pushed the door with my right foot, headed straight for a cubicle and let the sickness out of me. Out came my salad-and-cheese sandwich with Dr Pepper. I was on my knees, my stomach contents trying to come through my nose as well as my mouth. I gasped for air, feeling pain in my chest, while holding both sides of the cubicle. I wondered if someone in heaven was having a good laugh at my expense.

When I finished, I stumbled to the hand-sink and splashed my face with cold water. My hands were still trembling. I decided that a good walk down St Kilda beach would get my mind back on track. It was only mid-week, but the way things were going, I wondered how I was going to make it past today.

On my way out of the VIFM, I told the receptionist to tell Dr Main I had left for the day, if he could be kind enough to send me a copy of Tracy Noland's autopsy report as soon as he finished writing it up.

I slid behind the wheel of my car, confused and ashamed of myself. For someone who was supposed to be Victoria's foremost forensic expert, I wasn't doing too well.

I cracked the gears into reverse, did a u-turn and stepped angrily on the accelerator.

St Kilda beach was almost deserted at three o'clock on a Wednesday afternoon. With the entire beach to myself, I breathed in the soothing sea water while seagulls cried in unison above my head. I hoped to God none would have the brilliant idea of beginning target practice. The sun was high in the sky. Grey clouds peaked shyly at the horizon, and, according to this morning's weather forecast on Radio National, would take over Melbourne before sunset. A hot wind was still blowing from the ocean, causing my skin to dry.

I walked passed an ice-cream kiosk surrounded by white plastic tables and chairs, and Coca-Cola umbrellas protecting nobody from sunburn. I almost gave in to one of those rich chocolate-coated ice-creams advertised on TV where a female model seemed to be experiencing the ultimate orgasm at first bite. But then I recalled the extra kilos I had put on since I'd stopped going to the gym.

I loved St Kilda, a bay-side suburb attached to Melbourne, where shops were open seven days a week, and people worried more about quality of life than climbing the corporate ladder. There was a good mixture of successful artists, bums and students, searching for an ever-lasting holiday environment without having to move all the way up to Queensland. Prostitutes and drug addicts crawled down Fitzroy and Grey Streets at night and vanished during the daytime like zombies, except on weekends when they were visible at all hours. Like every big city in the world, Melbourne had its share of homeless, burglars, junkies and prostitutes. It wasn't a perfect world, but a perfect world would have been boring.

I strolled past Luna Park towards Acland Street, my mind

filled with homicidal hypotheses.

I knew the death of Tracy Noland could have been accidental. Maybe she screamed and someone tried to quiet her down. Maybe the killer held his grip too hard for too long until she could no longer breath. Maybe he didn't know what to do with the body once he found out she was dead. The girl hadn't been sexually assaulted, making it even more difficult to conjure the killer's motivation. What was it that she saw or heard to make someone desperate enough to kill her?

Because Tracy Noland had been found in Albert Park, an inner-city suburb, I concluded the killer had to be a local. No one would have taken a corpse from an outer suburb to the city and dump it there. It would have been easier to get rid of it in an outer suburb, where there were less people around and more open spaces available to dump the body without getting caught. Tracy Noland's murder didn't seem premeditated. And that gave me hope that the killer might have left enough clues on the way.

My next step was to conduct door to door interviews in the neighbourhood where Tracy Noland lived. From past experience, I knew that everything in life was related, like pieces of a jigsaw puzzle, and a murder was no different. Someone somewhere had to know something. What I had to figure out was who and where.

But before interrogating any of Tracy's neighbours, I wanted to have a chat to Mrs Noland. Although I didn't want to jump to any conclusion at this early stage of the investigation, I knew homicide was often a crime of passion committed by a person usually well-known or related to the victim.

# CHAPTER THREE

**M**rs Noland agreed to be interviewed on the ninth floor of the St Kilda Road Police Complex, home of the homicide squad and part of the Crime Department of the Victoria Forensic Science Centre. The Homicide Squad at 412 St Kilda Road in Melbourne investigates deaths or serious injuries ostensibly resulting in death in connection with criminal violence or assault; accidents, including criminal negligence, vehicle, rail-road, aeroplane and boat accidents; suicides; drowning; any sudden death, or death which occurred under suspicious or unusual circumstances; and all deaths during confinement in jail or in a detention cell. The Homicide Squad works closely with the Arson Squad, the Robbery Squad, the Special Investigation Squad, the Burglary Squad and the Drug Squad, and collaborates with various other departments in the building, including the Fingerprint Branch, Document Examination and Traffic Offences.

Mrs Noland was not a suspect at this stage, and the basis of the interview I was to conduct - unlike an interrogation where questioning involves a person suspected of having committed a crime, having complicity in a crime or having direct knowledge about a crime - was to establish whether she had any information which I believed would be of interest to the investigation.

Prior to the interview, I managed to acquire some background on Mrs Noland. She resided at 13 Vincent Court in Albert Park, was forty-four years old, born in NSW, had completed four years of secondary education, and had never

31

held a job in her life. She had no record of past problems with police or other legal trouble. According to Social Security records, she received adequate child allowance on the basis of being a sole parent. Payments were about to stop since she no longer had a child. I had no idea how she was going to make a living.

We were alone in a room especially designed for interviewing witnesses or suspects. To my eyes, the room was austere and sterile, not the ideal environment for interviewing potential witnesses. A green Formica table and three orange chairs stood in the middle, the walls were bare and painted white, and a video camera was mounted on one corner. Hardly a place to invite someone for a chat and a coffee.

For the past twelve months, I tried to explain to the Homicide Squad that transforming the interview room into a pleasant environment would produce different results. I found interviewees nervous and unwilling to cooperate fully. I was convinced that a room designed as a business office, with fish tanks, and pictures on the walls - other than police posters about doing the right thing - and other furnishing would produce the desired attitude with people. But traditional thinking and older police officers *knew* better and didn't want to listen to any suggestions from some female PhD who trained in the USA.

I had to make the most of what I was being offered.

Two cups of coffee sat on the table, untouched.

Mrs Noland looked the same as when I first met her. Her face was carved in stone, and she wore the same dark lipstick. She avoided eye contact as much as she could, resulting in me feeling slightly uncomfortable. Interviewing was not something I particularly enjoyed doing, but it was something I was good at. I read her her rights and began the tedious procedure with the video camera rolling.

'Did you have any problems parking?' I asked, trying to break the ice.

She stared at me for a few seconds, looked down at her hands and said, 'No.'

'Mmm... I always find it difficult to park around here. Where did you park?'

She gave me another look. 'You gonna get on with it or

32

what?'

Well, sorry for being human. Fine, I thought, you want to play it rough.

'Do you have any idea who killed your daughter?' I asked bluntly.

Her eyes locked into mine. 'No idea. This is a big, friendly neighbourhood. Kids always play with one another.'

'Have you seen any grown-ups in the area?'

'No one who's not supposed to be there.' Her tone of voice was non-committal, and I could tell she only wanted to get the hell out of here.

'Look, Mrs Noland, I know losing a daughter is hard, and I know how you must feel right now, but you don't seem to be willing to talk much. We're on your side. If you don't help us, we can't help you.'

'Do you have kids, Ms...?'

'You can call me Kristina. And, yes, I've got a twelve-year old boy.'

'How would you react if someone killed him?'

I stood still for a few seconds. 'To be honest, I'm not sure. I'd probably be angry, depressed, I don't know.'

'Exactly. I've haven't had the chance to practice this event. It wasn't a subject taught at high school. So if you feel I'm being irrational, it's because it's my first time.'

I swallowed, wondering if there was more to it than she was telling me. Not the type of response I expected from a grieving parent. 'Mrs Noland, did you have any reasons to want your daughter dead?'

'Of course not, but other people might have.'

'Were you angry at her?'

'No.'

'Did you fight at all?'

She pursed her lip. 'We had words now and then, but it doesn't mean I wanted her dead. Don't you ever have a disagreement with your boy?'

'Sure, I do. But did you ever hit Tracy?'

'Hit? I've slapped her once or twice. But that doesn't make me a murderer.'

'Of course it doesn't.'

'This questioning is absolutely ridiculous. Why don't you go and find who really killed my daughter?'

I sipped from my coffee cup. 'Mrs Noland, all I'm trying to do is eliminate the obvious. In cases like these, it's often the parents who kill the child. If I'm going to spend time and energy out there, I want to make sure I'm on the right track.'

Her eyes circled the room for a few seconds.

'I haven't killed my daughter,' she retorted. 'That's all you need to know. I'm leaving.'

She stood and left the room.

I looked up to the video camera and shrugged.


Ten minutes later I met with Frank in the same room.

'Goosh is pissed with you,' Frank announced, as he circled the table, deciding on which chair to sit on.

'So? Isn't he always?'

'Says he's tired of you jerking him around and would like to talk to you whenever you can make yourself available.'

'That might not be for a very long time.'

Frank took a chair opposite me. 'What's the story with her?' he asked, obviously referring to Mrs Noland.

'She seems very defensive and short-tempered,' I began. 'Kind of an unusual reaction. I expected her to break down at some point, but she didn't.'

'Do you think she did it?'

'A bit premature at this stage, but nothing would surprise me. Maybe she didn't do it so much herself, but got someone else to do it. Contract killing is becoming extremely popular, especially to solve family problems. All she had to do was establish a solid alibi and bingo.'

'What about her husband?'

'Checked the files. Doesn't have one. She's been a single mother since the birth of her daughter.'

'And where's the father?'

'Left one day without a word or a trace.'

'Do you think we should get a warrant to search her home?'

'There's not enough to get a warrant, and I don't want to scare her off. Maybe she didn't do it. And if it is her, she's not going to help us with anything. I'd like to talk to the neighbours first. See what they think. Maybe they saw something. Maybe they can tell me about the mother-daughter relationship. In a couple of days, she might come to accept what has happened and decide to cooperate.'

'This is only my personal opinion, but I think she did it. The way she conducted herself at the mortuary. I know, you're going to say I've got no proof, but this is just my instinct. She killed her daughter, maybe a freak accident, I don't know, and she dumped the body in Albert Park Lake. Happens all the time. Maybe she didn't mean to kill her.'

I looked at him without commenting.

He went on, 'Maybe she killed the husband too, who knows?' He scratched the back of his neck. 'Anything else I should know?'

'Yeah. She doesn't have a driver's license or a car. If she killed her daughter, someone had to help her bring the body to the lake.'

Vincent Court, where Tracy Noland lived, was well-maintained, filled with Victorian-style houses, manicured gardens, expensive cars and not an adult soul in sight, only a bunch of kids playing down the end of the court.

I parked my car two houses down from the entrance of the street and checked myself in the rear-mirror. Satisfied I looked better than I felt, I stepped out of the car, clipped my photo-ID to the breast pocket of my navy sports jacket, and assessed my surroundings.

At 5.45 p.m., most people were home after a long day at work, unwinding in front of the television or enjoying time with their family. I felt like the big bad wolf who was going to intrude into everyone's privacy, but life gave me no choice. I promised Tracy Noland's mother I would do my best, even if it meant annoying the hell out of ordinary citizens.

Although I didn't expect any dramatic encounters, not so early in the investigation, I tucked my .380 semi-automatic between my belt and the small of my back. It amazed me how quickly I depended on the gun to make me feel protected. I could honestly understand women in America who refused to walk alone at night without a piece. It was total lunacy, especially when one considered all the trigger-happy, feeble minds who carried weapons around, not to protect oneself where protection was freely available. There were those who argued that carrying a gun could potentially give my assailants the opportunity to kill me with my own weapon, but I'd like to think I'd still have a better chance of coming out alive than fighting with my bare hands against someone jabbing a knife at me. Morally, I felt uneasy about carrying a gun, but in the real world, morality didn't always go hand in hand with survival.

Before knocking at someone's door, I decided to have a quick chat to the kids who where playing at the end of the cul-de-sac. From a distance, they looked Tracy's age, and according to Mrs Noland, Tracy used to play with some of the kids in her street.

I walked casually, as if I belonged in the neighbourhood, but psychologically, I was bouncing from one foot to the other.

The group of kids consisted of three boys and two girls - the boys wore knee-length basketball shorts with oversized T-shirts and Nikes; the girls wore cute little dresses, one green and one red. Some could have been brothers and sisters, I couldn't tell.

The evening was warm and pleasant, making it ideal for kids to play outside instead of spending time in front of the box.

By the time I was five metres away from the group, I could feel them sensing my presence. Their chatting had turned to whispers, and it was clear I was trespassing.

I paced towards the children and forced a smile.

'You guys *hang* around here?' I asked, injecting warmth in my tone.

They nodded in unison without a word.

'Oh, that's *cool*,' I said, as if surprised.

Kids' language was different from grown-ups'. Everything was *cool* and *dude* and *digging*. I knew because my son Michael hung around with other kids of his age, and when they dropped in at home once in a while to empty the contents of my fridge, they spoke this foreign language.

'I work for the cops. I'm just talking to people about Tracy Noland. Any of you knew Tracy?'

They looked at each other, and one of the boys, a redhead

with more freckles than a poppy-seed bun, came forward.

'You really a cop?' he asked, his green eyes showing genuine interest.

'Certainly am.' I unclipped my ID from my breast pocket and handed it over.

He scrutinised the plastic card. 'What's the V-F-S-C stand for?'

'Victorian Forensic Science Centre.'

He licked his upper lip and said, 'Wow, cool, like an X-Files kind-of-thing?'

The other kids began surrounding me, passing my ID card from one to the other.

'Sort of. I don't do alien abductions, but you never know.'

One of the girls, blond hair, blue eyes, the one with the green dress, stood in front of me. 'I'm Chelsea,' she said, extending her hand. 'I knew Tracy.' I shook her limp, moist hand.

'Yeah, we all knew her,' the redhead added.

'Yeah, she used to hang around here, but not with us. She was kind of by herself all the time,' one of the other boys added.

Then the red-head: 'We didn't really like her. Never talked to us. She thought she was better or something. Treated us like we were kids.'

'Anyone who knew her well?' I asked.

'Yeah,' Chelsea said, 'she used to hang around this guy. Don't remember his name. He was older.'

'How old was he?'

She looked at the others for some kind of suggestion.

'Around seventeen,' she said, and the others nodded their approval.

'And you're sure you don't know his name?'

'Nope.'

'Do you know where he lives?'

'Yep. Number twenty-two. That's that one down there.' She pointed to the other end of the court, towards the T-intersection, but it was too far for me to see anything. I removed my notebook from my pocket and jotted down the information.

'Anyone else she used to hang around with?'

'Not that I know of.' To the rest of the group: 'Guys?'

'Don't know.'

'Nope.'

'Nope.'

'Nope.'

It was kind of weird watching these kids answer my questions as if they had one brain shared amongst them. In a way, it made me envious because I never experienced close friendship when I was a child until my last year of high school, when I met a girl named Evelyn Carter who went on to university with me but ended up choosing a career as a high-class prostitute. My parents were always moving from one place to another, making it impossible for me to establish meaningful relationships. Every year, I moved to a new school, saw new faces, faced new expectations. I admit the first time or so, it was kind of fun, but after a while, the novelty wore off and depression settled in. I concentrated on my homework instead, spending my lunch time hunched over newspapers and books.

I removed a bunch of business cards from my handbag and distributed them around.

'If you guys remember anything about Tracy, like anything at all, I'd like you to give me a call.'

They all stared at the cards as if I had just handed out fifty dollar notes.

'And we can call you any time?' the redhead said.

'Any time.'

'Wow, cool.'


The first house I chose was elevated and had a pretty front veranda and rose bushes in the yard, enclosed by a green picket fence. I climbed the steps to the veranda and straightened my jacket.

I knocked twice on the door, my stomach churning. I was used to talking to people I'd never met before, but this time it would be different. I anticipated everyone in the street had learned about Tracy Noland's death and would still be upset by it. And that made me more nervous than usual.

The advantage of conducting interviews so early on was

that everyone would be willing to help, to feel they've done their part in aiding the investigation. Also, if anyone did see something, then their recall of events would be more accurate than if I conducted interviews in another week. I was expecting the customary answers; how Tracy was loved by everyone, how intelligent, beautiful and bright she was; and how they were all going to miss her.

The door opened, and I introduced myself to a forty-something woman dressed in grey tracksuit pants and an apron with 'mum's kitchen' printed in large block letters on the front, overlapping onions, tomatoes, meat and a large carving knife. She told me her name was Susan Griffin.

'Come in,' she said, opening the door fully. Her brown hair was tied in a knot, and she could have done with ten kilos less. 'Excuse the mess. I was making dinner. The kids have gone to play tennis and Darren's still at work. Won't be back until around six-thirty. Maybe you'd like to talk to him then, but he spends all his time at work, so he wouldn't really know much about Tracy.'

I followed her down a wide hallway where arched corbels, ceiling roses, a candelabra light fitting and  blue carpet set the tone.

Packets and tins of food lay all over the kitchen table, and something was on the boil. Stock aroma filled my nostrils, reminding me how hungry I was. The kitchen was spacious with wooden bench tops, a slate floor, timber cupboards, built-in dishwasher, stove and microwave and plenty of storage space.

'I'm making beef goulash,' Susan said, clearing some of the mess from the table. 'You wanna a cuppa of something?'

'Actually, I won't be taking too much of your time. I've got to interview everyone in the street.'

'Sure.' She paused, puzzled for a few seconds and went on, 'What a terrible thing to happen to a child. I'm not going to miss her, but still, that was not a nice way to die.' She saw my inquiring glance and added, 'Oh, don't get me wrong. I didn't want the girl to die or anything, but the few times she came over, she was a real little bugger. Complained about everything. Always fought with other kids in the street. Had a mind of her own, and, God, did she know how to use it. She was so miserable, kind of broke my heart. I never understood how someone so young could be so old.'

Her comments took me by surprise. It never occurred to me that the girl was going to be unpopular. In the back of my mind, I had associated her death with someone cute and kind and sweet, like all the pre-conceived ideas society had about little girls.

'Was she in trouble at home?' I asked.

'Not that I was aware of. Her mother was nice, though. But the other neighbours, they'll tell you the same thing. She was not a nice kid, and no one wanted her to hang around. I'll be surprised if anyone says anything different.'

'Do you know why she was like that?'

'Don't know. You know what it's like. People have all kinds of personalities, and you can see that from the time they're kids. I guess if Tracy ever grew up to be a woman, she'd have been a real pain to live with.'

In the back of my mind, I disagreed with Susan, but I didn't feel like arguing. It was too early at this stage to figure out why Tracy Noland had an attitude problem. And it was certainly a bit premature to conclude she couldn't have changed. As a child, I always sulked and never spoke to anyone. My parents had branded me a problem child, although I'd rather have believed they were problem parents. But I didn't grow-up a misfit, or someone who had a grudge against the entire human race. Maybe Tracy had problems no one really understood or could help her with. Maybe she'd given up on finding someone to listen. And if she was still alive, maybe she would have found that person or sorted herself out one way or the other, like most of us did eventually.

I shifted from one foot to the other and said, 'Did she have any friends at all?'

'Nope. But then, if she did, I wouldn't know. She used to hang around the far end of the street. I only saw her now and then. I'm probably not the best person to talk to.'

I took down her phone number and thanked her for her time.

I visited another two homes after that, which also proved fruitless. No one really knew the girl. They were working people and only had time to mind their own business.

By the time I finished visiting my fourth, it was 10.34 p.m., and I decided it was too late to conduct further interviews. Most people would get annoyed if I knocked at their door late at night. I know I would.

I decided to leave the rest of the inquires for the following day.


Bright and early on Thursday the 18th December, I made my way to the VFSC in Macleod. The traffic was bumper-to-bumper chaos as usual, and it took me an hour and twenty minutes to drive all the way from St Kilda.

The VFSC was located next to Macleod Secondary Technical College and close to La Trobe University Bundoora Campus, where a Graduate Diploma in Forensic Science was offered to science graduates.

I turned left into Forensic Drive. A large blue sign with 'Victorian Forensic Science Centre' by the side of the road told me I was at the right place. The centre was surrounded with grass and bushland.

I drove past a blue, high steel gate and glanced at the security camera attached to the building. A ten-kilometre speed limit sign ordered me to slow down.

The main building was a brown-creamy colour. Gum trees lined the car park.

I parked in the main car park, between a red Toyota Cressida and a Ford Laser, and made my way to the main entrance, where I was greeted by glass sliding doors and a foyer which looked like a mini museum with its historical photographs, awards and trophies.

After clearing myself with Liaison, room C47, I went straight to Frank's office at exactly 7.54 a.m. I had to meet Dr Main at the mortuary by 9.00 a.m., and I hated the thought of being late. He was going to run over the autopsy report with me.

Frank Moore was sipping a mug of freshly brewed coffee when I walked into his office. He looked as if he could have done with some extra sleep. His desk was clutter-free, and there was nothing on the walls other than his degree from RMIT.

We greeted one another, and then he told me Goosh wanted a progress report on the investigation. Christ, we'd only found the body twenty-four hours ago, and already he wanted me to explain what was going down. I swear to God, this man's existence was designed to make my life purgatory.

Frank opened a cream manilla folder in front of him and lay it flat on his desk. He looked up and raised his eyebrows, a signal for me to go-ahead.

'The kids around the area where Tracy lived seem to think she was kind of a loner,' I said, pressing my buns into an orange, injection-moulded chair. There was a chill breeze from the air-conditioning, a nice change from the day's forty-two degree temperature.

Frank looked up and eyed me in a way I couldn't figure out. It was as if he was trying to shed some light on the comment I'd just made, but somehow he seemed lost in his own world.

He pursed his lips for half a second and said, 'Well, you have to ask yourself why. Where do kids learn most of their behaviour from?'

'Home, of course.'

'That's true. So, if a child's got a problem, then you have to look at the source. It a well-known fact that children learn to imitate behaviour and develop a sense of morality in the first five years of life.'

Gee, I thought, when did Frank suddenly became a child psychologist?

'Sure, but Tracy Noland was twelve-years old. Surely by the time you begin primary school, there are factors which influence your behaviour other than your parents. A teacher, whether good or bad, can make a difference in the way you look at the world. What about other school kids? There have been known cases around the world of children who committed suicide after being bullied around by school mates. That type of influence on a child's character can't be ignored, nor pushed on to the parents.'

He puzzled at my response for a few seconds and said, 'Okay, I agree. But I believe that if a child has a problem, it's always a parent-related problem. Jeez, you've done all this psycho-crap at university. You know that ninety-nine percent of people who have problems adapting to society have had problems with their parents. If a child lets himself be bullied at school by other kids, then surely it's the way he's been brought up which is going determine how he will cope with the situation.'

It was hard to argue with Frank, because he was right. I've never met a maladjusted person who didn't come from a dysfunctional family. But was there such a thing as a non-dysfunctional family?

I shifted on my chair, realising I was going to be late for this morning's autopsy at the VIFM. 'Okay, so, maybe she did have problems with her mother. It doesn't mean she killed her. Most people have problems with their mothers. I bet you had problems with your mother. Does this make every mother a killer?'

'I didn't say that.'

'No, not directly. But you're implying it. You're pushing me into a corner. You're trying to make me say the reason Tracy was a problem child was because she was going through hell at home. You want me to confirm her problems at home were the reasons why she was killed. And I don't think I can agree with you. It's far too early to make this type of hypothesis. You're closing your eyes to other possibilities.'

'Yeah, well, I like to think things are black-and-white. Why do *you* people always look for complications when everything can sometimes be so damn obvious?'

I told him about how the kids in the street told me about the seventeen-year-old-or-so Tracy used to hang around with.

'I still think she did it,' he said, refusing to consider what I'd just said. He closed his manilla folder instead.

I stared at him for a few seconds, wondering if he deserved a reply.

Finally, without any warning, I stood from my chair and aimed for the door.

'I'll see you at the mortuary,' I snapped angrily.

# CHAPTER FOUR

I met with Dr Charles W. Main in his office at 9.24 a.m., late for my nine o'clock appointment. He hadn't sent me the autopsy report on Tracy Noland and had suggested by phone the previous night that I come to get a copy at the VIFM.

'I've got some things I'd like to discuss with you,' he said when I called him on my mobile phone on my way to South Melbourne to inform him I would be late.

I parked in the VIFM car park and entered the blue-grey building complex through a glass door. I showed my ID to the front desk and went down a corridor and straight to Dr Main's office.

Before I had time to greet him, he said, 'So, didn't have the stomach for the autopsy?'

I felt heat on my cheeks. 'I never wanted to be a doctor, and watching dead people being split open is not my idea of a good time either.' I also didn't want to explain to him the backbone of every decision I made. That was as much as he needed to know, I felt, even though there wasn't much more I could have added because it was the truth.

He did a quarter turn on his chair and said, 'It's just that you were supposed to be present at the autopsy. You realise your departure from the procedure might cause some problems later in court?'

I nodded embarrassingly, aware that some god-damn defence attorneys would do their best to discredit everything we ever collected as evidence to mount up a solid case. Not to mention that my reputation would be on the line, and some smart alec would suggest that I sit in a few autopsies just to toughen my stance.

'I really didn't mean to walk out. I was sick. What was I supposed to do? Throw up all over your work?'

He smiled, making me glad he had a sense of humour.

'Okay, don't worry too much about it. We've got the entire autopsy on videotape.'

He reached for a twelve-by-fourteen inch yellow envelope, which contained all the paperwork, photographs, legal identification records, fingerprint cards, and autopsy report to date. 'I've finished the preliminary autopsy report. I'm still waiting for analysis on the stomach contents. Other than that, I can already confirm a few things, but this is only preliminary observation.'

I nodded for him to go on.

'Well, I've found no major bruising, laceration or any other kind of injuries on her body, which you would have heard me mention the other day during the autopsy, if you were listening. Other than that, I'd say she died of asphyxiation, lack of oxygen to the brain. Some bruising and slickness of skin in the mouth and nasal area support my findings. She was smothered to death. No doubt at this stage.'

'So, poisoning is out of the question?'

'Can't confirm either way. I'm still waiting for the toxicology results. There's nothing to say she wasn't drugged prior to the killing. Maybe she was put to sleep first, that's definitely a possibility.'

'Anything else?'

'Yes, actually. When I removed and opened the stomach to check its content, I noticed an unusual smell of rose water. The contents were just half-digested food; greens, carrot and chocolate.'

'Any idea what the rose water smell came from?'

'Once again, don't know. Couldn't find any indication. I did make a note of it in my report.' He passed me the pages he'd removed from the manilla folder. 'I've made a copy for you. As soon as I get the toxicology results, I'll have them sent to you.'

'Thanks.' I was truly grateful that Dr Main had bothered with me, especially after I'd been such a nuisance to him the previous year when I broke into his office. Maybe if I'd asked him for what I wanted back then, he would have gladly given it to me, but at the time it felt as if I was on my own and no one would lift a finger to help me.

He flicked through some pages of the documents he had with him. 'Note that the autopsy report is not complete at this stage. What I've given you is something to work on. Be aware that the final report and opinion might differ to what's in there. I wouldn't go and arrest someone just yet on the basis of what's in this preliminary autopsy report.'

I acknowledged his comment by nodding.

I took the duplicate autopsy report, which he handed across the desk, flicked through its contents and thanked Dr Main for his time.

I spent the rest of the day going through the autopsy report. Dr Main had conducted a thorough examination of Tracy Noland, and other than the bruising in the mouth area and the rose-water smell in the stomach, nothing was suspicious, at least nothing which Dr Main hadn't pointed out.

Late afternoon, I returned to Vincent Court where Tracy lived. Before going door-knocking for the second time, I decided to visit Mrs Noland to see how she was coping and also because I was a little curious. I didn't like the way our interview at the St Kilda Road Police Complex had ended, and I was hoping we'd be able to hold another on more civilised grounds. I wasn't sure whether she killed her daughter at this stage, not like Frank who always jumped to conclusions without waiting for enough tangible evidence.

I believed in the way our justice system worked, how someone was innocent until proven guilty. It certainly didn't make it easy for the police, who had to accumulate enough evidence to be able to justify an arrest and mount up a case. But the police were here to help us with truth and justice, and the complexity of their work was to ensure innocent people wouldn't be sent to jail over something they didn't commit. Even though at times there were too many on-going cases, it didn't give police the right to speed up the process just because they wanted to get the work over and done with.

During my years of involvement in criminology, I had seen good cops and people who had no place investigating crimes. Their work was sloppy, and they had no interest in justice, only in advancing their careers and exerting their power. These people were giving the Police community a bad name, clearly undermining the reason they'd been employed in the field of investigation in the first place. And at times, I felt Frank was bordering on that type of behaviour, although I'd never be brave enough to tell him to his face. My idea of justice was not merely to brown-nose everyone above me, or in my case anyone who'd have something to say when my contract would be up for review, but to serve the people of this country, the survivors, the victims and those whose lives had been abruptly shortened by another human being.

When Mrs Noland opened the front door, she didn't seem surprised to see me.

'Come in,' she said, while pushing the fly-screen towards me.

I followed her down the hallway with its arches, corbels and ceiling roses.

'Would you like something to drink?' she asked as we stepped into the kitchen.

'Coffee would be nice.'

I commented on her home being nice with its pale-green carpet and pale tones, and she began a monologue about how the three-bedroom house had been re-stumped, rewired, re-plastered and partly re-plumbed five years ago. The fireplaces and high ceilings had been reinstated, highlighting its Victorian heritage. The kitchen was modern and very functional with plenty of cupboard space. A skylight above my head kept the room bright and cheerful. The kitchen opened to a living room, which opened to a courtyard garden, where I noticed a large covered deck area, a brick barbecue and parking space for two cars.

While she was busy filling two mugs of instant coffee with hot water, I said, 'I talked to some of your neighbours yesterday. They told me Tracy wasn't very friendly with the other kids.'

She didn't respond, obviously waiting for me to make my point.

'They said she spent a great deal of time by herself and

with a kid down the road. He lives at number twenty-two.'

Without turning around, she said, 'I know.' Her tone had changed from warm and mellow to sharp and snappy. She didn't seriously believe I came here for coffee and biscuits?

I pushed on. 'Did you know the young man Tracy used to hang around with?'

'No, but I've seen him with her now and then.'

'And that didn't worry you?'

She turned around and locked her eyes into mine, 'Why? Should it have?'

I grabbed the mug of coffee she handed me. 'Doesn't it strike you as strange that a seventeen-year old boy spends a lot of time with a twelve-year old girl?'

'Should it? No one else talked to her.'

I didn't know if she was playing me or was truly naive.

I went on, 'Well, I feel that if it was my daughter, I'd be damn worried.'

'Well, you're not me,' she snapped, 'and frankly there was nothing admirable about Tracy. I'm sick and tired of people putting her on a pedestal when she was nothing more than a sulky child. It's my daughter, and I'm devastated that she was killed, but she wasn't the angel you're trying to make her be. All I want you to do is find the killer and stop poking at me. Just because I'm a housewife, you think I must be dumb. I know what you people are playing at. You think I did it, so you're going to bombard me with all those silly questions until I crack under pressure and confess. Well, I tell you now, you're wasting your time. I didn't kill her, so you better start looking somewhere else.'

I stood speechless with my mug of coffee untouched. I had never been certain that Mrs Noland had killed her daughter. But her relationship with Tracy seemed somehow unorthodox, not what I would call in my books a typical mother-daughter relationship. Now I more or less understood where Frank was coming from. Her defensive attitude didn't portray her in the best light. If I hadn't known better, I'd think the next thing she'd tell me would be that Tracy deserved to die.

I sipped a mouthful of coffee while thinking carefully about what I was about to say next. I really wanted to get to the bottom of this, to clear the air and get everything out in the open. Whether she killed Tracy or not, making her an enemy would only complicate the investigation.

'I didn't mean to offend you, Mrs Noland,' I said. 'It's just that with cases like these, we always have to look at the parents of the victim first. It's a procedure we must consider before pushing further. Surely, you can understand that.'

'I understand,' she said as if cued, but not giving away what was really on her mind.

'There's no indication that you've killed your daughter. All I'm trying to accomplish at this stage is to establish a list of people who knew her. It's unlikely, I believe, that she was killed by a complete stranger. It does happen, but in the majority of cases I've worked with, the victim has always been known to the killer.' I took another mouthful of coffee. Then: 'In your opinion, do you have an idea of who might have been interested in getting rid of your daughter?'

Her eyes softened. Obviously she was relieved I wasn't just pointing a finger at her.

'I can't think of anyone. Tracy didn't have family other than me. She never met her father, and my parents live in Queensland. They never call, so I don't bother.'

'Have you begun a relationship with anyone recently?'

She seemed puzzled.

I elaborated, 'You know, a boyfriend, someone staying over?'

'I wish. I'm a single mother, and believe me, single mothers don't get to have many men coming in and out of their lives.'

Now didn't seem like the appropriate time to tell her I was also a single mother, who had more men after her than she could handle.

'What about friends? Could anyone have been jealous of you or Tracy for any reason? Can you think of anyone who might have wanted revenge of one kind or another?'

Mrs Noland stared vacantly at the empty space in front of her. 'I don't think so,' she finally said, emptying the rest of her mug into the sink. 'I really don't think I can help you. My life is so bare of other people, I can't see a connection between who I know and what happened to Tracy. I'm really not that important for someone to want to revenge themselves against me. All I want is the killer to be found so I can get on with my life.'

'I understand,' I said.

When Mrs Noland walked me to the door, I added, 'I might come back some other time. Maybe I'll need you to come down to the station to answer more questions.'

She gave me a stern look. I thought she was about to hit me.

'Look, Dr Melina,' she said, surprising me by remembering my name and title, 'I don't have anything else to say to the police. I've already told you everything I know. I'm getting tired of repeating myself. Don't you keep all this stuff on record?'

'It's procedural stuff.'

'Yeah, well, procedural, my arse. Get that sonofabitch and stop harassing me.'

She slammed the door in my face.

She could have punched me in the nose, the effect was the same.


It was 9.32 p.m. when I finished visiting my sixth house. As anticipated, everyone came up with the same story: Tracy Noland didn't deserve to die, but, hell, was she a troublesome and miserable child.

All that my findings had achieved was to get me depressed. Not only was I investigating the death of child, but to add to the difficulty, the child was detested by everyone who ever met her. Hell, for all I knew so far the killer could have been any of the people I had interviewed. My list of suspects was now inconclusive because there were far too many people who could have been the ideal killer. I was looking for some kind of inconsistency of character, something in a person which would trigger my mind.

I decided to make house number seven the last one for the day. I would continue the rest of the interviews first thing the following morning.

The entire street was plunged into darkness, giving it a creepy feeling.

A mild chill rippled down my body, despite the high-twenties temperature.

Not a soul in sight.

Did people sneak in and out of their homes through the back door? If Tracy Noland had been abducted in her own street, it was easy to understand why.

House number seven was actually the biggest one in the cul-de-sac—a double-storey Edwardian house with grey rendering and French windows and a front yard which made the botanical gardens look like a backyard. Whoever lived there must have had a lot of money to burn or invest, and nothing much to do other than gardening.

There was a new, grey Mazda 626 parked in the cobblestone driveway, one which I had seen recently advertised in one of the weekend newspapers. Dual air bags and some kind of steel vertical crash-proof column to save the occupants from turning into sardines in sauce if the car ever rolled over.

According to the size of the house, the maintenance of the front yard, and the late model of the car, the occupants had to be retired. When the front door opened on the fourth knock, I realised I'd been right. I hadn't expected the door to be answered so suddenly, and, as a result, I felt my pulse race.

'I saw you coming from down the street,' said the old man with white hair. 'Great view from the living room. I can see the entire street from there. Come in, I'll show you.'

The old man's face was loosened by extra flesh, and I guessed he must have been overweight at a younger age. Even though he was at home, he wore a blue shirt and a mismatched brown tie with slacks. He reminded me of those old people at the Balaclava Hotel, where I usually had my Sunday lunch, hunched over the bar, drinking as if they were in a Guinness Book of Record challenge, dressed in their slacks, shirts and ties, which they'd been wearing for the last forty years.

I was surprised that he didn't even ask me who I was and why I was here.

My high heels sank into a thick burgundy carpet, as I followed him down the hallway.

'This way,' he said before I had time to say a word.

Three ceramics ducks hung on a wall, following each other on their way to the other end of the hallway.

The inside of the house smelled of recent cooking, but I couldn't figure out exactly what the familiar sweet aroma was.

I followed the old man past an entrance to the right into

what I presumed was the living room. The furniture was a mixture of new and old, mismatched dark woods and pines with frames and useless bric-a-brac dangling from every conceivable place. I immediately sensed no woman lived in the house.

The old man was standing erect in front of a huge bay window, which I'd noticed when I'd walked up the stairs before. His white hair was thinning at the back, giving way to pink flesh and a mild skin rash.

'See what I mean. Look at that.' He waved his arm across the window as if he was a presenter on *Sale Of The Century*. 'The entire street, I told you.'

I rattled my throat and said, 'Do you have any idea who I am and why I'm here?'

He turned around. 'You're a cop or something. It's about little Tracy. I saw you going from house to house, so I figured out it had something to do with Tracy. Plus I rang the police yesterday to talk to them. They took a message and said the person in charge of the investigation would get in touch with me.' Now I remembered the phone message Frank mentioned. So, this was the person who called.

The old man smiled with all his teeth, which surprisingly did look as if they were his. His face was pleasant and looked as if it had been etched from leather. I kind of liked him straight away. There seemed to be something honest about him, like a no-nonsense, no-bullshit attitude, which is hard to find in this day and age.

I presented my hand which he shook vigorously. 'I'm Dr Kristina Melina from the Victorian Forensic Science Centre. You're right. I'm investigating the murder of Tracy Noland.'

'I'm Jason Harvey.' His grey eyes gazed into mine for a few seconds. 'An awful tragedy, Dr Melina. She was such a lovely little girl. Always playing with the other kids, always friendly.'

I froze for a few seconds, puzzled by what he'd just told me. 'I heard she didn't get on that well with other kids.'

He shrugged and said, 'You know what people are like. Gossip. She was just a young girl. Say, you wouldn't want anything to drink? I can make you a coffee. Tea, maybe? How about a glass of water.'

'I'm fine, thank you.' I looked down the darkened street

52

from his window. He was right about being able to see the whole street. Maybe he did see something that would help my investigation. It was interesting that he found Tracy a friendly person. Maybe he never really spoke to her. If he saw her from his lounge room window, the impression must have been that she was getting on fine with everyone else.

'Did you see much of Tracy Noland from your window? I heard from the other kids that she was friendly with a seventeen-year old.' I removed a notebook from my handbag, flipped a couple pages and added, 'who lives at number twenty-two, down the end of the street. Ever heard of this young man?'

'Oh, yes. She was always hanging around Malcom, especially in the evening. That's why I called the police. Don't really like him. He's kind of old for her. I mean the girl was only ten or eleven, and he's seventeen. Don't understand why no one said anything. If you ask me, I reckon he did it. Was too fond of her. And I think she kind of liked him too. Straight after school, she went and sat on his fence, waiting for him to come back from god-knows-where. Then they stayed outside, talking for hours.'

The plot was thickening. I had to admit this was not common behaviour for a twelve-year-old and a seventeen-year-old. I certainly would be more than concerned if Michael hung around a twelve-year old girl at the age of seventeen. I wondered if his parents were aware of the friendship.

'Did he ever take her inside his home?'

'Haven't seen him do that. But then, I'm not in front of the window twenty-four hours a day. There's a rumour going around that he has an extensive amount of photographs in his house, things he'd taken himself. Pictures of kids, I heard.' He winked at me, but I wasn't sure what it meant.

'And who told you?'

'Just a rumour. People talk. I've never seen the pictures, but you know, rumours usually come from somewhere.'

I agreed with him on that point. The kids in the street had already told me the same thing. 'And do you think he took pictures of Tracy Noland?'

'I don't know. I shiver at the thought. It made me want to turn away and not think about what he was up to. I guess I should have, but then there was nothing much I could have done. She chose to befriend him. Don't know what she saw. The kid is good for nothing. Wastes his life. Today's generation. Computers, television and sex. It wasn't like that when I was a young man. We used to go out, get some fresh air, live our lives. But today's kids, they're just so messed up inside. Kind of sad, if you ask me.'

Although I didn't agree with his analysis of today's generation, he'd been so helpful that I hated to contradict him. The fact was if less people complained about youth and alienated teenagers, the less problems we would have with them. But on the other hand, I could understand Jason's frustration. Having lived an entire life, it wasn't always easy to reject the ideals and beliefs accumulated over the years.

'You're sure you don't want anything to drink?' he added. 'It's really not a problem.'

'No, thank you. It's actually getting quite late, and I should let you get some sleep. I still have to get home and eat something.'

He waved his hand. 'Ah, don't worry. I haven't eaten either. Tell you what, I'll make something for the two of us.'

I thought about Michael at home all by himself and said, 'I really have to get home. I've got a son waiting for me.'

He shrugged. 'Oh, well. It would have been nice to have some company.'

I noticed the wetness in his eyes and couldn't help feeling sorry for him. He reminded me of my mother who died of a sleeping-pill overdose two days before I turned sixteen. My father had been convicted of child abuse six months prior, making me a ward of the state. Jason Harvey wore the same expression my mother did when my father was found guilty, and it broke my heart knowing this old man was probably spending a good deal of his time all by himself, feeling alone and isolated like my mother must have felt when she knew what my father had done. Human loneliness had a way of etching itself on its victims' faces.

'I'd love to have a bite one day,' I said, 'but tonight is really not the right time.'

'What about tomorrow?' His eyes glittered with excitement.

'Mmm...'

'That would be great. We could talk more. I'd love to help.

It broke my heart when I heard the poor girl got killed.' He's face creased, and I could feel his pain.

He walked me down the hallway and to the front door.

'How do you keep busy during the daytime?' I asked as he unlocked the door.

'I worked as a banker for thirty years. Now I'm a professional entertainer.'

'An entertainer?'

'I do mind reading acts at the local RSL club two night a week and on the weekend.'

'Well, that's great. I better keep my thoughts on the straight and narrow. And all this time I was thinking you'd be spending most of your time between these four walls.'

He laughed gently and said, 'You're a nice person. It's written all over you. I knew it the moment you walked into my home.'

I blushed. 'Thank you, Mr Harvey, that's a lovely thing to say.'

'You can call me Jason. Out there with the formalities. Why don't you come back for some lunch? We can talk some more.'

'All right, Jason. Saturday, lunch. You've got a date.' I wasn't sure why I agreed, but it must have been him insisting. It was a gut-feeling, impulsive response. Although he wanted to have lunch the following day, I thought I'd give myself an extra two days, just to ensure I wouldn't be tied up with important work. The reality was that I'd probably be up to my neck with this investigation, seven days a week for the next few months.

He smiled and said, 'Wish I was thirty years younger.'

I was about to shake his hand, but he took me by surprise and gave me a hug instead. I don't know why, but I felt all mushy inside, tears coming to my eyes. Something about Mr Harvey kept reminding me of the father I never had. Maybe it was the gentleness in his smile or the warmth in his eyes. His citrus aftershave smelled familiar, but I couldn't place it. Probably one of those cheap bottles from K-mart or Safeway that my son was using.

While making my way down the stairs and towards my car at the opening of Vincent Court, I could feel his stare roaming from the large bay window of his living room. I glanced over my shoulder a few times, but couldn't see a thing.

And yet I knew he was watching me walk off into the darkness of the night.

# CHAPTER FIVE

I jumped out of bed when the telephone on my side table went off at 9.02 a.m. I couldn't believe I'd slept in, but since I'd suffered from insomnia from the moment I hit the sack, it didn't exactly surprise me that I felt as if I'd only slept for a couple of hours.

At 11.32 p.m. the previous night, I turned off the light of my bedroom, my mind filled with all the interviews I'd conducted during the day. Perhaps the strangest thing was that everyone felt Tracy Noland had been a bad person, except for Jason Harvey. Maybe it was because of his mind reading ability, a skill I didn't truly believe he possessed, but it sounded nice to theorise that only he could see goodness in Tracy Noland because he could read her mind.

And then there was that Malcom person who took pictures. I knew that the very next morning I would have to make a priority visit to his place. The rumour of his photographic collection matched the unusual personality characteristic I'd been hoping for. At least now I had a probable suspect.

I'd fallen asleep at 1.22 a.m. believing this case would be resolved in no time.

But this morning, Friday the 19th December, my sleep was interrupted once more by the damned telephone.

'Dr Melina?'

'Yes?'

'Goosh. I'd like to see you in my office at ten o'clock.'

I rubbed my eyes with my left hand. 'This morning?'

'Yes, this morning. It's about the Tracy Noland case. Is there a problem?'

'No, no, I was just—'

'Good, then, I'll see you at ten.'

He hung up before I had time to say another word.

Not a nice way to wake up in the morning.

I showered and dressed in under twenty minutes. Breakfast consisted of a multivitamin and an E-supplement, washed down with a cup of coffee, no sugar, no milk. Not a breakfast rich in fibre, but as far as fat content was concerned, it wasn't something I had to worry about.

I made my way down from my second-floor apartment on Chapel Street, checked the letter-box for mail, even though I knew the mail wouldn't arrive until late afternoon, and slid into the driver's seat of my Lancer.

I cracked the gears into reverse, did a u-turn in the driveway, and came out on Chapel Street, between the kerbside and a green tram stopped at a red light, dropping off passengers. When the light went green, I sped and overtook the tram. I took a left on Princes Highway, where the Astor Theatre resides and headed towards the police complex on St Kilda Road.

I unwound the driver's window fully, letting a cool breeze roam through my auburn hair. Grey clouds hovered over the South-West, giving me hope that it wasn't going to be another thirty-five-degree day. Although I was wearing marine pants with matching jacket and a white blouse, I'd taken the precaution of packing a dress in the boot in case the weather turned Melbourne into something which resembled the inside of a baker's oven.

A fresh smell of seawater blended with exhaust fumes, and I could see the deadly smog slowly rising above the skyscrapers, turning city dwellers' lungs into two charcoal sponges, which would eventually claim many lives in the form of asthma and heart attacks.

The traffic was slightly congested, but not as chaotic as it would have been half an hour ago. By nine o'clock most office staff had parked their cars somewhere and begun sorting through their in-trays or gossiping over their first cup of coffee, leaving the main roads to late risers, the unemployed, housewives, company directors, CEOs and self-employed people like me.

It was 9.53 a.m. when I parked in front of the building at 412 St Kilda Road. There were no parking spaces left outside, so I pulled into a police-restricted parking area, even though I wasn't actually a police person as such.

After passing the security check-point, I climbed into the elevator, realising it was not even ten o'clock. It kind of annoyed me that I made it on time. Goosh would think more of his power over me now. He clicked his fingers, and I was there on the spot. Oh, well, I didn't feel like waiting in a sandwich shop with an over-priced coffee and stale croissant from the previous day.

Goosh's secretary, a pretty twenty-year-old something, with hair the colour of winter wheat and striking blue irises, did a sensual thing with her lips, letting out a high-pitched noise I couldn't make out, and with her hand directed me through to his office. Bad mistake employing personal assistants who are too good looking, I thought. People always wondered why this woman had been hired by Goosh in the first place. She looked more like someone you'd find on the cover of *Dolly* -and yes, she did look *that* young and girlish- than the personal assistant to the Deputy Commissioner of Police. As my feet sank into the deep red, carpet of the Commissioner's office, I wondered if his wife had ever met his come-and-fuck-me assistant.

'Take a seat,' he commanded before I had time to say greetings. Hallelujah, it was going to be one of those days, I could feel it. 'Do you want to tell me what's going on?' His face was flushed, as it always was whenever he got into a confrontation with me.

I knitted my brows and remained on my feet, arms crossed over my chest, a ping-pong ball in my throat. I knew he didn't call me up to his office to have me decorated with a bravery award.

He began matter-of-factly, 'I believe you've begun work on the Noland murder.'

'That's what we agreed on.'

'Don't have a problem with what we agreed on. It's the after development which is complicating matters. You told Frank Moore you were going to investigate this case *after* you told me

59

you wanted someone to replace you. And *after* I already arranged for an alternative investigator, you decide, all by yourself, that you'll keep on investigating. What are you trying to do? Make me look like an idiot?'

*That wouldn't be too difficult.*

I shifted from one foot to the other and did a juggling act inside my head. 'I analysed the situation and deduced that since I'd begun working on this case, I might as well finish it. I thought that's what you'd wanted all along. Plus Mrs Noland begged me to find her daughter's killer when I saw her at the mortuary. I promised her I would do my best. I can't let her down.'

He gave me a look school teachers reserve for students who come late to class, especially those who came up with the most pathetic excuses, stories they made up thirty seconds before walking into the classroom.

'On the subject of Mrs Noland,' he retorted, 'she's placed a harassment complaint against the department and against you.'

'Really?' I was genuinely surprised.

'She says you've been at her place, throwing all these accusations at her, calling her a murderer. Now, that's a really intelligent thing to say since Frank has reason to believe she might well be the one who committed the crime.'

I felt my brain drilling through the back of my skull. If there ever was an example of mindless exaggeration, that had to be it. Problem was I didn't know who was stretching the truth by half a city block. Mrs Noland or Goosh? And why was Frank reporting to Goosh every five minutes? I was in charge of this investigation, not him.

'Sir, let me assure you that I did not intimidate Mrs Noland in any way.' I forced myself to remain in control of my so-called temper. I've been known to blow off steam in front of people I should have respected.

'Look, you can stand here and tell me all you want. Fact is she's out of reach.' He pointed to the chair opposite him. 'And take a seat while I'm talking to you. You're giving me a head-spin.' His complexion had turned a deeper red and became even more obvious in contrast with his crop-styled salt-and-pepper hair. I knew he was trying hard to push me beyond my threshold point so that he would have something else to complain about.

I took the seat because I began to feel awkward standing up and not because he told me to do so. 'What do you mean out of reach?' I asked, elaborating on his last question.

'What do I mean out of reach?' he said, imitating my tone of voice. 'What I mean is that she got herself a solicitor, and we can't ask her any more fuckin' questions with him around telling her *you don't have to answer that* every thirty seconds! That's what I mean. What I mean is that Frank Moore felt she was a number one suspect, and now we can't even touch her.'

'Get a court order.'

'With what? You haven't given us anything yet.'

I wanted to jump over his desk and dig my nails into his whitish, fleshy throat. How this man ever got this high in rank was beyond any common sense. Why was it that only assholes made it to the top?

'I've only been on this case for a day and a bit. Will you give me a break?' My voice began to lose its confidence. I felt my hands shaking and made them into fists.

'I'll give you a break, all right. You've got two weeks to solve this damn thing, or I'll have you replaced before you get time to harass someone else.' To himself: 'God dammit! Do I have to go through this every time?'

It was all uphill from there.

I stood from my chair and glared into his eyes. 'Thanks for your help, Mr Goosh, I don't know where I'd be without you.'

He stared at me, a confused expression on his face, trying to figure out whether I'd just given him a compliment or insulted him. His lips were about to form a syllable, but I never gave him a chance.

'Have a good day, sir.'

I spun on my heels and headed straight for the door.

I was halfway down the hallway when I heard the sound of my name coming from his office, followed by the squeaky voice of his secretary.

I ignored both and hurried to the elevator.

When I got back home, I felt bewildered that Mrs Noland had put in a complaint against me. Why would a mother of a murdered child refuse to cooperate with the investigator-in-charge? If it was my child, I would have spoken to anyone who asked just to find the bastard who did it. She didn't seem to mind me talking to her early on when I was at her place, until the last minute that was, when she slammed the door in my face. Sometimes it felt as if this whole damn world was running backwards.

I slipped off my shoes and went straight to the lounge room where I played *Look to the East*, an album by the Los Angeles Jazz Quartet, an acoustic-based group of a younger generation that specialises in a mixture of older standards by jazz greats and their own original material written by each member of the group. The space drowned in an atmosphere of jazz I would normally associate with Sundays and cappuccinos.

I poured myself a Dr Pepper with ice in a large glass in the kitchen, walked back to the lounge room, and threw myself on the floral sofa, trying to shake off my anger.

And it worked

I loved this place. I moved into the apartment complex when I came back from the USA eight years ago, after graduating from the FBI's National Academy. The real estate agent advertised it as New York living, with its graffiti on the walls and its nine parking spaces for eighteen apartments. But the inside of my apartment was filled with imaginative furniture and items. I spent a great deal of time making sure it was done to my taste. Decorating an apartment was not a cheap thing to do, but I wanted to feel comfortable in a world where comfort was becoming more and more a luxury rather than a right.

In the main bedroom, a pine-bed-platform was built at cupboard floor level. The mezzanine had been lowered to give enough height for standing. Away from the wall, a flight of stairs created a screen for the bathroom entrance and extra storage space. Additional storage space nested beside the bed. Next to the bathroom was my study with a magnificent panoramic view of Chapel Street through a corner bay window.

Michael's room was next to mine and was kept shut most of the time. He was rarely home during the week. Often he stayed over at his Chris's, his buddy from school, and now that he was on holidays, he spent most of his time there.

I loved Michael so much, but I don't think he realised. Maybe I didn't show it enough. The previous year we had a fall-out because we never saw enough of each other. And although I promised to make an effort to devote more time to our relationship, so far my promise had only been half kept.

I could hear a tram outside, a car blasting its horn, and construction workers renovating apartments across the street, which had burnt down two months ago in the middle of the night. I never heard the five fire engines and other emergency vehicles because of my habit of sleeping with ear plugs. The only thing which woke me up was the telephone or the alarm clock, which were both at close proximity.

I drank half my Dr Pepper in one-go. I loved the stuff more than black coffee, especially on hot summer days.

I stretched my legs across the two-seater and wondered how much more I could take. Things were meant to be easier in your thirties, but I was only a year away from my forties, and I'd never felt so alienated in my entire life. I thanked God that at least I had a man in my life who took me as I was and didn't ask me to change. Although I didn't see much of Phillip, no thanks to my unorthodox choice of career, I was always looking forward to the weekends when he, Michael and I spent some time together. But even though it was almost twelve noon on a Friday, the weekend felt like miles away. Phillip was at work, Michael at his friend's, and I felt like the most dejected person on this end of Chapel Street.

I extended my hand and reached for the tortoise-shell telephone on a side table next the sofa. I punched in Phillip's work number, which by now I did automatically without remembering what number I was dialling. The Los Angeles Jazz Quarter was playing track six on the album when I paused it with the remote control.

'It's me.'

'I was hoping you'd call,' he said almost in a whisper. His voice felt so close to me, I could almost feel his warm breath on my neck, smell his Paco Rabanne whisking out of a shirt I could only visualise. 'What's up.'

'You busy?'

'It's cool. We can talk.' Then: 'You sound worried.'

'I'm just having a hard time.' I explained what went on that morning at Goosh's office.

'Don't worry,' he reassured me. 'The guy's a jerk, anyway.'

'Doesn't make him more bearable.'

'Hey, look, everyone has to put up with at least one asshole in their lives. It's not the end of the world, baby, cheer up.'

It felt strange listening to him calling me baby. I was used to Katrina, Dr Melina and some derogatory terms, but not baby. I wasn't sure if I liked it or not. It made me feel loved and secure, but at the same time I couldn't help thinking he was referring to some kind of Barbie doll.

We made small talk about his project. I remained polite, but it was hard for me to get interested in telecommunications. I did some investigative work for his firm last year, and it was kind of boring, but it paid the mortgage between homicides. I wished at times Phillip had a more interesting job, something in my line of expertise, but I knew I was being unfair. I would have hated it if he wanted me to be any different, and that made me realise I shouldn't expect anything from him. That's how my first marriage ended soon after I gave birth to Michael. We expected so much of each other, promised we would change, become better, but in the end, one can only be oneself. It took me a long time to realise that alone we're born, and alone we'll be for the rest of our lives, and the more we expect from each other, the more we grow apart. I just wanted to enjoy someone else's company now and then, someone who made me feel like a woman and not some god-damn thumb-pushed computer chip on a circuit board. Nearly forty, and I've never felt so much the need to be loved and make love.

We agreed to go to Camberwell Market on Sunday, just to let off steam and enjoy some parts of our lives.

At around 11.30 a.m., I walked up Chapel Street to the Prahran Post Office. I checked my postal box for mail, but there was only a white, sealed envelope with a window addressed to the box holder, asking me if I wanted to become a winner this year. I dropped it straight into the plastic bin provided. Sometimes I wondered what was the point of having a postal box when half the time it was filled with junk mail.

While eating a Vegie Whooper from Hungry Jack's at the corner of High and Chapel Streets, and washing it down with a Coke and ice, I decided to resume my interviews in Vincent Court. I was uncertain on how to approach Malcom, the seventeen-year old kid whom Jason Harvey, Mrs Noland and the kids in the neighbourhood mentioned. Maybe I would need to talk to Frank first and come up with a clever way of conducting the interrogation. I didn't want to frighten the young man, just in case he was the murderer. The last thing I needed was someone defensive and unwilling to cooperate. It was bad enough Mrs Noland kicked me in the back. Maybe Frank did see things clearly. As current statistics stood, in eleven out of twelve child cases, a direct family member was the culprit. And the way Mrs Noland had barricaded herself with defence solicitors and wild accusations, I was now uncertain she had nothing to do with her daughter's death.

As I walked back down Chapel Street, I reasoned it would be better if I interviewed Malcom in his own environment, preferably at home like the rest of the neighbours. In fact, all I had to do was pretend this was just a routine chat rather than an interview, just like the ones I conducted with the other neighbours.

By 6.00 p.m., I had seen fifteen of Tracy Noland's neighbours, all of them with the same opinion. In general, they agreed Tracy Noland was an unpleasant child, who went out of her way to be disliked. I decided to give it a rest and continue the interrogations the following morning. I wanted to spend some quality time with Michael when I got home. I only had five more houses to go, other than Malcom's, which I would cover just before lunch the following day. I had promised Jason Harvey a visit and intended to keep my word. It would also give me the opportunity to pick his brain a little deeper.

The evening was uneventful, so Michael and I borrowed 'Witness' from the video shop. I'd seen it before, a story about a cop played by Harrison Ford who gets caught in the middle of police corruption and finds himself responsible for the life of a young Amish boy and his mother. I told Michael it was good because I had seen it at the cinema when it came out in 1984, but he found it too slow for his taste. I had to admit it wasn't as good as I'd remembered. Michael said we should have taken out 'Alien 3' because he hadn't seen it yet. I told him he was too young to watch that kind of mindless violence.

We shared a litre of Sara Lee chocolate ice-cream before hitting the sack.

# CHAPTER SIX

There was one woman who seemed to be of the same opinion as Jason Harvey. Her name was Linda Coleman, and she lived down the other side of Vincent Court, close to where the street began at the T-intersection. She was the last person I had yet to visit, other than Malcom.

Linda Coleman received me at around 11.30 a.m., giving me just on half an hour before I would join Jason Harvey for lunch. As soon as I walked inside her brick veneer home, she made me sit in the lounge room while she raced to the kitchen to make a 'cuppatea', despite my insistence that I'd already swallowed two cups of coffee at her next door neighbour's.

While she was busy with her tea-making, she yelled from the kitchen, without me asking, that she was currently working as a nurse at St Patrick's hospital. It wasn't easy doing shift work at her age, she pointed out.

I wrestled with a green cushion pushing into my lower back on the brown, leather couch. Finally, after punching it into shapes a few times, I tossed it on a chair next to a fish tank. My eyes wandered around the lounge, observing its gas-log fire, French doors and ornate beams in the ceiling. The contents reminded me of a garage sale assembled into one room. I'd never seen so much junk under one roof. Empty cereal packets, various plastic dolls, including three versions of Ken and Barbie, plants, hundreds of magazines piled up like Towers of Pisa, a brown box of chocolate with gold lettering half open, enough miniature plastic animals to fill the Melbourne Zoo, posters of Neighbours' characters pulled-out from TV Week and other soap magazines, unopened six and twelve packs of toilet rolls (in the lounge room!), and three television sets, including one being used to house an assorted candle collection. Sunlight filtered itself across the dirty window pane, highlighting particles of dust so large and numerous, I wondered if they would trigger an asthma attack.

'I did notice young Tracy was waiting after school not far from Malcom's home,' Linda Coleman volunteered as she walked back in the room with two cups of tea on a yellow plastic tray. 'It was as if she actually had arranged to meet with him. Malcom seemed fond of her, which I found rather worrisome when you take their age into consideration.'

She placed the tray on a coffee table, amongst various copies of Women's Weekly, Who magazine, TV Week, and That's Life.

Linda Coleman was a generous woman with a round face and arms bigger than my thighs. Her dark-brown hair was short and spiked with gel, making her look like a fashion victim from the mid-eighties. When she handed me my cup of tea, I noticed a tattoo of a rose bush on her left arm, half-concealed by a lime-coloured fleecy top with sleeves pulled up to her elbows. There was something very masculine about Ms Coleman, and the overall effect was kind of overwhelming. She certainly had presence, enough to make me shrink in my seat with my red floral dress, little black shoes and auburn hair sculptured into a ponytail - it was Saturday so I wore my casual gear. The word 'bloke' came to mind as I sipped from my cup.

'Do you have any idea who could have killed Tracy Noland?' I asked, having suddenly decided I didn't want to spend more time than necessary alone with that woman. It wasn't that I had something against large woman, but I feared this one might have the sudden impulse of making a pass at me, a thrill which I cared not to experience. I was a man's woman, no doubt in my mind. No two-way street in my bedroom habits, not that I was aware of to date.

She turned around and locked her grey eyes into mine. 'I think Malcom did it,' she said as if cued. 'Of course, it's only my word, but since you're asking, don't waste your time anywhere else. Men like him scare the shit out of me.'

I hadn't met Malcom yet, but I wondered how anyone could scare the pants off Linda Coleman without fearing for his life first. One smack with that king-sized fist of hers, and the result would be major facial reconstruction and on-going psychological counselling for the next twenty-five years.

She went on, 'I'm telling you, this young man is up to no good. Hell, she was only a little baby. What are you guys doing anyway? He should be behind bars by now. Aren't you going to arrest him? The whole street knows he did it. It's immoral to let him come and go as he pleases.'

I spilled some of my tea on the floor, but she didn't seem to notice. Her assertive tone took me by surprise. Not only did she seem certain the young man killed Tracy Noland, but she was even willing to instruct me on investigative procedures and my moral duties to the world.

'Did you know Tracy well?' I asked.

'Me? As well as anyone else in the neighbourhood. I work eight to ten hours a day, so I guess some people got to see her more often than I did. But, hell, you had to be blind not to see what was going on.'

'What *was* going on?'

She gave me a sheepish smile. 'You're not playing games with me?'

'I'm sorry?'

'You know about the photos Malcom took?'

I raised one brow and replied, 'Someone mentioned he took pictures, yes, but I haven't had a chance to look at them to date.'

She gulped the contents of her cup in one go and said, 'Well, I suggest you get your arse over there ASAP and check out the evidence. There's enough shit in his room to bring back the death penalty.'

'Have you ever been to his room?'

'What the hell would I be doing in his room?'

'Then how do you know about all the photos?'

She puzzled for a few seconds and said, 'The same way as you do. People talk.'

People did talk, indeed.

Maybe too much.

There was a pause.

'And who told you about the photos?' I probed. I could tell by the look on her face I'd asked a question she wanted to avoid answering.

'Well, now, there are things which are better kept between friends.'

'I respect your integrity, but when it comes to investigating the death of a twelve-year-old child, secrets have to come out of the closet.'

'I don't see how the identity of who told me about Malcom's photos would help in any way. Would you like to be known as a snoop around the neighbourhood?'

I placed my empty cup of tea on the coffee table, amidst the magazines, and swallowed hard. 'I think you're missing the point here. If you're so forward and certain about Malcom's guilt, why don't you help me and point me in the right direction?'

'I've already done that. Go and knock on his door. He's as guilty as hell.'

'Well, I don't know that for a fact. I like to work out things for myself —'

'Long enough for someone else to get killed?' she interrupted. 'You cops are all the same. You talk and talk, and take so much time to work out the *ifs* and *whys* and *hows*, nothing ever gets done. It's like the other day, some dickhead in the street threatens me, says he's going to chop my head off and kill all the Asians. I go to the police station to report it, and you know what they tell me?'

I looked at her, puzzled.

'Come back when he's done something. So, I say, should I fill in a report? And they go no, there's no need to, the guy hasn't done anything. And I say, well, what am I supposed to do? Wait until I'm dead before you do something? And they look at me like if I'm some kind of moron. I tell you, the way things are becoming around here, nothing surprises me any more.'

I was left speechless.

I thanked her for her time and made my way to Jason Harvey's home.

Jason Harvey made ham, cheese and salad sandwiches for

lunch. I chewed on my white sliced bread with little enthusiasm, but without the nerve to tell him what I really thought of white bread sandwiches. The last time I ate white sliced bread sandwiches was at high school. The agonising daily routine of finding the same thing inside my lunch day-in, day-out put me off white sliced bread forever.

A chunk of bread stuck to my palate. I struggled to open my mouth.

'I visited one of your neighbours this morning, and she told me about Malcom's photographs as well.'

Jason took one big bite of his sandwich, his eyes gleaming, and said, 'I told you. I knew he was up to no good.'

'But I haven't seen the pictures yet.'

'Yes, but trust me, when he took these pictures, he had something in mind. I'm telling you, from where you're standing, it might look like an innocent pastime, but I know what goes on in his head. I've seen young men like him all my life. Fired up on the inside with a burning desire to appease his burning lust. Believe me, it wasn't just pictures he had in mind.'

'What was it then?' I finished my sandwich and immediately emptied my glass of water.

'What do you think? You're the cop, Dr Melina. You tell me. What do *you* think it means?'

I wasn't a cop, but I didn't feel like explaining my job again, so I let it go.

Jason stood from his chair, pacing angrily from one side of the kitchen to the other, his hands buried deep inside the pockets of his beige chinos.

I put my empty glass down on the kitchen table and said, 'I know what you're getting at. And I know that the pictures might indicate that Malcom could have killed Tracy Noland. But—'

He interrupted me. 'Get him arrested! Throw him in the slammer before he kills someone else. You want evidence? Find the evidence afterwards. In the meantime, lock him up!' He removed a coin from his pocket and began rolling it between his thumb and forefinger. He seemed agitated, almost angry.

I stood from my chair. 'Mr Harvey...'

'Call me Jason.'

'Jason, you're getting all worked up for nothing. So, maybe the young man did kill Tracy Noland, and then maybe he didn't. There is no clear indication here. All we've got is assumption, certainly no grounds to get a warrant for his arrest. This young man has as much right as you have.'

He shook his head. 'I don't believe you people. You always wait until the last minute before you do something. And most of the time it's too late, and someone else has to die. What is it going to take for you to open your eyes?'

It was difficult to argue with him because I felt his anger and frustration were well-grounded. Over and over, the police seldom listened to complaints from the average citizen with any seriousness. Details were written in reports and filed away, and by the time some tangible proof came along, it was too late. On the other hand, having worked as a banker and now a small-time entertainer did nothing to increase his awareness of police and legal procedures. He was letting fear cloud his judgement, and I sympathised with him. When a murder takes place, it's often difficult to react rationally.

'Jason, I know you're angry. But making blind accusations is not going to solve anything. If I was as certain as you are that Malcom killed the young girl, I would have had him into custody and got a warrant to search his home. It's not that I believe Malcom is innocent, but I don't believe he is guilty yet. Certainly, there seems to be a lot of clues pointing in his direction, but nothing concrete at this stage. We have to take our time on this.'

'Sure, and then someone else dies. What will it take?'

I gave up and stared at the coin he was still rolling between his thumb and forefinger.

'What's this?'

He smiled, looked at the coin and held it up. 'It's my lucky coin. I believe in luck.'

I wish I did too, but so far the only luck I had was the one I had made for myself.

He tossed the coin from one hand to the other. 'This coin has brought me more luck than anything else. Everyone should have one. There's too much bad luck going around in this world. And everyone thought Albert Park was a safe place to live. Not in my worst nightmare would I have imagined something so horrible could have happened in this neighbourhood.' He jabbed his forefinger in the air. 'There's no justice left in this world. No justice. Too much bad luck going around.'

I never thought of the world as a place filled with unlucky events. To my mind the world was what you made it. But if carrying a coin made Jason Harvey believe he was in control of his life, he should have carried a pocket full of them.

'Well, maybe you're right,' I said. 'Maybe this world needs more luck. I wish I had some to find out what the hell really happened to Tracy Noland.'

He settled down a bit after that and asked if I wanted another sandwich.

'That's enough for me.'

We talked shop for a good hour, and I found myself liking the old man more by the minute. He could carry a good conversation, reminding me of my friend Ken from Terry Bennetts' gymnasium on High Street. He also had that interesting aura around him. He had an opinion about everything and seemed so alive and interested in the world around him. Even young people I met weren't so full of life.

'I've got to go to the RSL this afternoon,' he said, while rinsing glasses in the kitchen sink. 'Why don't you come and join me. I'm a hell of an entertainer. I'm sure you'll enjoy the show.'

'I'd love to, but I've got a son to go home to.'

'Bring him along. I'm sure he'd like to see a magician, I bet he's never seen one.'

'I'll ask him. If he's interested, we'll turn up.' I doubted because the only magic Michael wanted to know about was Sony Playstation and the Internet.

'I'd love to have you come along. I can introduce you to a few of my friends. Hey, who knows, maybe someone will be able to give you some information on Tracy Noland.'

He got me on alert for a few seconds, realising this might be a good idea. 'Sure, I'll see what I can do, but I can't promise anything. If I don't turn up, you'll know why.'

He walked me to the front door, his hand on my right shoulder. 'I do hope you get moving quickly on that Malcom boy. I don't have kids of my own, but I'm sure other parents in the neighbourhood will be really angry when they find out the police haven't done anything to date. You saw it yourself. There are other kids playing in the streets. Why take a chance?'

There was fear in his eyes.

I promised to do everything in my power to get the investigation rolling.

As soon as I jumped in the car, I dialled Frank on his mobile.

'Me busy?' he asked. 'Well, you know I don't have a family to go home to.'

'So, can you make it to my place this afternoon, yes or no?'

'Sure. What's it about?'

'Tracy Noland. I need your opinion on something, plus I'm thinking of interrogating the Malcom kid this afternoon. Maybe It would be a good idea if you came with me.'

We agreed to meet at two-thirty.

Michael was out when I arrived at the apartment. I threw my bag on the floral couch in the living room and went straight to his bedroom. I saw little of him these days, and it was tearing me apart. He was the only person who truly mattered in my life, and yet, we always managed to rank each other as second priority in our ever-busy schedules.

The door of his room had been left ajar, but before I even stepped in, I could see the mess. I pushed the door open, my eyes circling the room. Clothes were thrown all over the bed and floor. Posters of various pop and movie stars, whose names I could not recall, hung on every bit of wall space available. Compact discs, music and cd-rom varieties, were scattered on his desk and side table. Two recent copies of *Sports Illustrated*, with bikini-clad girls on the covers, were thrown on top of his bed, reminding me that every day he grew more into a man and less into a boy.

Five years from now, Michael would be eighteen. I felt nervous about this fact. I still hadn't got used to the idea that he wasn't five-years old, and soon I'd have a grown man living in my home, someone whom I'd know little about unless I kept our communication channels fully open. Male hormones were frightening. All I wished was that he'd grow into a healthy young man, not someone filled with neurosis and overwhelming sexual impulses. But nature had to take its course, and I knew that my job as a mother was to learn to love him no matter who he became.

I closed the door to his room and made my way to the kitchen where I poured myself an icy-cold Dr Pepper in a large tumbler filled with ice. In the lounge room I played my Los Angeles Jazz Quartet album at half-volume.

I walked up to the balcony, opened the windows and breathed in the fresh smell of seawater. The sky was clear. It was just another sunny day in St Kilda, where people came from all over Melbourne to experience the holiday-atmosphere of Acland Street, experience its exquisite cake shops, street entertainers, flocks of in-line skaters and the enchanting sight of Luna Park. Despite the druggies, prostitutes and bums, this was the best Melbourne had to offer, if you could afford a nice house in a cul-de-sac, in walking distance from all the main attractions.

Living on Chapel Street, where trams travelled almost around the clock, and the traffic was never-ending, I began to feel an increasing urge for quietness, to find a place where I could sit outside, and all I would hear would be the sounds of birds singing and the wind blowing in the trees. The need for peace was proof that I was becoming older without realising it. When I moved to St Kilda eight years ago, I wanted my environment to be vivid and full of life. At thirty-nine, entertainment consisted of sharing a nice glass of Chardonnay with Phillip and watching a video in the comfort of my own home. The irony of life is that you laugh at everything your parents did when you were younger, and a few years on, you end up enjoying the same things.

The door bell interrupted my stream of thoughts.

I paced down the hallway and unlocked the door.

Frank stood there. He wore denims, a white cotton shirt and brown-leather shoes. I got so used to seeing him in a business shirt and tie, it was strange to see him dressed casually. The effect was the same as if he'd shaved his eyebrows, or something similarly drastic.

He smiled as he walked in. 'I hope I'm not coming to hear you whining about Goosh again,' he said in a non-provocative manner.

'Not a chance. I've got better things to do with my time than worry about him.'

He followed me to the kitchen.

'Do you want anything to drink?' I asked, already pouring pure filtered water from a five-litre cask into a large glass.

He moved forward and grabbed the glass. 'Thanks.'

We sat in the lounge room, making small talk for the first five minutes. Then we changed gears and moved on to the Tracy Noland case.

'I've been putting some thought into it,' he said, 'and I can't helping thinking that the mother has something to do with it.' He emptied his glass and placed it on the pine coffee table in front of him.

'I'm not saying anything yet' I said. 'There's always the possibility she did it. But you have to look at all the other leads.' I ran through my encounter with Linda Coleman, and how she also mentioned the name Malcom.

His brow creased and he said, 'Well, that does change the perspective.'

'How do you think we should interrogate this guy?' I asked, still wondering whether Malcom's home would be the best place to conduct an interview.

He massaged his chin, puzzled over my question and suggested, 'I think you should just go in there by yourself, ask him the usual routine questions, you know, where he was the night prior to Tracy Noland's death, and then mention something about the photos he's taken.'

'Sure, and then what?'

'That would depend on what you get out of him. Whether he did take photos or not. And so on.'

'So if the photos do reveal an unusual pre-occupation with children, can we get him in for questioning? Do you think that would be enough?'

'I think getting a warrant to search the premises could accelerate the process and give us a good reason to have him interrogated officially on police premises.'

I knew what Frank was getting at. By conducting the initial interview at the suspect's home, the accused might say something off-guard. I also knew that if we took him in for questioning, he would feel more pressure and maybe crack up and admit to his crime. The only problem is that to conduct a proper interrogation, we would have to advise him that he had the right to talk to a solicitor. That would delay things, and his solicitor might refuse to have Malcom answer any questions on the grounds that his client would only incriminate himself.

'Okay,' I said, 'so I go in there, get all friendly, find out what he's all about, you know like I'm on his side kind-of-thing. And then on what basis do we get the search warrant?'

'The photos he'll show you and the testimony of Linda Coleman and Jason Harvey. They both saw him hanging around the girl.'

'And so did her mother and the other kids in the neighbourhood.'

'Okay, so that makes more than two. I think if he did it, we can corner him pretty quickly. Maybe you will have this whole thing wrapped up in less than two weeks. Do you think Goosh would still want your cock on the block?'

We both laughed at his joke, which I didn't find particularly funny. It was the idea of wrapping up the case in less than two weeks, and the face Goosh would make when I'd succeed in finding the killer, that sent me into stitches.

Frank wiped a tear from his face and added, 'You know, after all this time we've been working together, I've never understood something.'

'What's that?' I asked, between two chuckles.

'Well, you know, we work well together as a team, and, you know, we kind of get on pretty well too, and like, you know, we're good friends...'

'When we're not fighting,' I added. The seriousness of his tone wiped the smile from my face.

'Yes, well, everybody fights now and then. But, you know, what I meant to say is that, well... we make a pretty good pair.'

I laughed and took his hand in mine. 'Ah, Frank, stop asking me to marry you. You know how I feel about us. You know it's never going to happen.'

Frank was persistent but harmless. He still hadn't gotten over the fact that I wasn't interested in a relationship with him. Maybe he thought it was a phase I was going through, and then one day, when my eyes would open, I would see the light, take him into my arms and be happy forever after.

But it was never going to happen.

I didn't love Frank, not in a sexual sense, and never would.

'I'm sorry,' he said, looking down to the carpet. 'I don't want to be a nuisance. You know, it's just so hard being me, and then there's you—'

'You don't have to explain yourself. It's okay, I understand. I'm really flattered. I wish I could make it up to you.'

He smiled like a little boy, and I wanted to hug him but was afraid it would only encourage him to carry on like a love-sick puppy.

Suddenly, I grabbed his empty glass, stood from the couch and walked back to the kitchen bench. 'Do you want another drink?'

'I—'

'Yeah? Cause I'm having one. You know, apparently, if you drink two litres of water a day, you don't have to worry about your cholesterol.'

'Really?' He forced his interest.

'Yeah, cause apparently, it cleans up all the shit you've been eating all week out of your system. And in your case, being a bachelor at the age of... how old are you now?'

'Forty-eight.'

'That's right, forty-eight. At forty-eight, you must have a lot of blocked arteries. Do you actually cook something when you get home? Or are you like one of those TV cops who eat on the run all the time?'

'I drink a lot of water, Katrina. You know I drink a lot of water. You're only trying to avoid the conversation we were having.'

I brought him back the glass of water filled to the brim and said, 'I'm not trying to avoid anything. It's just that we've gone through this over and over, and I don't see the point of pushing it further. And, anyway, you know I'm having a relationship at the moment. I've got enough problems as it is without having to think about what the hell I'm going to do with you.'

He stared at me blankly, searching for a response. He looked hurt, but hell, I was tired of his nonsense. He was nearly half a century old and not mature enough to face defeat.

'You know, Frank,' I went on, 'if you want my opinion, maybe you should advertise in one of those singles' magazines? What about the newspapers? I see ads every day in there.'

'I'm not desperate. You make it sound like all I need is just anyone out there.'

I paced to the other side of the lounge room. 'Okay, okay, forget I said anything. It's none of my business. What about interrogating that Malcom kid? Can we do it this afternoon? Phillip's not coming until tonight, and I don't know where the hell Michael is.'

He glanced in my direction, but I was avoiding eye contact. I just wanted to get on with my work.

'Sure. Maybe you'd like me to wait in the car.'

'That would be good.'

# CHAPTER SEVEN

It never crossed my mind that Malcom lived with his parents. Of course, he would. He was only seventeen. What seventeen year old would live in Albert Park all by himself unless he inherited a home or a ridiculous amount of money?

Most homes in the area fetched not less than $300,000, but half a million was the average. This realisation made me wonder how Linda Coleman lived in the area. She dressed like someone who would look more at home in Footscray or Dandenong, two Melbourne suburbs not known for setting fashion trends.

Mrs Sternwood, Malcom's mother, received me at the door.

It was 3.02 p.m., and I was tired from lack of sleep the previous night. As usual, heart-wrenching cases drained me mentally and emotionally, so much so that my nights were spent tossing and turning.

Frank was waiting in the Lancer, just in case something went wrong, although I couldn't imagine what at such an early stage. He suggested Malcom might try to make a run for it once I got him cornered into admitting he killed Tracy Noland. A possibility, but Frank always had an over-zealous imagination from watching too many cop shows and reading too much crime fiction.

When I came knocking on the front door of the free-standing single-fronted Victorian home, I could hear the sound of a vacuum cleaner in the hallway.

The vacuum cleaner stopped at the same time as I swallowed.

When the door opened, a tall, slender woman with dark hair, dressed in an elegant white cotton dress, gave me a look which clearly indicated I was unwelcome. Her eyes were grey and emotionless, and her lips pinched together as if she had already decided I was someone who deserved to be treated second-best.

I introduced myself, flashing my ID in front of her face.

I explained I wanted to talk to Malcom in regard to the death of Tracy Noland. She gave me a cold glare and I added, 'I'm trying to get as much information as possible. And that means interviewing as many people as I can.'

I could tell she knew I was lying from the crease on her face. Her hands jumped to her hips, blocking the entrance to her home, protecting her family from the enemy.

'You're not going to try to frame him?' she said tartly, 'Cause you'd be wasting your time. He didn't do anything. Malcom is not that kind of person. I know, I'm his mother.'

Well, that wasn't very convincing since I had a twelve-year old son and knew little about him. Being his mother certainly didn't make me an expert on what was going on in his mind. Maybe it was different for other mothers.

'So you don't object if I talk to him?' I asked.

Silence.

She crossed her arms over her chest. 'That's up to him, isn't it?' she finally said.

I moved forward up the steps. 'Let's ask him.'

'No, no,' she protested, one hand in front of my chest. 'You wait here. *I'll* ask him.'

'Sure, whatever.'

She disappeared, slamming the door in my face.

I glanced around me, noticing the immaculately-kept rose bushes along a picket fence which led to the doorway. The grass had been freshly cut, and everything in the front yard looked as if it had been prepared for a display home. These people must have had nothing to do during the day, or they had a landscape gardener attending to their every wish.

The woman came back within two minutes and reluctantly led me into the house.

Malcom agreed to see me in his room.

He was a short guy for seventeen. Brown hair, sparkling blue eyes and a bit of fluff on his upper lip. He wore green cords, which I hadn't seen since the seventies, and a v-neck T-shirt. He smiled and gave me a limp handshake.

I sat on the edge of his single bed for lack of anywhere else to sit. In a glance, I examined my surroundings. The room smelled enclosed, as if the windows had been sealed since the beginning of time. Other than that, everything was well kept, and in its place, just like the front yard. Maybe he was the landscape gardener.

A large wardrobe stood in one corner of the room, next to the main window. I noticed neatly piled, grey cardboard boxes on top of the wardrobe. There was a study desk free from clutter or any hint of disorder. The white-painted walls were bare from pictures or posters of any kind. Was this normal for someone who was seventeen? Straight away I thought about compulsive behaviour, an attitude which tied in with serial killers and other criminals, according to my eighteen-month training at the FBI in Quantico. The room showed a need for control, a need to manipulate one's surroundings, to be in command of one's environment.

Malcom's big blue eyes looked into mine, trying to figure out what kind of person I was. He seemed at ease with himself as if I was none other than a second-hand dealer evaluating the contents of his room.

We introduced ourselves and smiled at each other, the way strangers do when they're forced to meet for the first time. He mentioned something about the weather, and I said that indeed it wasn't a day to stay indoors. This purposeless conversation went on for another three minutes. But it was all part of the process of interrogating or interviewing someone, making them feel at ease, letting them realise that you were just another person doing your job.

'I hear you knew Tracy Noland quite well,' I said suddenly, deciding to cut to the chase.

He was only seventeen, but the way he checked me out from head to toes sent a chill down my spine. There was young lust in his eyes, and that reminded me of Jason's warning that the young man had only thing on his mind. Maybe I was being paranoid, I wasn't sure.

'I wouldn't say quite well,' he mumbled. 'Yeah, I knew her. We hung around and talked. She was interesting to talk to.' He played with his fingers. 'We had a lot in common. I know it sounds strange, especially when she was so much younger than me, but, yeah, we had very much in common, which is far more than most people I know.'

Immediately I figured out the young man wasn't half an idiot. He had already assessed the situation and was leading the way. Or maybe it was his mother who lectured him properly before I walked in the room.

'What did you talk about?'

'Everything. Life, you know, problems. Kind of stuff us guys talk about all the time.'

'And did you ever get the impression that she was in some kind of trouble?'

'Nope. No one really liked her. I thought she was okay. Kind of felt sorry for her. But that's not why I talked to her. I liked her, that's all. Like I said, we had a lot in common.'

'How's that?'

'I don't know. We just thought people were a pain in the arse in general.' He placed on hand on his mouth and added, 'Oops! Not you, of course.' And then he smiled, breaking the ice.

I smiled back. 'It's okay. I think people are a pain too.'

He blinked timidly as if we were now from the same side of the fence. But a smile never fooled me. I knew he could still be the one who killed Tracy Noland. Woman's instinct. I've seen many lunatics in my line of work, and it was the shy or over-friendly types you had to watch out for. His reputation in the neighbourhood certainly kept one step ahead of him, and I was always curious as to how someone built any form of a reputation. Nothing came from nothing.

I stood from the bed and said, 'Someone told me you're into photography.' I stared purposefully at the top of the wardrobe, guessing the grey cardboard boxes I had spotted earlier on were filled with photographs.

'Yeah, that's right.'

'Can I see them?'

'See what?'

'The photos.' I looked at him and back at the cardboard

boxes.

'Well...'

'It's okay, I'm useless at photography,' I lied, knowing I was quite competent because of the crime-scene photos I took. 'I'm sure you're better at it than I am. I promise I won't say a thing, no matter what.'

He hesitated, fear in his eyes, and said, 'Okay, then.'

I could tell he was embarrassed as he reached for a pile of photo albums from inside one of the cardboard boxes.

God only knew what was in there, and soon I would know too.

He passed me one of the photo albums, which I nestled in my arms and began flipping the pages. I looked at him and back at the pictures. They were all pictures of children, all playing or gathered somewhere on Vincent Court. A chill jolted my body. Mother of God, if he wasn't the killer, it was a hell of a coincidence. Jason Harvey had been right.

'I know what you're thinking,' he quickly volunteered. 'This is a good street to take pictures of kids. No traffic. And they're always playing outside.'

I didn't say a word. The shots were accomplished, in fact quite amazing for someone who was only seventeen years old.

'Do the parents mind you taking pictures of their kids?'

'No one knows, I'm discreet.'

I bet you are, I thought.

'Did Tracy like to have her picture taken?'

'Most kids don't mind. I shot while they're not watching.'

I began to feel increasingly uncomfortable alone with this young man. I knew he wouldn't do anything to me. If he was indeed the killer, of which he seemed to fit the profile like a glove, he only attacked people weaker than himself. Tracy Noland would have been the perfect prey, someone he'd easily have control over.

Despite my over-zealous desire to handcuff the teenager and throw him in the slammer, I knew it would take more than bare instinct to prove he was the murderer. I had to find out if Malcom Sternwood had a violent past. Although the girl seemed to have died peacefully, killers have different M.O.'s, and maybe little Tracy died from a passion killing. Maybe the killer made a pass at her, and when she objected, he felt as if he had no other choice but to kill her. Maybe this was the killer's first victim, making it difficult to match a precedent M.O.

'When did you begin taking photographs?' I asked, hoping this would eventually lead me to deeper dark secrets. I continued flipping through the album until I froze at a page filled with pictures of Tracy Noland. These were not pictures he took while she wasn't watching. They were posed photographs, and her eyes clearly indicated she was aware of the camera.

'When I was thirteen my father bought me a 35mm. Always wanted to be a photographer since then. It's in me. It's my passion.'

I looked down at the photos in front of me. In one of the photos she was standing with nothing on but her underpants, playing with a white, fluffy rabbit. The shots were not straight pornography, but they did send a chill rippling down my back. I could see how some perverts would feed their lust on this type of material. On the other hand, it wasn't much different from the back pages of a Target catalogue with this year's latest undergarment fashion for kids advertised over two colour spreads.

'Why children? Aren't your worried about what people think?'

'My tutor told me to take as many different types of people as possible. Children are not an exception, although I do find them extremely easy to take. They possess an innocence which is easier to capture on film than with grown-ups. Plus grown-ups don't like to have their pictures taken. When they pose, it looks fake. And I can't afford to pay professional models.'

I puzzled for a couple of seconds. 'Did you say you have a tutor?'

'I'm doing a part-time Diploma of Photography at the Melbourne College of Photography.'

'Really?'

'Yeah. It's really expensive, so my parents won't pay for it. I work as a night filler at Coles to pay for the course. And the paper, chemicals and films cost a fortune as well.'

I was surprised because I knew you had to be at least eighteen to be admitted to the college. When I pointed that out, he admitted he lied about his age on the application form. He wrote down he was eighteen.

'But I thought you were unemployed?' I went on.

'Who says?'

'One of your neighbours.'

'They wouldn't know. I don't start until eleven at night, and by then everyone is asleep anyway. Either way I take my mountain bike to work. It's not as if someone's going to hear me take off.' He grabbed one of the other photo albums and handed it over to me. 'Take a look at those.'

I opened the album and flicked through the pages quickly, surprised at what I was seeing. These were shots of various people working in a supermarket. Foolishly, I began to realise Malcom's photographic interest wasn't children only, but people in general. It just happened that he stored the same type of subjects in the one particular album. Or maybe that was a way to eliminate any suspicion of him taking pictures of children. It was hard to figure out where he was coming from. Perverts and killers can be very cunning and clever in their habits. They always find some reason to explain their unorthodox behaviour or unusual pastimes.

I didn't know what to conclude. What I wanted was to search the bedroom, but I wouldn't be able to do that without a warrant or his authorisation. I knew he would not give me a go-ahead since I hadn't told him he was a primary suspect in the death of Tracy Noland, and if I did tell him, well, I doubted he would have invited me into his room with open arms.

'You don't mind if I take these pictures with me,' I said, grabbing the album with the photos of the children in it.

'Well, it's kind of... a collection. I wouldn't want them messed around or anything.'

'Oh, no, it's not like that whatsoever. It's just that you've got good pictures of Tracy, and they might come in handy to solve the case.'

He stared at me silently for five seconds, shrugged and said, 'All right. But I trust you with those. Don't you dare lose them.'

'I promise I won't.'

I walked out of the room, the photo album tightly gripped

85

against my chest, the beginning of a headache slowly creeping from the back of my skull.

When Frank saw the photos, he leaped up and down like a dog wanting to go for a walk.

'Jesus Christ, Katrina. That sonofabitch did it. Look at these picture. This is child pornography.'

We were in a room on the ninth floor of the Police Complex on St Kilda Road, home of the Homicide Squad.

I took a closer look at the pictures of Tracy Noland, which were now spread over a large mahogany conference table. I'd never seen child pornography before, but somehow this didn't strike me as pornography.

'I don't know,' I said, going from one picture to the other.

'You don't know? Open your god-damn eyes! What am I looking at here? A near-naked girl trotting around in her underwear, flashing her front and her back, grinning for the camera. I bet you the little bastard is jerking all over those pictures when he's alone in his room. Oh, man, this is good. This is really good. We're going to nail him, and you don't have to worry about a search warrant. We're definitely going to get one with shit like this.'

Maybe Frank was right. There was something abnormal about taking pictures of a twelve-year old girl trotting around in her underwear. It certainly wasn't art, and I couldn't imagine what the purpose of it would be.

'You know,' Frank went on, 'for a while I was on the wrong track. I really thoughT it was the mother who did it. You have to admit she did act out of character. In all my years in homicide, I have never seen someone so rigid at the death of a child, especially her own child. But there, it goes to show you never know.'

While talking he was waving one of the pictures around.

'Be careful with those,' I said. 'I promised him I would take good care of them.'

He looked at me as if I was insane and laughed. 'You're going to take good care of his pictures? Well, you don't have to worry about that. The only place he's going to see those pictures is at his trial.'

I tilted my head and said, 'Frank, you know, maybe you're

jumping to conclusions. Why don't we get a warrant and search his room before you get too excited.'

'What are you talking about? It's obviously him.'

'Yes, and you said the same thing about Mrs Noland the other day.'

'But this time, I'm sure.'

'You were sure about it then as well.'

He stood on the spot and moved his jaw a few times before something came out. 'Don't do this shit with me, Katrina. Why do you always do this?'

'Do what?'

'Act as if I'm some incompetent asshole, and you know everything.'

'That's not true.'

He pointed at me. 'You know, not everyone had the opportunity to train at the FBI. You think you're some hot shot profiler. You're not Douglas or Ressler,' he said, referring to the two FBI agents who invented criminal profiling. 'You're not with the Bureau any more. This is Australia. This is Melbourne where big shit never happens. So don't bring me all your chip-on-your-shoulder attitude and talk to me as if I'm some fifth grader. If you're in this job, it's because I fought tooth-and-nail for you after the Wilson investigation. Don't you ever forget that!'

He raced out of the room and slammed the door before I had time to reply.

That was a damn lie. The only thing he did for me during the Wilson investigation was run away to Sydney when things were getting a little tough.

I sat on a chair, the pictures of Tracy Noland sprayed in front of me, tears coming to my eyes.

And he had the nerve to tell me that together we'd make a perfect couple.

I gathered the pictures, placed them in a manilla folder, swallowed my pride and left the room.

# CHAPTER EIGHT

**P**hillip came at seven, just after I finished washing my car downstairs from my apartment. I needed to do something which had nothing to do with investigating Tracy Noland's death. Thank God it was Saturday. I intended to get all this murder stuff out of my mind and recharge my batteries. I felt like a wind-up doll who's travelled around the world twice in the luggage department of a Boeing 747.

The sun was turning into a large orange while clouds peaked shyly at the horizon. There was a mild wind coming from the ocean, soothing my nerves. A news broadcast coming from the radio in my car announced a Sunday filled with sunshine and a top of thirty-four.

Phillip's green Mazda pulled into the driveway just as I finished sponging off the last water marks from the duco of the Lancer. If cars had personality, this one would have given me a hug. It seemed filled with joy, anxious to go for its next ride to show the world what a beautiful make-over it had just undergone.

I threw my yellow sponge into a plastic bucket filled halfway with soapy, murky water, and paced towards Phillip, a broad smile on my face. I was glad to see him. I needed someone to fuss over me tonight, to tell me what a wonderful person I was, to emphasis how I looked sexy in my summer dress, someone to take me for long walks down the beach and buy me an ice-cream from a kiosk along the Esplanade. I needed someone full of life next to me, to take me away from the people I worked with, those who made my life more a burden than a challenge.

Phillip parked his car between mine and a white Cressida.

As soon as he stepped out of the car, I wrapped my arms around his neck and kissed him passionately. He smelled of Paco Rabanne and hair gel. I closed my eyes so I could feel more of him.

'Hey, hey,' he said, 'I'm glad to see you too.' He pulled a bottle of white wine from behind his back. 'I thought you might need something to help you relax.'

I seldom drank, and only began when I started going out with Phillip. He knew his wines better than I did. But after spending time with him, I knew the difference between a Chardonnay and a Riesling. Though I was still a bit rusty on my reds, I began to develop a mental catalogue of good vintage years. Phillip told me once that vintages were like 18th century battles in Europe. The French won most of them, the Germans grabbed the occasional brilliant victory, and the Italians never bothered. According to his encyclopaedic knowledge of fermented grape-juice, good vintages often came in pairs, 1928 and 1929, 1961 and 1962, 1970 and 1971, 1982 and 1983, 1985 and 1986, although there had been some good single years such as 1945, 1959 and 1966.

We made our way upstairs, him with his bottle of wine, and me with my plastic bucket, sponges and car detergent.

'I wanted you to try some Chenin Blanc,' he said. 'It's not my favourite, and in fact I'd say it has a bouquet close to vomit.'

I laughed.

He went on, 'But if I'm going to teach you about wines, you have to know the good and the bad. Chenin Blanc is made from grapes which are grown in the Loire Valley and also in South Africa, and are, without doubt, probably the most revolting grapes in the world. But this little baby,' he raised the bottle above his head so I could clearly see it, 'is an exception. In favoured corners of the Loire, grapes are somehow turned into some of the best dry and sweet wines in the world. And this 1986 vintage is a perfect example of how one can sometimes turn a bad omen into something sweet and victorious.'

His wine-to-life philosophy impressed me. Phillip had a great body, and although he was not intellectually gifted, he did have a zest for life which scored high in comparison to mine. He seemed motivated by the pleasures and joys of life, while I was content to go through it with my sleeves up and my hands deep in shit.

While I put some Diaboli on the boil and began slicing onions and tomatoes, Phillip uncorked the white wine and poured us a glass each.

'You can put some music on if you want,' I said from the kitchen.

Thirty seconds later, he said, 'Wow! Have you got enough CDs here or what?'

'Around seven hundred.'

'Shit, I'd love to have a collection like that.'

Collecting CDs was one of my obsessions. Frank collected cigarettes, Philipp wine, and Michael Playstation games. I just loved music in all its forms other than heavy metal. My collection consisted of classical, jazz, blues, eighties music and some contemporary stuff by eighties artists. I admit openly that I was an eighties music freak, and it was just a dream finding all these albums, which I loved so much when I was younger, going out for a song in music shops bargain bins.

He went about his task, but my interest was somewhere else. As much as I promised myself I wouldn't think about work, Malcom kept coming back to mind. I knew that at this very minute, a search warrant was being written up, and Goosh had been given the good news.

The apartment was filled with Mozart's Symphony No. 40 in G minor, a masterpiece written during the summer of 1788 in which a low, agitated accompaniment on the strings sets the mood for the *Molto allegro,* where initially the violins lead, urging the music on to the lyrical second theme, which is shared between woodwind and strings.

Just as I was tossing sliced onions in a large frying pan greased with a film of olive oil, and Phillip was telling me about the new telephone card system his company had developed, the phone rang.

I tucked the receiver between my ear and my shoulder, a wooden chopping board still in one hand and a knife in the other.

'Yeah?'

'Katrina, it's Jason.'

My mind did a juggling act, and for a few seconds I couldn't place the name.

'Who?'

'Jason Harvey. We had lunch together.'

'Ah, yes,' I said, trying to sound joyfully surprised, but at the back of my mind I wondered how the hell he got my home number. I place the chopping board on the kitchen bench, but kept the knife in my hand. 'How are you, *Mr* Harvey?'

'I'm fine. Look, you didn't come to my show this afternoon. So I thought maybe you'd like to bring your boy with you tomorrow.'

I changed from one foot to the other. 'Well, I'm sorry, I haven't seen Michael all day. He must be at a friend's place. I'll ask him.'

'I saw your car today.'

'A big your pardon?'

'You were parked in front of Malcom's home.'

'Uh-huh?'

'Did you arrest him?'

'All I did was talk to him.'

'When are you going to arrest him?'

'Well, we did find the photos you mentioned, so we're getting a warrant to search his premises.'

'Well, I'm glad. I knew that boy was up to no good.'

Phillip gave me a glance as if to say, 'who the hell is that?'

'Look, Mr Harvey, I'm kind of busy at the moment. Why don't we catch up some other time?'

'Tomorrow?'

'Maybe. I don't know. Give me your number, and I'll have a talk to Michael.'

He gave me his number, which I scribbled on a notepad next to the phone and tossed it aside immediately.

'Don't forget to call,' he insisted. 'I'll be expecting you.'

After he hung up, I felt a bitter taste in my mouth.

If Frank had given him my home number, I was going to slice him up just like an onion. I didn't mind Jason Harvey, but my private life was just that, private, and I liked to be the one to pull the strings when it came to my after-hours activities.

'Who was that?' Phillip asked while passing me my glass of Chenin Blanc. I explained and he added. 'So, if he was doing a show at the local RSL in the afternoon, how did he see your car parked at Malcom's?'

I puzzled over this for a few seconds. 'Maybe he was leaving for the RSL when he saw the car. He never told me what time he would be performing. I don't know. I just hate people giving away my phone number without my authorisation.'

'You sure you didn't give it to him?'

'No.'

And maybe I did.

But with all that had been happening in the past few days, I would have been quite unwilling to pass a memory test.

Phillip lifted his glass and said,' So, what do you think?'

'About what?'

'The wine.'

I took a sip and said, 'Hmm...'

'Looks a bit amber for a Chenin Blanc.'

He was right. The green bottle never indicated the colour of its contents.

He went on, 'Mmm... this is not as bone dry as I would have expected.'

It did have a tang of sweetness, but was somehow well-balanced. And on an empty stomach, it went straight to my head, giving me some relief from all that was happening in my life. But still, no amount of white wine could completely cure one's anxieties, at least not in the long run without causing irreversible damage to skin, liver, brain and other vital organs. I never drank wine as a remedy to life's challenges, and I wasn't about to. This was an exception. Phillip brought the wine, and it was Saturday night after all.

I closed my eyes, letting the alcohol simmer in my brain, but all that came to mind was the face of Tracy Noland at the mortuary. Her death had effected me more than I realised, but then, I had expected it on that hot December morning when we found her on the banks of Albert Park Lake.

Flashes of other children's cases I had worked on in the

past few years, most of them not as an investigator but as a consultant, came to mind. I never coped well with child abuse and never would. Maybe it was my own childhood which made it difficult for me to come face to face with the horrors of what men could do to their own children. After all, it was easier to live in a world of denial than having to face the harsh reality that evil was not something to be found in hell after we died, but something that lived on this planet, in the streets, amongst us, in the form of another human being.

There seemed to be no factor which could point out why a person would sexually abuse a child, although a large number of offenders had been abused themselves as children, or so they claimed. I began to wonder if this wasn't a front so that the judge and the jury would become more lenient when it came to sentencing. After all, who would be heartless enough to punish someone who had been sexually abused or battered as a child, no matter what type of monster they turned out to be in the future? The average person found great comfort in the knowledge that evil could be cured from men, that it only took a bit of counselling, some form of prison term or a couple of months at a mental health facility.     Me, I wasn't that cynical. They put these men and women in prison for life, but release them after ten years, sometimes less, and nine times out of ten, they re-offend. I've always held a strong disbelief in the death penalty, but after having seen what people did to children, it had been damn easy to change my mind. I would challenge anyone who called me cruel to go to visit a mortuary or a crime scene and come out unaffected. Unfortunately most people who are against the death penalty tend to be sitting comfortably in front of their television, thinking themselves some type of Messiah, while investigators are the ones dealing with the horror of homicide every day. Those same people turn a blind eye when a child killer is re-released into the streets, naively believing that somehow a man whose actions have been dictated by savage lust from an early age would suddenly change overnight to a saint because some Christian has given him blessing and a bible, from which he memorised as many verses as possible for lack of anything else to do for ten years, confined between the walls of a three by four prison cell.

I opened my eyes, partly blinded by the fluorescent light on the kitchen ceiling.

Phillip must have read the look on my face because he said, 'You're not still thinking about the investigation?' He shifted from the lounge room Indian rug, circled the kitchen bench and planted himself in front of me. 'Try to relax. Don't bring your work home. Look at me, once I leave work, I leave it all behind. I don't try to analyse every problem once I'm out of the joint. No one is paying you for doing mental overtime. No one gives a damn if you worry twenty-four hours a day about your job. You can't go on living and enjoying life if you keep on dragging all this stuff with you.'

I took another sip of wine. 'Well, your line of work is not exactly mind-teasing.'

He looked at me stunned. 'And what's that suppose to mean?'

'That if I think of work after hours, it's because I'm dealing with people in the real world who have horrific things happening to them. It's not like I can just separate myself from reality. This is not a television show where one can just switch off whenever it gets too unpleasant to watch.'

'And how do I do it?' There he was again, comparing apples with oranges.

I glared him straight in the eye. 'Setting up telephone booths is not as melodramatic. You can just hang up at the end of the day.'

'Ah, ah,' he answered sarcastically. 'You know, Katrina, your attitude can be irritating. You think you're the only *woman* on the planet who has to worry about other people. How do you think the rest of the world lives?'

I swallowed the contents of my wine glass in one gulp. 'You know, *Phillip*, I don't ask you to change for me. So stop asking me to be someone other than who I am.'

'I'm not asking you for anything.'

'Yes, you are.'

'No, I'm not.'

'Whatever.' I slammed my empty glass on the bench top. 'I thought we were going to have an pleasant evening together, not a gender war.'

He moved forward. 'We are going to have a pleasant evening. This is just foreplay. It builds up tension.'

He came close and kissed me at the back of the neck, while Mozart's Symphony No. 40 in G minor had returned to the mood of the first movement with its rising arpeggio of the opening theme in *Allegro assai*.

I closed my eyes, letting the warmth of his hands massage my stomach and Mozart's melody fill my mind, pretending to be enjoying the moment.

Phillip spent the night at my place. We were in bed when Michael came home at 12.42 a.m. the following morning. I hadn't closed an eye, wondering where the hell he'd been. A couple of times, I thought of calling his friend Chris in case he happened to be there. Finally, just before going to bed, I did make the call, but Chris wasn't home, his mother told me, and yes, she did see the both of them earlier in the day. She thought they went to the Jam Factory to see a movie - apparently, a new James Bond movie came out, and they'd been hanging out to see it. I'd never met Chris's mother, but had spoken to her on the phone several times.

Phillip and I made love, but my heart wasn't in it. I couldn't disassociate sexual intercourse with what had happened to Tracy Noland, even though at this stage there was no indication that she'd been sexually molested.

My mind kept shifting back to Malcom, and the more I thought about it, the more I realised he must have been the killer. But I didn't want to turn into Frank and pass sentence before due time. Monday morning, Frank and I would head straight to Malcom's home and serve the search warrant. I was still uncertain as to what we would find there, but nothing would surprise me. And as much as I didn't want Malcom to be the killer, since he seemed to be such an obvious target, I hated to leave the premises empty-handed. I just hoped to God we would find something that would push us in the right direction. The sooner this case was over, the better I would sleep at night.

After we made love, Phillip rolled over and went to sleep. My eyes were glued to the ceiling, my brain actively anxious about everything in my life. With all those loonies out there, I couldn't deny being scared not knowing where Michael was. He was the only person who gave me strength to carry on when life seemed so complicated.

Early on in the year, just after Easter, I promised him we would spend more time together. So far, all we'd managed were Sundays, but even that was scattered and irregular. Tossing and turning, I was wondering where I was going to take him. Then I thought about Jason Harvey. Maybe Michael would like to see a magician. I didn't remember him ever seeing a real one other than on television, which wasn't the same. It amazed me how many things children learned from television alone. Kids growing up without ever seeing a real-life cow or sheep. That was the danger of living and growing up in the city, where nature was something mythical found inside the box.

When morning came, I was as tired as when I went to bed. I managed to get some sleep at around four in the morning - at least that was the last hour I remembered seeing on the digital clock by my side-table before daylight woke me up at 7.02 a.m. Phillip was still asleep, naked between the sheets, looking like a little boy with his unkempt hair and long eye lashes.

Quietly I stepped out of bed, pulled on a pair of grey flannel shorts and a white T-shirt, and made my way to the kitchen. I realised I'd been hard with Phillip, perhaps even unfair. Maybe he'd been right when he told me not to take my work home. I decided to make an effort and try to think about other things over the weekend, even if it seemed like thoughts were random things which bombarded my brain without me having any control over them.

While water was boiling for some coffee, I stepped outside the apartment and grabbed my copy of the Sunday paper, which was conveniently delivered to my door. The morning was fresh and crisp, but the sky was cloudless as far as the eye could see. Traffic was already heavy for so early on a Sunday morning. I heard someone swear in the distance, and then the tram coming down the track, on its way up Chapel Street.

I took a deep breath of carbon monoxide, wondering how in the world I was going to last another ten years in a place filled with so much pollution. I remembered watching an autopsy of an elderly woman last year whose lungs were so black, I immediately assumed she was a smoker. But Dr Main explained that these were merely lungs of a person who has spent the past twenty years living in the city, and that in fact

96

her lungs looked quite healthy for someone her age. If I hadn't known better, I would have thought the poor thing died of lung cancer.

After getting rid of the shrink-wrap, I unrolled the newspaper while making my way upstairs.

Tracy Noland's picture with the words STRANGLED TO DEATH were splattered all over the front page. The banner at the top stated that here was a 'special report' from pp.23-43, with lots of pictures and interviews. The funeral would be conducted on Monday morning. No one had invited me, and it never crossed my mind to ask. I guess I'd just have to invite myself.

Over a cup of virgin black coffee, I poured over the pages one at time, absorbing everything the public was being told. So much for trying to forget about my work. It was the first thing I read about in the morning paper.

When I turned to page thirty-five, I saw myself in black and white staring back at me. It was a small photo, but it made me look ten years older than I was. Or was that the way I looked in the eyes of the public? There was a caption underneath which read: 'Dr Kristina Melina nearly pulled out'. Someone had written a two-hundred-and-fifty-word piece on how I was going to drop the case but changed my mind at the last minute. The article included a quote which I didn't remember saying: 'There is no justice left in this world. I intend to bring some back.' That's creative journalism for you.

Fully absorbed in my reading, I didn't even notice Michael sneaking up behind me, reading over my shoulder.

'Your photo's in the paper again,' he said, his voice fresh and young. I'd almost forgotten what he sounded like.

I closed the newspaper, but that only displayed its front page with the picture of Tracy Noland, so I turned back to front, flashing a colour photo of Andre Agassi, smiling after winning three straight sets.

I told him about Jason Harvey's invitation, and he said, 'Yeah, Okay,' without hesitation.

We had breakfast together, but had little to say to one another. His world of Playstation, MTV and basketball seemed so far away from mine. I wondered what he was going to do with the rest of his life. I knew he was only a twelve-year old, but I couldn't help worrying that he had no particular interest, and that would make his choice of career a little more difficult. Mind you, I didn't know I was going to work in criminology until I reached eighteen.

Phillip joined us fifteen minutes later. He was in a cheerful mood after 'getting some' the previous night.

Michael and he exchanged opinions about the forthcoming Australian Open. I didn't share in the conversation because I cared little about tennis.

By ten o'clock, we were all showered and dressed, ready to make Sunday the best day of the week.

I called Jason Harvey, and we agreed to meet at lunch time at the Esplanade. He told me he wouldn't be performing at the RSL today after all, but he'd put on a little show at the Sunday market in St Kilda instead.

I parked my Lancer in the car park of the French Alliance, the only place I could be certain of finding a vacant spot without earning a pink slip. St Kilda's grey ghosts were the worst in Melbourne. With parking restrictions from 9 a.m. until midnight in most areas, I'd hate to be a tourist who hadn't read the signs properly and as a result copped a lovely forty-five-dollar ticket at the end of the day.

We spent some time crawling up and down Acland Street, experiencing its many eateries, novelty shops, buskers and colourful citizens. The atmosphere was fizzing with a carnival ambience, and it was hard to hate this place unless one hated people in general.

I bought Phillip and Michael two chocolate eclairs from one of many European-styled cake shops, which they consumed without saying a word or taking time to breathe. I settled for a freshly-squeezed orange juice.

At 11.45 a.m., we made our way up the Esplanade, in front of Luna Park, where street entertainers had a lot of room to perform their silly but amusing acts.

We watched Jason Harvey, dressed in black with a cape like Zorro, perform a trick with a rope, where he made the rope shorter or longer depending on how he was moving his hands. Michael seemed fascinated by the whole thing, which was quite amazing since it wasn't something he saw on television or on his Playstation.

Jason continued with some card tricks and a silver ball. He

then used his lucky coin and made it disappear out of his hand. I had to admit I was impressed and wished it could have been that easy to solve a murder investigation.

After he finished his performance, people dropped coins in a wooden box he had sitting in front of him. It looked as if he'd made about thirty dollars, which wasn't all that bad for a fifteen minute act.

When we approached him, his face beamed with excitement.

'I'm so glad you could make it,' he said, looking different in his black outfit rather than his chequered shirt and slacks. He moved towards my son. 'So, you're Michael. Your mother told me a lot about you.'

'Hey, that was really cool, the thing you did with the rope,' Michael said.

'I can show you how I did it.'

And before I could say anything, Michael and Jason had become the best of friends.

# CHAPTER NINE

Monday the 22nd of December, heavy banging on the door woke me up from a deep sleep.

I jumped out of bed, covered myself with a white bathrobe from the en suite and raced down the hallway. I was still tired from having gone to bed late and reading Sue Grafton's *L is for Lawless* until one o'clock in the morning.

Bang! Bang! Bang!

'Hang on, I'm coming.'

I felt dizzy from being woken up in the middle of a dream. I didn't even take the time to check the alarm clock on my side-table. I had no idea what the time was, but I noticed it was still dark outside when I stepped out of bed. Whoever it was, he or she had a nerve to come banging at someone's door so early in the morning or the middle of the night, whatever the time was. I hurried so that the person wouldn't knock on the door again. I feared Michael would be woken up, if he hadn't been already.

It was warm in the apartment, and I smelled like night sleep.

I opened the door, not bothering to ask who it was.

Frank stood there, all excited, words pouring out of his month like a fountain. His hair was still wet from a morning shower, and he smelled of cheap aftershave and cigarettes. His eyes were heavy, but the tone of his voice was filled with excitement. 'You're not ready yet? Come on, hurry up and get dressed.'

When I realised it was him, I scratched the back of my head and said, 'What are you doing here? Jesus, what's the time?'

'Five-thirty, and you better make it snappy.'

I zigzagged back down the hallway, letting him close the door behind him. He seemed fully awake, while I was battling to keep my eyes open so as to not crash into walls and doors.

'Why are you here so early?'

We moved to the kitchen where I automatically switched on the kettle and removed two mugs from the cupboard. I threw in a spoon of instant coffee in each mug, and removed a long-life carton of milk from the fridge. I didn't bother asking if he wanted coffee. At that time of the day, I was on automatic pilot.

'We're going to search bright and early before the bastard has the chance to realise what's going on. And Tracy Noland's funeral is at ten o'clock, so we want to get the Malcom interview over and done with ASAP.' He talked so loud, I thought he was going to wake up half the neighbourhood. I asked him to keep it down because Michael was asleep, but he went on, 'I've got the search warrant right here. You get ready while I load your stuff in the car.' He scanned the kitchen. 'Where do you keep your camera and PERK?' As if I would keep it in the kitchen.

We left our coffees untouched while I took him to the spare room, where I kept all my forensic equipment under lock.

'Okay, okay, you get ready,' he ordered while jabbing his finger. 'I'll get all this shit sorted out. I haven't slept half the night thinking about this.'

I shook my head in disbelief, but rather than argue, I did what I was told and headed straight for the en suite

The shower was short and sweet, but woke me up from my slumber. While blow-drying my hair, I began to feel the contagious excitement Frank was experiencing. Although I'd tried hard to keep my mind off the investigation over the weekend, I knew I had to face Malcom Sternwood for the second time this week. Now that the moment was drawing near, adrenalin began pumping in my through my veins. As much as I hated crimes, the reason why I chose a career in criminology was because of the excitement that came with it.

Unfortunately, there was also a lot of bureaucracy, which I wasn't aware of at the time I joined the FBI Academy.

I brushed, flossed and used a mouth-wash. After seeing that dreadful picture of myself in the Sunday paper, I was determined to look my best. I dressed in long pants and matching jacket over a white blouse. I looked as if I'd just stepped out of the Police Academy in Mt Waverley.

All the way to Albert Park, Frank couldn't stop babbling.

'I haven't slept all bloody night. This thing is eating me alive,' he said while tossing a cigarette between his lips. He flicked his lighter on, ready to inhale.

'Do you mind?' I protested.

'Oh, sorry,' and he butted out before the flame had time to reach the tip of the cigarette.

I had nothing against smokers, but I breathed in enough crap during the day without having to endure somebody else's vice. Frank was a two-pack a day, and his breath smelled like a lounge room after a Saturday-night party.

Traffic at 6.02 a.m. was mild, making it easy for us to get to Albert Park in under five minutes.

The cul-de-sac was awfully quiet at that time of the morning, and it felt wrong to wake up someone at the crack of dawn, even to serve a search warrant. Surely, Frank could have waited until eight or nine o'clock. It would have made no difference. He was probably going to get a kick out of shocking these people out of their socks. I told him so.

'The warrant gives me the right to do what I want.'

'Well, actually, you should only serve this paper during daylight, unless you've got a damn good reason to do it at another time.'

'What do you call this? Night time?'

It wasn't night, but it certainly wasn't full daylight either.

'You know this is going to fall back on you if this kid's innocent.'

'Don't make it sound like I'm doing this on purpose to piss anyone off,' he protested as we stepped out of the car. 'Point is there's no one around at the moment. Everybody's in bed, which means we're not going to have nosy neighbours waiting in the front yard and a television crew rolling down the street within five minutes.'

His point was partly valid, but it didn't stop me feeling like an intruder, especially if Malcom was innocent. I'd hate to be in the kid's shoes.

'I'll get the stuff out of the car, and you can wake up this mob,' Frank ordered. I was going to protest that I was in charge of the investigation, but it was too early in the morning for an argument. I could have done with at least another hour's sleep, and Frank was so bottled up with anger, I didn't want him to take it out on me. Sometimes it's better to let events take their own course.

Frank slipped the envelope with the warrant in my hand and circled the white Ford Falcon. The warrant gave us authorisation to search Malcom's bedroom, and Michael's bedroom only. It had been issued on the strength of the photos I took with me from his room.

I made my way past the front gate, recognising the manicured front yard and the freshly painted picket fence.

*Wakey, wakey, it's the Avon lady!*

God, I hated my job sometimes.

Three knocks on the door, one ring of the bell.

It didn't take more than that.

The door flew open within thirty seconds. Mrs Sternwood looked as dreadful as I felt, like someone who could have done with another two hours sleep. After I told her we were here to search her son's bedroom, I thought she was going to slam the door in my face.

'You've got a hell of a nerve coming with your papers at this time of the morning,' she snapped. 'The boy is still in bed. He's just come back from work. What am I supposed to do? Wake him up?'

I managed a smile and said, 'That would make it easier to search his bedroom.'

'You've got a smart mouth, you know.' She glared at me for a few seconds and added, 'You wait here while I get him out of bed.' She slammed the door in my face as I dreaded she would.

I turned around and saw Frank walking up the path.

'So?' he said, his hands loaded with the PERK and the camera equipment.

'She's waking him up.'

'Mmm...'

We stood there for a while without saying a word.

Three minutes.

'How long does it take to wake someone up?' Frank asked.

'Give her time.'

Five minutes.

'Another minute and I'm breaking in.'

'Frank, be patient. If you came to my door at this time of the morning, I'd do the same to you.'

'Well, damn it. For all I know the bastard could be running out the back door with all the evidence.'

Seven minutes.

'That's it, I've had enough,' Frank snapped.

And so did I.

Frank banged on the door so loud, I glanced to the houses on my left and right to see if he'd woken up the Sternwoods' neighbours.

No one bothered answering the door.

And then we heard people arguing inside. I couldn't make out what they were saying, but I recognised Malcom's voice and that of his mother.

Frank banged on the door again and yelled, 'Police. Open the door.'

Finally, the door flew open for the second time. Mrs Sternwood stood there, tight-lipped and fully dressed in stone-washed denim and a blue T-shirt. 'What's the matter with you? Can't you give us time to get dressed?'

Frank pushed his way into the hallway. 'Frankly, I couldn't care less. We're investigating a murder, and as far as I'm concerned, you can be walking around naked, it makes no difference to me.'

She made a sound with her throat, which implied Frank was the rudest person she'd ever come across, although with her attitude, I doubted it. She must have made a few people angry in her lifetime with her delusion-of-grandeur attitude.

We passed the kitchen to get to Malcom's room. He was having breakfast, looking morbidly petrified. Immediately, I wondered why he was having breakfast if he'd just come back from work and slipped into bed.

His eyes met mine, and he yelled, 'I didn't do it! I didn't do it.' He threw his chair to the floor and came running down to the doorway, where I was standing. He stood right in front of me, grabbing me by the shoulders, words spitting out of his mouth. 'I didn't kill Tracy. Believe me, I didn't do it. You know I didn't do it!'

My heart was drilling through my chest. For a split second, I thought he was going to beat me.

Frank moved in on him fast, grabbed him by the collar of his red pyjamas and yanked him back. 'Hands off! Go back to the kitchen and stay there.'

'But I didn't do it,' Malcom whimpered, trying to maintain balance.

'Hey, no one said you did,' Frank lied. 'We're just doing our job here. You're not being arrested or charged.'

'Why are you searching my room?'

Frank and I looked at each other, searching for the right answer.

'To make sure we've covered every angle,' I suggested.

'But...' Malcom went on, moving two step towards us.

'Back off!' Frank ordered and gave him a push back towards the kitchen. 'One more step and I'll arrest you for assault and obstruction.'

The young man looked as if he was going to need an ambulance any minute. Blood had drained from his face, and his hands were shaking. He moved back to the kitchen, muttering to himself. 'I didn't do it. Oh, God, you know I didn't do it.'

The whole scenario sent a chill down my spine. It would have been better if we'd done the search when Malcom wasn't around.

Mrs Sternwood stood there the whole time without saying a word. She didn't try to defend her son, nor did she try to stop us from arguing with him. She knew there'd be no point. Or maybe she knew we were wasting our time, and that we'd walk out of here empty-handed.

Malcom's room was what I remembered, except that his bed had been slept in. I could understand his frustration. At his age, and living at his parent's place, the bedroom was his sanctuary, the only place in the world where he felt at home.

And now we were going to invade his private territory. But at the back of my mind I had the face of Tracy Noland, and if it meant turning the whole damn street upside down, then I was willing to do it.

Frank shut the door, not wanting Mrs Sternwood to stand there and watch us throughout the operation.

I unzipped one of my soft bags and removed various packaging - brown paper, vinyl bags, cardboard boxes, plastic containers and vials of different sizes. I also pulled out five sheets of continuity labels to mark the packaging.

We both slipped on a pair of surgical gloves, just to make sure we wouldn't leave our prints everywhere.

Frank begin searching the obvious places, such as the inside of the wardrobe, under the bed, in the grey cardboard boxes where the photographic albums were hidden.

I looked through his study desk, but came up with nothing but books on photography, slides and various writing pads. Then I noticed a stack of black computer diskettes next to his computer. The computer was an older Standard model, probably a 486DX2 or similar. I flicked through the diskettes, but none were labelled. I counted them. Twelve in all.

Meanwhile Frank had turned the wardrobe inside-out. Clothes were thrown on the floor, and books and papers scattered around. Frank was on his hands and knees, searching every item of clothing, looking through the pages of every book and magazine, trying in vain to find evidence which would point to Malcom as the killer.

'Damn it!' he said to himself without elaborating. I guessed he'd found nothing, and his frustration was mounting. He obviously didn't want to go back to the office and report we made an error.

And neither did I.

I flicked the computer on, waited for the system to boot up and inserted one of the small black diskettes in the A-drive. The system was still running on DOS 5.0 and using Windows 3.1 at a speed of 50MHz. As far as computer technology was concerned, this was already a dinosaur, even it had been the latest model two to three years ago. By the end of this year, they were talking about all computers operating at a speed of no less than 400MHz. It was mind-boggling how far we had come in so little time.

I went to DOS and typed: *a: [enter]* followed by *DIR [enter]*. The black screen shot back a list of ten files with a .gif-extension from *jen0.gif* right through to *jen9.gif*. The volume number was *CHILDREN_001*. Apprehension crept at the back of my neck. I knew I'd found Ali Baba's cave.

The gif-extension was a graphic file. And *jen* kind of spoke for itself. The name of the girl on the graphic files was probably Jenny or Jennifer.

I removed the disk from the drive, and inserted another one. I typed *DIR [enter]* and watched the screen spill back a new list of gif files, but this time they were from *sue0.gif* to *sue9.gif.* under volume *CHILDREN_002*.

It tried the next four diskettes. I found *sha0.gif* to *sha9.gif*, *mic0.gif* to *mic9.gif*, *kar0.gif* to *kar9.gif* under volume number *CHILDREN_003, CHILDREN_004* and *CHILDREN_005*. and finally what I had been hoping for, *tra0.gif* to *tra9.gif*. under volume number CHILDREN_006.

'Fuck, fuck, fuck!' I heard Frank say behind me, still, battling with the wardrobe contents. 'There's fuck all in here.'

Without taking my eyes off the screen I muttered, 'Get over here. I think I've got some stuff you'd like to see.'

He shifted his weight behind me and responded in a dead-pan voice, 'What?'

'See these files?' I pointed to the computer screen:

```
A:\>DIR/P

Volume in drive A is CHILDREN_006
DIRECTORY OF A:\

   .                              <DIR>
      06-06-97          3.55P
   ..                             <DIR>
      06-06-97          3.55P

TRA0                    GIF    112304      07-28-97
            7.32P
TRA1                    GIF    115627      07-28-97
            7.34P
TRA2                    GIF    126782      07-28-97
            7.34P
TRA3                    GIF    117967      07-28-97
            7.35P
TRA4                    GIF    104564      07-28-97
            7.36P
TRA5                    GIF    128765      07-28-97
            7.38P
```

```
TRA6                        GIF      128990        07-28-97
              7.40P
TRA7                        GIF      127767        07-28-97
              7.41P
TRA8                        GIF      119980        07-28-97
              7.42P
TRA9                        GIF      107865        07-28-97
              7.42P
                                                   12      file(s)
1190611       bytes

                        209567 bytes free
```

He stared for a few seconds, but the look on his face indicated he didn't know what he was looking for.

'Look at that,' I went on, indicating the first two columns on the left side of the screen. 'All those files are graphic files. You can tell by the gif-extension. There's about twenty other formats of graphic files, but gif, along with bmp and pcx are the most commonly used. Now you see this file,' I pointed to tra5.gif, 'the first three letters stand for a name. And *tra* is...?'

'Tracy?'

'Correct. The number simply indicates what picture it is, and the extension that it's a graphic file. My guess is this is the fifth picture of Tracy Noland collected by photographer/computer whiz Malcom Sternwood.'

Frank puzzled over my finding for few seconds.

'Oh,' I added, 'and it's not just this one.' I grabbed the stack of diskettes. 'These are full of them as well, not the same girl, but same file formats. He classifies each diskette with a volume number that has the letters C-H-I-L-D-R-E-N, children, and follows it up by a three-number digit, so he knows the number of diskettes under his collection.'

He eyes followed the diskettes then returned to the screen.

'Ingenious little devil,' he said.

'Actually, this is quite basic stuff. The way these files are labelled, he never thought someone else than himself was going to check those diskettes. I mean, if you're going to collect child pornography on computer files, you wouldn't label the volume number CHILDREN. That's kind of obvious. You'd label the disks under numbers only, or something which looked like part of an operating system or a file-utility program.'

'Okay, so, you're telling me all these files are pictures of some sort?'

'Yep. According to their sizes, they're quite small and poor in quality, but large enough to view and get excited over. It's unlikely they're in colour, since colour graphics take a lot of space. You're barely be able to fit a picture on a three-and-a-half-inch diskette.'

'Can we bring these pictures up on the screen?'

'As long as he's installed software that can read gif-extension files, then we can do it right here.'

I returned to the C-drive, and typed the command *WIN* [*ENTER*] to access windows. Since Malcom had diskettes with graphic files in them, I excepted him to have a program on his computer that would be capable of reading those files.

The Microsoft 3.1 window came up followed by a series of icons. I looked for any icon which looked like the key to a graphics program. There was one labelled WinGif, which told me straight away it was a windows program designed to view gif-files.

'This is it,' I said, pointing the mouse on the WinGif icon and double-clicking the left button.

Frank wasn't saying a word. He just stood behind me, his hand clutching the back of the chair I was sitting on.

When I entered the program, I chose FILE and OPEN, conducted my search in the A-drive, and a list of the gif-files on the diskette I had inserted earlier in the drive came up. I double-clicked *tra0.gif*.

Before the picture came up, I knew what I was going to find, but I wasn't sure how bad it was going to be. Maybe these would be the same pictures I'd seen in his photo-album collection, but he'd decided to store them in digital format.

Inch by inch, a black-and-white picture of Tracy Noland came up, her head first, then her bare chest, then the rest of her body.

We froze, staring at the picture.

I recognised the picture as one of those from the photo album, except that in the album, Tracy Noland was wearing white cotton underwear, while in this picture she was stark naked.

'Holy shit!' Frank said.

But something else about the picture wasn't right. The

pubic section of the girl was covered with a dark bush. When I attended the autopsy, I remembered clearly that Tracy Noland had not grown pubic hair yet in spite of her being twelve-years old. But I knew this was normal. Puberty happened at different ages for different people.

'Something's not right here,' I commented.

'What?'

I explained what I noticed during the autopsy, and how it compared with what we had on the screen.

'So?' he asked, obviously wondering what point I was trying to make.

'Well, it means Malcom didn't actually take naked pictures of Tracy Noland. He probably wanted to, but she refused. So he had to settle for her wearing underwear, and then, to complete his fantasy, he transferred the pictures to computer graphics so he could manipulate them and do whatever he fancied.'

'And how did he do that?'

'A graphics program such as PhotoShop let's you transform pictures. He could have got the pubic section from somewhere else, maybe scanned from a magazine, and super-imposed it on Tracy, making sure to match her original skin tone and border lines. Or he could have simply used Paintbrush and zoomed in close enough so that he could work on one pixel at a time. That's the way computer game graphics are designed. It's a long process, but it works. Newspapers tend to do that these days, so sometimes pictures don't tell a thousand words, but a thousand lies.'

Frank shook his head. 'Well, new-age, child pornography.'

'Easy to produce. Hard to detect.'

'Sonofabitch!'

'Welcome to digital technology.'

We packed, sealed and labelled the diskettes as evidence.

Frank thought the evidence was as good as gold, but deep down he must have known as well as I did that it didn't mean Malcom killed the girl. We needed something more concrete, evidence that would stand in a court of law.

For the next half hour we ransacked the rest of the bedroom and found such evidence.

# CHAPTER TEN

**M**rs Noland wanted the body of Tracy cremated. This was cause for concern for the investigative team, knowing that once the body was cremated, there'd be no chance of performing further forensic tests or searching for trace evidence originally overlooked.

It was straight after the search of Malcom Sternwood's bedroom that I found out what the funeral arrangements were. Jason Harvey had the courtesy of giving me a call on my mobile phone while Frank and I were on our way to the VFSC to deposit the evidence we'd collected from Malcom's room.

When Frank and I arrived at the funeral home in South Melbourne, I found out that the paper work had already been done, and there was little chance of changing Mrs Noland's mind.

The funeral home lobby resembled a five-star hotel in the City, with plush carpet; courteous and well-dressed staff; a waiting room which seemed more like a lounge; and everybody looking glad to see us. For the dearly departed, this might have been the nicest place they'd stayed at for a long time.

Prior to the service, I spoke to the funeral director, Mr John Stanley, an overweight man with dyed brown hair and a friendly face. His dark suit was impeccably cut, and his white shirt and black tie crease-less

'It's her decision,' he said in a relaxed, low-voice, as if he was scared of waking someone up. 'Cremation is becoming more common every day.'

'But you do understand my concern as an investigator?' I protested.

'Sure, I do. But it makes no difference.'

John Stanley went on discussing the history of cremation, and what happens to a body when it is cremated. I never asked for the details, but he seemed glad to deliver his speech, which he must have memorised line-by-line for curious people like me.

'Once the casket is rolled into the cremation chamber,' he explained, 'incineration occurs at a temperature of 1800° Fahrenheit or higher. Natural gas is commonly used to produce the heat desired, but we prefer to use electricity for safety reasons.'

'Do you ever incinerate two people together?'

'Can't do it. The combustion chamber is only big enough to hold one coffin at a time. To do so would mean placing two bodies in the one coffin, which has never occurred as long as I've been working here.'

I only asked the question in the hope that whatever remained of Tracy Noland would be kept separate for further analysis if required.

'So, we could still use the remains of the body if the need occurred?' I asked.

'You wouldn't be able to conduct any worthwhile examination once the body has been subjected to such temperature. All that remains are ashes and pieces of bones, weighing six to seven pounds, depending on body weight. Bone fragments are collected and pulverised in a grinding machine. The remains are then placed in an urn and ready for the funeral. The combustion chambers are not kept at the funeral home. We keep them at another location, once again, for safety reasons.'

'And how long does the process take?'

'Sixty to ninety minutes, once more depending on the weight of the body. She was only a little girl, so it took just over fifty minutes.'

'You mean Tracy Noland has already been cremated?' There was genuine surprise in my tone.

'Of course. I thought you knew. The ashes were delivered

to us two hours ago, ready for the funeral.'

The funeral ceremony was uneventful, and not many people attended it. Jason Harvey, Linda Coleman and Susan Griffith, the first person I interviewed at Vincent Court, were present. I left half way through, unable to digest the whole procedure. I surprised myself by being too weak to sit with mourners, crying at the loss of the young girl.

Frank stayed behind, chatting to people with the hope of developing further leads. Three photographers, pretending to be relatives taking pictures, were taking records of everyone present at the funeral. Later on, Frank and I would analyse the photographs and interview people whom we hadn't interviewed to date.


The Forensic Biology Unit began in the 1960s as a small team at Melbourne University in Parkville, then moved to a small laboratory in Spring Street, in the city's CBD. In the mid-1970s, the Spring Street building was too old and too out-of-date to accommodate the ever-increasing need for accurate and dependable forensic testing. Scientists had to work in dreadful conditions, especially in summer when the temperature indoor swelled to forty degrees Celsius and above. It took until 1986 before the unit moved to newly-built labs at the current VFSC building under the watchful eye of State Premier John Cain.

The biology unit was arguably the third best in the world with every staff member holding a degree, which hadn't been the case ten years ago when people could walk straight in from secondary school. But this was about to end since all forensic services were currently being shifted away from the police force and moved into the private sector or other government departments. I was a product of this gradual change, working for the Crime Scene Unit at the Centre, which was overlooked by Directors, the Business Manager and the Quality Management Branch, a section of the Centre also dedicated to training new and current staff.

John Darcy was a forensic biologist and branch manager at the VFSC Forensic Biology Unit. John looked younger than his fifty-three with his blond locks and sparkling blue eyes. He bore a straight, small chin with a neatly-trimmed beard, and would look more like a beach bum than a scientist if he wasn't wearing a lab coat.

Like me, John hated office bureaucracy and was also willing to help a fellow scientist whenever the need arose. But last year, while investigating another murder, John had disappointed me. Just when I needed him the most, and when Goosh and his mob were putting pressure on everyone, he gave up on me. I'd forgiven him after the case was over, but one never forgets. I tried not to hold a grudge against him because he was my eyes and ears to test results conducted at the centre. Being on the inside and working all day in the building also gave him the opportunity to befriend anyone in the Centre and access documents by friendly request.

He was playing with a Bunsen burner and a rack of test tubes when I walked into the lab. John was forever conducting tests which dealt with fibres, blood grouping, DNA and any other matter classified as of biotomy. He was proud that his unit was the only one in Australia which attended crime scenes, and that all his staff were trained to conduct DNA testing.

'Come in, Katrina,' he said, acknowledging my presence. He had a pair of safety goggles on and a thousand and one pens sticking out from the pocket of his lab coat, which was now stained with various ink colours.

I circled the room with my eyes, observing with interest the hundred-thousand-dollar scientific equipment, including serology, liquid and gas chromatographers; mass spectrometers; four or five compound microscopes with a wide range of power; laboratory ovens; and various other optical and analytical instruments. Galvanised benches were hugging the walls around the room. Near a sink, glassware was waiting to be washed. Tens of hexagonal, yellow containers made of cardboard, approximately thirty centimetres tall, and labelled with a biological-waste-hazard symbol, were scattered around the benches. The ceiling was a multitude of fluorescent tubes.

The air conditioning made the room pleasant to be in, if one didn't mind the smell of various chemicals. It could have been the ideal environment to work in, but I preferred to move around than stay in the same place all day.

'How are the kids?' I yelled across the room, hoping he

114

would remember I was still here.

'They're fine.'

John had marital problems which he solemnly discussed. I'd met his wife on a few occasions when I went to his place for work reasons, but now I avoided his home all together. I was scared of being thought as the other woman and of complicating matters further.

'What about the Mrs?'

'She's okay.'

I could tell by the tone of his voice he didn't want to discuss his private life. He turned the Bunsen burner off, slid off his safety goggles and walked towards me. Bags hung under his eyes, and it was obvious he'd missed passing a comb through his hair that morning. His lab coat had two buttons missing in the middle, exposing a yellow T-shirt with a logo I couldn't quite make out.

'Now, you're here for that Tracy Noland case?'

'That's right.'

'Well, I haven't done the test yet. Too much back log. Seems like criminals are doing overtime during the holiday period. Probably boredom more than anything else.'

I had only given him the material six hours ago, and to expect to have it all done by now, well, that was just me. I shifted from one foot to the other. 'So, how long will it take?'

He rolled his thumb and forefinger over the stubble on his chin, looked up to the ceiling and then behind him, towards a bench where a clock indicated it was just on two o'clock.

Back to me: 'I tell you what: if you hang around I can do the test right now.'

'How long will it take?'

'Five minutes.'

'Okay.'

He passed me an oversized lab coat. I rolled up the sleeves, feeling like a university student who shared whatever lab coat was available because I'd left mine at home. The damn thing smelled like an ox, and I wondered if it had ever seen the inside of a washing machine.

We circled the lab and stopped in front of a large galvanised bench, on which I had seen John perform forensic tests in the past.

I plunged my hands in the pockets of the lab coat and felt bits of paper and paper clips, which I didn't bother removing.

He grabbed a brown paper bag with a continuity label attached to it. On a writing pad, he recorded the time, date, VFSC-ID product number and his name. I was aware that everything had to be immaculately recorded at the Centre, and in fact anywhere where evidence had the potential of being presented in a court of law. One day some defence lawyer would look at the evidence presented and question its handling from the moment it had been collected to the moment he held it in his hands.

And then he would ask, 'So, you're saying that those DNA tests were performed from the exhibit I'm holding my hand? When did that happen?'

Some scientist would answer with uncertainty, 'Um, on the second or third of March.'

'On the second or third of March?'

'Yes, that's right. I'm pretty sure it was then because it was just after my son's birthday.'

'And why isn't the exact date recorded somewhere?'

'Well,...'

'If you can't remember who handled the exhibit on a particular day, how does the jury know who handled what, when? How do we know for a fact someone hasn't been tampering with the evidence?'

The scientist would look completely dumb-founded, realising this would probably be the last time he'd ever appear in court, and praying he wouldn't lose his job over the incident.

And then the defence would ask for the exhibit to be thrown out of court, terminating the prosecutor's only chance of building a water-tight case.

After slipping on a new pair of surgical gloves from what looked like a box of tissues, John Darcy carefully cut the continuity label with small pointed scissors. Gently, he lifted the flap at the top of the bag, and pulled the bag open.

Meanwhile, I was reading at a dot-matrix computer print-out which came with the bag, observing John from the corner of one eye:

116

VICTORIA FORENSIC SCIENCE CENTRE LIAISON ITEM RECEIPT
                    Printed on 12:15   22 DEC 1997
Case Number 2189/967

Time & Date Entered      08:06          22 DEC 1997
COURIER

      Reg No              :HODS         Melina,      Katrina
Oliveira Dos
      Rank                     :Contractor Class 4
      Station             :CRIME - VFSC

INFORMANT

      Reg No              :HODS         Melina,      Katrina
Oliveira Dos
      Rank                     :Contractor Class 4
      Station             :CRIME - VFSC

NAME (S) INDEX

      NOLAND, TRACY (complainant - deceased)

offence                 : HOMICIDE

ITEM (S)

Item ( s ) received at Liaison Store on 07:55    22 DEC
1997

No        Description
                                  Property No.
_____


Item (s) retained by VFSC member on 07:55   22 DEC 1997

No        Description
                                  Property No.
_____


Item (s) retained by a NON VFSC member on 07:55    22 DEC
1997

No        Description
                                  Property No.
_____

1         PANTIES

      124/97



                  sign:  *BVeitch*

After placing the scissors on the galvanised bench, John removed a pair of small, cotton underwear with faded flower patterns from the brown paper bag.

Frank had found the underwear inside Malcom's pillow when we conducted the search in the boy's room. It was definitely girl's underwear, and seminal-like stains were spread throughout the front and the back of the material. If the stains were in fact semen, and if the semen was that of Malcom Sternwood, he was in bigger trouble than he'd ever dreamed he'd be. What intrigued me was that Tracy Noland hadn't been raped. Was the underwear a souvenir he jerked on just to remind him of the killing? The whole idea made me feel nauseous.

I knew of killers who kept souvenirs from their victims just to remind them how good it felt when they raped and killed. This was especially true of serial killers, who not only collected killings, but objects to remind them of their great achievement.

With the invention of the video camera, I knew of one offender in South Australia who went to great length to produce, edit and distribute real-life torture, rape and killing b-grade movies. The movies sold particularly well in the United States and the former USSR. It took a while to track down the film maker, who turned out to be the killer and director, a thirty-three year-old, frustrated National Institute of Dramatic Art drop-out, a former student with a fascination for ultra violent torture films, but couldn't find anything real enough to ease his appetite. As a result he built a state-of-the-art video studio in the basement of his home in Adelaide, where he would perform the most savage rituals on his female teenage victims, whom he'd kidnapped on their way back from school. The films were digitally recorded and posted through the Internet in chunks to a b-grade studio in America, whose owner thought the visual effects, especially when the girls were cut from breast to groin, were amazingly realistic. When his day in court came, the buyer of the snuff movies insisted he didn't know he was distributing real-life footage. On that statement, he only got sentenced for distributing unclassified material.

John took handwritten notes on a white, A4-sized notepad. He commented at the same time for my benefit.

'One pair of white cotton underwear with flower motifs, size 4/6, labelled Target - all cotton girl brief - no visual tear or damage. Yellow, creamy stains in the front and the back. Grass particles and dirt present.'

'What do you think the stains are?' I asked, already knowing what the answer would be.

'Seminal, I guess, but I'll have to conduct an acid phosphatase colour test to confirm.'

'What's that?'

'Basically, the presence of semen is indicated by a purple-blue colouration on a test strip when the acid phosphatase enzyme in the semen reacts with napthyl phosphate under acidic conditions to form napthyl and phosphate to which the naphthyl reacts with the brentamine fast black dye.'

'Okay,' I said, not wanting further explanation. I managed sixty-two percent in Chemistry in my last school year, nothing to gloat about, and had little interest in the subject beyond basic crime-scene analysis and associated testing.

From another brown paper bag, John removed a pre-stained white handkerchief.

'What's that for?' I asked.

'Part of the procedure in case someone challenges the accuracy of the tests in a court. Prior to conducting the test on the underwear, the method and reagents should be validated by using a known seminal stain.'

I nodded.

With the help of an eye-dropper, John placed two drops of the calcium alpha-naphthyl phosphate and Ilnaphtalin diazo blue-B mixture on the stain from the handkerchief. He immediately peeled off the adhesive strip cover and applied the strip with pressure of his thumb onto the stain.

He repeated the procedure on a stained and clean area of the underwear with two separate strips.

'What's the other strip for,' I asked, referring to the test conducted on the underwear, but away from the stain.

'We need to compare the final test to something, and the method calls for a control test to do the comparison. Like if you did a drawing on a blank sheet of paper, and when you finished it, compared it with another blank sheet identical to the one you drew on.'

After thirty seconds, he removed the control test, which had turned purple, and wrote 'control test: Phoshotesmo Km +ve' on his pad. He then removed the other strip, which had also changed colour. He scribbled in his pad and said, 'Positive as fuck. Seminal stains confirmed on item 2189/967, item one, sample one.'

I glanced over his shoulder and realised that he hadn't really written the word *fuck*.

'So, this is semen?' I asked.

'Yep. The guy's jerked all over the girl's underwear.'

Before the test had been conducted, I'd known there was a good chance it would come out positive. However, I was still shocked to realise Malcom was *that* type of person. He just seemed so innocent, the way his big eyes looked into mine, begged me, assured me that he didn't do anything. And now, faced with the most discriminating evidence, there would be little he would be able to do to save himself. I was disappointed in him. At the back of my mind I wished it could have been someone else.

It always nagged me when a young person was guilty of a violent crime, and, as a result, his life would be ruined. If only someone had gotten through to the young man when he was still building up to the crime. If someone had realised he had a fascination with prepubescent girls early on, he would have received counselling on time, saved the life of a young victim, and in the process saved his soul.

But there were so many frustrated young people who learned to cope with the difficulties of life through drugs or other unhealthy obsessions. It scared the hell out of me that Michael would experience similar frustration in years to come. I just hoped he would come out of it un-scarred like the majority of people.

But sometimes, someone, somewhere slipped through the

net. The mind goes bang, and a pact is made with the devil.

As I walked out of the lab and down the hallway, a cold sweat took over my body. I had to face the truth.

Jason Harvey had been right after all.

# CHAPTER ELEVEN

**W**hen I told Frank the results of the seminal tests, he reacted with a stern face, but anger crept into his eyes.

At 4.23 p.m., we were sitting in the conference room on the ninth floor of the Victoria Police Complex on St Kilda Road, home of the Homicide Squad, print-outs of Malcom's digital photo collection of teenage nudes spread all over the table. There weren't just photographs of Tracy Noland, but other girls as well. He must have been doing that for a while, although the photos gave no indication that they were taken in his bedroom. We'd tried to come up with a location where he may have taken the girls to do his work. At first we thought it might have been at the Melbourne College of Photography, but we knew this would have been impossible. Anyone could have walked in on him, and if they'd realised he was taking pictures of semi-naked, under-aged girls, he would have been in deep trouble, perhaps even expelled from the college. Maybe he rented a room somewhere, but I did recall that he could hardly afford to do the photography course, let alone renting motel rooms.

Frank stirred his coffee slowly, staring at an empty spot in front of him. He wasn't himself, and I'd been working with him long enough to know when an investigation was taking over his life. Me, I just wanted the culprit to be found and thrown in jail so no one else would get hurt. Him, he wanted revenge. And that was typical of men. They felt so angry towards the aggressor that a slap at the back of the head was never enough. If Frank had it his way, he'd probably take Malcom into a room and beat the living daylights out of him. It was just as well I was the one in charge of the investigation.

'Okay,' he went on, 'so now we have evidence in the form of child pornography and soiled underwear. How does that prove he killed the girl? We know he did, but we're going to need something really solid. The court is not going to punish someone because of soiled underwear hidden under a pillow and some manipulated digital photography. This is no proof he killed someone. All we've got is circumstantial evidence, and you know as well as I do that we'd be crazy to charge him with so little to go to court with.'

I sipped from my Victoria Police mug and said, 'I've asked John Darcy to do a DNA test on the seminal stain. We're going to have to get a warrant for Malcom's blood sample and do a comparison. There's no doubt in my mind that the stains on the underwear are his, but that still needs to be proven.'

'And then what?'

'And then, when we prove he's the one who jerked in the underpants, we'll place him under arrest. After that, it's a matter of finding a link between what we've got and what we're yet to find.'

Frank ground his teeth, obviously unhappy about my proposal. He slapped one hand on the mahogany table and raised his tone, 'This is bullshit! I'm not going to wait here to get another court order for a blood sample. I say we bring him in and get the truth out of him. He's a damn immature kid, and I doubt he can lie for much longer.'

I could understand Frank's frustration, but I didn't want to rush into the interrogation. If we weren't careful and calculative in the way we proceeded, we'd be more likely to make a mistake. And the last thing I wanted was to get reprimanded by Goosh and provide him with another opportunity to have my contract terminated.

But on the other hand, I shared Frank's frustration with balancing a load too heavy to carry. I needed to ease my mind like everyone else who was involved in this case, maybe even more since I hated working on child murders in the first place. But most of all, there was the underlying fear that another girl might get killed, although at this stage there was no indication that we were dealing with a repeat offender.

'If,' I said, 'and only *if*, we go ahead with an interrogation, I'll be the one handling it.'

'Don't have a problem with that.'

'Good, cause I'm gonna have none of this violent type of interrogation.'

He shook his head vigorously. 'What are you talking about? I didn't say I was going to kick the truth out of him. I said we were going to *ask* him.'

I didn't recall Frank using the word *ask*, but as it was, I knew his methods of interrogation were not always up to scratch. There were other means of interrogating a suspect other than resorting to violence. And since I'd seen Frank perform in the past, he was not someone I'd put in charge of interrogating criminals. As much as I wanted the truth to come out, beating it out of someone was always suspicious. You never knew if what you were told was some tale made up because of the victim's desire to get it over and done with. Nobody likes to be pushed around and beaten up, and if lying was the fastest and best way out of it, then the police had a lot to learn about interrogation techniques.

Other than that, it was completely illegal, and the admission would be thrown out of court before it could pass the front door. Not to mention the risk of being charged with assault and abuse of police power.

'And, anyway,' he went on, 'don't make it sound like I'm the bad guy. This bastard killed the girl, and even if he didn't, which I bloody much doubt, then he's got a lot of explaining to do in regards to all the shit we found in his room.'

I didn't bother with an answer.

Two hours later, we brought Malcom Sternwood in for interrogation. We made him aware of his rights, but he refused to have an attorney represent, which was just as well because the last thing we needed was some hot-shot solicitor making the interrogation a nightmare.

Because of the seriousness of the allegation, the interview had to be videotaped in a closed room, connected to a live monitor in another room. Later, Malcom wouldn't be able to deny anything he had said since it would be recorded.

Before Malcom walked in the room, I had carefully laid Tracy Noland's blue dress on the table of the interrogation room. The dress was the one she wore when we found her body. It was still covered in mud and botanical residues, but additionally tagged with a VFSC label. Squares had been cut from the dress in various places to conduct forensic tests.

I was hoping to get a reaction from Malcom the moment I re-entered the room. If he killed Tracy Noland, there'd be no way that he could just stand there and ignore the dress. Maybe he would try to avoid looking at it in an obvious manner, or maybe he would break down and want to run out of the room. Either way, if he'd killed the girl, I expected some type of reaction.

I was watching from one of the video monitors in a room adjacent to the interrogation room when Malcom was brought in. The door opened, and a uniformed police officer led him in.

'Just take a seat,' the officer said. 'Someone will be with you shortly.'

The officer left the room immediately.

Malcom looked confused and devastated. At first his eyes circled the room, but suddenly he stopped at the dress on the table. He approached the table, took a close look at the dress and moved back a couple of steps. He seemed puzzled by what he was looking at. And then he began to sob quietly. He walked to one corner of the room, sat down against the wall, his face in his hands and cried.

'What now?' Frank said, over my shoulder.

'We'll wait and see,' I answered, my eyes glued to the monitor. 'Give him a bit of time by himself. He'll be thinking of a thousand-and-one options. If he killed the girl, right now he's trying to come up with his best version of the event. Or maybe he doesn't care any more, and he's going to tell us the truth.'

Frank didn't answer. I could feel his breathing behind my neck. I'd forgotten how accustomed we'd become to each other, and if he'd put his hand on my shoulder, I probably would have let him.

Half an hour later, Malcom was still in the corner of the room. He was motionless and had stopped crying.

'What now?' Frank asked again.

'He's coming to terms with what's happening to him. He looks in control on the outside, but my bet is that he's feeling really confused at the realisation of what he has done and how he's going to cope. It's not always easy to face your own demons. If I walk in now, I might lose him. Give him another half hour. I want him to be so ripe, the truth is going to fall on the table like a rotten apple.'

Frank shifted his weight. 'I'm going to get coffee. I'm tired of standing here watching this jerk dealing with his conscience. He should have thought about it before he killed the girl. If you'd let me walk in there, I'd get the truth out in five minutes.' I was about to pass a comment, but he must have sensed it and smartly changed the topic. 'Do you want anything from downstairs?'

'Coffee, black, no sugar.'

Frank left, and I was alone in the room, watching Malcom huddled in one corner of the room, getting myself psyched-up for the interrogation. To make this a success, I had to get friendly with him, make him believe I was on his side. If he thought for one minute I was here to frame him and throw him in jail, he'd refuse to talk to me. Or he'd come up with the biggest lies just to get me off his back.

Fifteen minutes later, just when my elbows were getting sore from resting my head on the palm of my hands, Malcom finally stood up. He looked around, dazed as if he'd just discovered he was alone in this strange room. He circled the room and for the first time noticed the camera attached on the east wall. Then he observed the dress up-close without touching it, and finally took a seat at the table, an expressionless mask hiding his fear.

The last hour must have felt like an eternity, and I'd have hated to be in his shoes right at this moment. Knowing he was going to be asked about the digital photographs of naked teenagers we found in his computer, and whatever else he knew we'd found in his room, must have been hard to accept. He'd built this secret lie around him, indulging in his own fantasies, probably believing nothing would ever go wrong, and now his world was being shattered. People jabbed an accusing finger at what he had done. I wasn't sure what was going through his mind at that moment, but it certainly wasn't visions of freedom.

As much as I wanted to burst into the room because I felt we were both ready, I waited for Frank to come back with his coffee. I needed someone to watch over this on the monitor, just to give me that extra mental support while I was performing.

Ten minutes later, Malcom was still sitting at the table when Frank walked back in the room with three coffees.

'Thought I'd bring him one too, just to set his tongue loose,' he said as he placed two paper cups next to the monitor.

'Thanks.'

I stood from my chair and headed for the interrogation room.

The interrogation room, painted white, felt smaller than it looked on the monitor. The camera gave it a distorted wide-angle effect, giving the impression that at least twenty people would fit in the room, when in fact five would have been a crowd.

When I stepped in the room with a bundle of files twelve-inches thick, Malcom's eyes shot to me straight away. The files were a bluff, but he didn't know that. They were padded with blank photocopy paper just to make him believe we had more on him than he thought. I was trying to create an atmosphere of 'big brother is watching you.' I wanted him to feel hopelessly unable to deny what he had done.

I looked straight into his eyes. 'How are you handling it?' I said, placing his coffee on the table.

He glanced at the steaming coffee, then at me with a look that said he'd never asked for a brew. I read him his rights once more under video-taped eyewitness, but he declined having a solicitor, saying he didn't need one because he was innocent.

'I know you just want to go home,' I went on. 'But I'm here to help you. It's late, and I'd like to get home too. So, the sooner we get this over and done with, the sooner we can leave this place.' I took a seat next to him, close enough to get friendly, but not so close that he'd feel uncomfortable.

He just stared at his coffee.

'Drink it,' I continued. 'You haven't swallowed anything for the last hour. It'll make you feel better.'

He grabbed the cup and gulped half its contents in one go. After placing the cup back on the table, he took a deep breath and said, 'Am I being charged with murder?'

'No one's being charged with anything. We're just here to talk.'

'Talk about what? I didn't kill her.'

I tilted my head and said, 'Look, Malcom, I know you're pretty angry right now. If someone had locked me up for an hour in this room, I'd be angry too. The fact is that I'm not here to frame you. I'm here to find out the truth.'

'But I didn't kill her.'

'I'm not saying you're lying. It's just that... well, let's face it, even if you haven't killed the girl, evidence points to you. With the photos we found in your computer and the underwear stuffed in your pillow, people are asking questions. You're going to have to explain yourself just to get your name cleared.' I opened one of the manilla folders and retrieved three A4-size, colour print-outs of Tracy Noland in the nude retrieved from Malcom's computer. I spread them on the table, hoping to get him stressed.

'It's not a crime to take photos.'

'Some types of photos, I'm afraid it is. But that's another matter, and I certainly wouldn't worry about it at this stage. What I'm concerned about is how a jury is going to connect naked photos of Tracy Noland stored in your computer, and a girl's underwear in your possession, without believing you had something to do with her death.'

His eyes deviated to the blue dress, but he didn't talk about it. I was certain he was dying to know why the dress was on the table. I was waiting for him to make a slip of the tongue, to say something about the dress. And since he claimed he never killed Tracy Noland, how would he know that was the dress she was wearing when she got killed? Of course, he could have guessed because, after all, whose dress was it going to be other than Tracy Noland's? But the way he would deliver his questioning would more or less be an admission to his guilt. If he'd asked me what that dress was, nothing would be clear. But if he asked why Tracy Noland's dress was spread on the table, then I'd ask him how he knew it was Tracy Noland's dress, after which he might get confused and eventually admit to the murder.

But he never asked.

Malcom continued to proclaim his innocence. 'You know I didn't do it. I would never hurt Tracy. Never.'

I shifted on the chair. 'You know, Malcom, I'm going to be honest with you. I don't know whether you killed Tracy or not. I know we found enough circumstantial evidence in your room, and personally I'd like to believe you haven't killed her. Unfortunately, that's me. I tend to have some basic faith in human nature. But Senior Sergeant Frank Moore, you know, the man who searched your room with me?'

He nodded.

I went on, 'Well, he believes you did it. And other people believe you did it too. Everyone's going to come down on you like a ton of bricks. And when it happens, I won't be there to uphold your version of events. Which means if this whole thing goes to court with what we've got at the moment, you'll probably get life either way. You have to talk to me and convince all of us you didn't do it, if that's the truth. Is that the truth, Malcom?'

Anger crept into his tone. 'Why doesn't anyone believe me? I didn't kill the girl!'

'And if you did, I'm sure there's a reasonable explanation.' I paused. Then: 'You liked Tracy, didn't you?'

'Yes.' His tone lessened by a couple of notches.

'And why Tracy and not the other kids?'

'I like other kids too. But Tracy and I had a lot in common. I already told you the other day when you came to visit.'

'But you never said what.'

'We both liked photography. I'd like to take them. She liked to be the subject.'

'Did you like to take pictures of Tracy?'

'She enjoyed it. So, yes, I guess I enjoyed it too.'

'And that's all you felt about Tracy. She was just nice to photograph.'

'Yeah... that's all.'

I looked at him for fifteen seconds without saying a word. The look on his face told me he knew what was coming.

'See, Malcom, we're having a problem here. You're telling me you liked taking pictures of Tracy because she liked to have her picture taken, and that was more or less the extent of your relationship with her.'

'Friendship.'

'I beg your pardon?'

'It wasn't a relationship; it was a friendship.'

'Okay, friendship. Problem is you have naked pictures of Tracy in your computer, which implies you wanted more from her than just friendship.'

'They're only pictures. They're not even real pictures. I never took pictures of Tracy naked.'

'But you did convince her to strip to her underwear?'

I could feel his frustration building up. 'Ah, come on. You're making it sound like she didn't have a mind of her own. You talked to people. You know she could think for herself. I didn't force her to do anything she didn't want to do. When I asked her, she said yes straight away. It didn't take any convincing.'

'Okay, okay. So let's say she agreed. Now, you're a young man, and you've got a young girl near-naked in front of you, and you're telling me you didn't feel anything?'

'No.'

'Come on, Malcom, what about the photos in your computer? If you didn't want to see Tracy naked, then why did you bother enhancing the pictures and adding pubic hair to her groin when there was none in the first place?'

He blushed embarrassingly.

I continued, 'I know how hard this is Malcom. Most people don't understand. The girl was there, she was willing to play games. She was willing to have her picture taken, willing to take all her clothes off, except her underwear. And you began feeling something for her. I mean, she is a pretty girl, isn't she?'

He didn't answer.

I continued, 'I think she's pretty. I think she's young, but I can tell that one day she would have turned into an attractive young woman. Is that what you thought too? Is that why you added the pubic hair on the photographs? Because you didn't want to see her as a child?'

He looked at me relieved. 'Yes. I'm not into child

130

pornography. It's just that Tracy was there. And I changed her. She wasn't a child any more.'

'You changed her?'

'On the photographs. You can tell she's not a little girl any more.'

It was getting increasingly difficult to agree with him, but I felt I was breaking through. 'That's true, Malcom. She does look older, especially in the pictures you've stored in the computer. So you liked the idea of Tracy being older?'

'Yes, that's right. That's why I wouldn't have killed her in the first place. She was only a child.'

'So, if Tracy had been a grown-up, would you have asked her to have sex with you?'

He hesitated for a few seconds as if I'd asked him a trick question. Finally, after puzzling over an appropriate answer, he said, 'I guess so.'

'And you haven't asked her?'

'She's a child. I know the difference between a child and an adult. You're trying to make it sound like my mind is confused, but it's not. There's a difference between fantasy and reality. And I know the difference. I mean, look at all those magazines out there. Every time a man flicks through the pages of a porno mag, does that mean he's having sex with another woman? It's a bloody fantasy. And that's what these photos of Tracy were, a goddamn fantasy. Enhanced, manipulated pictures of Tracy. I didn't have sex with her, I didn't ask her to have sex with me, and I certainly didn't kill her.'

I wasn't giving in. 'What about the underwear? How does that fit in?'

'It's not hers. I stole it from Target.'

'Why?'

'To bring the fantasy alive.'

'And did it?'

'Did it what?'

'Bring the fantasy alive. Did you at any time believe Tracy wanted to have sex with you? Did you ask her, and she said no? Did you force yourself on to her, but she refused, and then you tried to shut her up? Is that what happened?'

'No.'

'You tried to shut her up, but she wouldn't, so maybe you

covered her mouth with your hand and didn't realise how strong you were?'

He shifted on his chair and said, 'I don't want to talk about this any more. It's private, and I don't have to talk about it.'

Now was not the right time to lose him. 'You're going to have to talk about it at some stage. Now, you can talk to me, or you're going to tell your story in front of a judge and a jury. I'm sure you don't want to tell this story in front of twenty strangers. Why the underwear? Was it the same as the ones Tracy used to wear?'

He nodded. 'But it wasn't hers. She wouldn't have given it to me in the first place.'

'Did you ask her?'

'Of course not. Do you think I'm crazy?'

'I don't think you're crazy. I think you liked Tracy, and something didn't go according to plan. I think you might have killed her by accident. If you killed her by accident, I can help you. I can talk to the prosecutor and work out something. It matters how and why she died. But if you say nothing to me, you're going to sink all the way to the bottom.'

'You know what I think? I think the only thing which didn't go according to plan was you guys turning my room inside out. That's what went wrong. And now you're trying to pin me down with a murder.'

'So, who do you think killed Tracy if not you? Do you agree that you're looking like the most likely suspect at the moment? What am I supposed to believe? What would you believe if you were in my shoes?'

'I don't want to talk any more.' He shifted uncomfortably in his chair while emptying his cup of coffee. 'Can I have a break?'

I stood from my chair. 'Sure, you can have a break. Take whatever time you need, but the sooner we finish this, the sooner you can go home.'

He didn't answer and threw his head between the palms of his hands.

'Do you want another coffee?' I asked while grabbing both empty paper cups and my stack of files.

He shook his head, and I left the room.

'For heaven's sake, he's as guilty as hell,' Frank barked as soon as I returned to the monitor room. 'You're playing around with him. Rough him up a little. Push him a bit. Jesus, you're talking to him as if this whole thing was an accident. He killed a child for heaven's sake!'

'Mind your own business, Frank,' I snapped. 'You do your job, and I'll do mine. I'm in charge of this investigation, and you're only here to watch. If you're going to tell me how to do my job, then you might as well leave. I've already got Goosh on my back doubting every move I make. I don't need you as well.'

He pursed his lips and made a whistling sound. 'Oops, sorry. I didn't realise you were so touchy. Fine, go ahead with your method of interrogation. Just don't expect me to sit there all night holding your hand.'

'I'm not expecting anything from you, Frank.' I looked at his empty paper cup. 'Do you want another coffee? I need some fresh air. Let him simmer in his own juice for the next half hour.'

'Sure.'

I snatched his cup and walked out of the room.

# CHAPTER TWELVE

**I** stopped at the ladies' room to refresh myself. I let the tap run while checking my reflection in the mirror, surprised at how tired I looked. Gently, I splashed water on my face, feeling the cold liquid enter every pore, bringing some relief to my exhausted mind. Just as well I had no foundation on, or it would have run down my neck.

The interrogation wasn't going as well as I had anticipated. To begin, Malcom hadn't reacted to Tracy's dress whatsoever. I was hoping he would eventually break down and confess. In the past, I found the method to be effective. Usually, I would put the weapon of the crime on the table with blood still left on it. The reaction was always the same. The accused would feel extremely uncomfortable faced with the weapon he used to kill his victim. And then, throughout the interview, he would keep glancing at the weapon. Eventually, he would give in and admit to the crime. The problem with Tracy Noland's death was that there had been no weapon found. According to Dr Charles W. Main, the young girl died of suffocation, so whoever killed her didn't use a weapon but his own hands.

I finger-brushed my auburn hair, trying to give it a lift so as to look more alive than I felt. I straightened my marine skirt, glanced once more in the mirror, forced a smile, and walked out of the room.

I took the elevator to the ground floor and passed the security check-point on my way out of the building.

The sky was overcast, but it was still hot and sticky, probably in the low-thirties. In that part of the city, five minutes from Swanson Walk, traffic was heavy all day long, even on a Monday evening. My breath of fresh air turned out to be a breath of freshly-squeezed carbon monoxide.

Around the corner from the Police Complex, there's a sandwich shop for people who don't have time to bring their own lunch, or those who'd rather have a real coffee than instant powder in a tin can disguised as coffee. I ordered two coffees to take-away, none for Malcom since he didn't want one.

I stepped back outside and took a sip from one of the polyester cups. Freshly brewed coffee, no milk, no sugar. Within thirty seconds I could already feel it working in my brain. I was ready to go back in the building and wrap up the interrogation.

I ended up finishing my coffee before I passed the security check on the ground floor. After walking through the centre of a metal detector, I climbed into the elevator, my ID clipped to my breast pocket, and pushed the button for the ninth floor.

When I stepped back inside the monitor room, the monitor screen was turned off. No one was in the room. At once, a high level of adrenalin rushed through my brain. Fully alert, I knew something had gone wrong. I place Frank's coffee next to the monitor, but it fell to the floor, the hot brew spreading itself all over the grey tiles. I stared at it for a few seconds, and thought, 'what the hell' before I stepped out of the room.

I threw open the door of the interrogation room.

Frank was sitting there all by himself.

I looked around.

Malcom was gone.

'What the hell is going on here?' I asked.

'He's been taken into custody.' He said that matter-of-factly, but I could register tension in his tone.

'What?'

'He confessed to the murder while you were downstairs, so I've placed him in custody.'

'What do you mean he confessed? Who did he talk to?'

'Me.'

135

'Why you? Did you go in there?'

He didn't answer.

I went on, feeling heat on my face, 'Did he ask you to talk to him, or did you just walk in there?'

He hesitated for a few seconds. 'What's the difference? He confessed. He was ready to spill his guts by the time you left. So, all I did was push him a little more.'

'You did what?'

He stood up and said assertively, 'You heard me. Don't play dumb and deaf. I went in there, had a little chat, and he confessed.'

I stood, speechless, not certain how to respond.

He continued, 'Point is he confessed, and now it's all over. Congratulations, the case has been solved within two weeks. I guess you'll get to keep your job.'

I approached him, slapped him on the face with full force and yelled, 'You bastard!'

His neck twisted sideways, his eyes expressing surprise. 'What was that for?'

'You've got a fuck of a nerve, Frank. I go downstairs for ten minutes, you have the arrogance to take over my interrogation, and then you stand there as if nothing happened.' He was about to say something, but I cut in. 'You know what? This is going down on the record. I'm filing an official complaint. It's over. I'm not working with you any more. You're worse than the rest of them. Just because you think you know me doesn't give you the right to do shit behind my back.'

I did a half turn and headed straight for the door.

'Katrina,' I heard him whimper, but I was already out of the room.

Half way to the elevator, I turned around and paced back to the monitor room. The coffee was all over the floor. Carefully, I tiptoed over it, and got closer to the monitor. I pressed the eject button on the video recorder. The unit spat out a black, VHS tape which I slipped in my handbag. If I was going to bother with an official complaint, at least I had evidence with me.

When I got home, I was in tears. I quickly made my way up to the second floor, opened the door of my apartment and went straight to the fridge. From there, I withdrew a bottle of Chenin Blanc, which Phillip and I had half consumed on Saturday night. I poured myself a full glass and swallowed it in one go. This was followed by another glass. So much for not resorting to alcohol when the pressure was getting too high. I was somehow aware that I was over-reacting, but I had to let the steam out of my system. Bottling up anger was a health hazard, anyway.

I stepped into the lounge room, flicked the television and video recorder on with the remote control, and inserted the tape which I'd just slipped out of my hand bag.

I crashed on the floral couch, a glass of white wine in one hand and the remote control in the other, and viewed the tape in rewind-playing mode. I stopped it when Frank walked into the interrogation room and pressed PLAY. I increased the volume until the conversation was loud enough for me to hear every whisper.

Malcom was still at the table, unaware Frank had just walked into the room. When Frank approached the table, Malcom jerked slightly as if he had been zapped by a low-voltage electrical current. He just stared at Frank, obviously wondering what the hell was going on.

Frank circled the table with *my* twelve inch files under both arms. He placed them on the table and announced, 'I'll be conducting the rest of this interview. Dr Melina has been called to an urgent job.'

I could read the discomfort edged on Malcom's face. He lowered his eyes to the table. I'd told him before that Frank believed he committed the crime, so he must have guessed this was not going to be a two-way, friendly conversation.

Frank took his seat next to Malcom, where I previously sat. Immediately he opened the top manilla folder and spread the naked pictures of Tracy Noland on the table.

'Recognise those?' Frank sounded like an army-drill sergeant.

Malcom shrugged.

Like thunder, Frank slammed his hand on the table, making me jump on the couch. 'I don't have time for your farty little games. Now, you're going to answer my questions and stop playing the sensitive new-age bullshit. Do *you* recognise those pictures?'

Without looking at them, Malcom said, 'Yes.'

If there was a scale which measured harassment of a suspect, Frank had already scored an eleven out of ten. He selected one of the pictures and placed it right in front of Malcom's eyes.

'Have a good look,' he ordered.

Not knowing any better in regards to his rights, Malcom looked at the picture.

Frank went on, 'Fancy her, do you?'

Malcom didn't answer.

'Answer the goddamn question!'

'Yes, I did. But it's not like the way you're trying to make it.'

'Oh, yeah? Well, what way was it then?' Frank placed the picture back on the table and moved his head really close to Malcom. 'You know, you can fuck around with Dr Melina and everyone else if you want, but between you and me, we both know you did it. You're playing this bullshit game just to gain time. But I'm telling you now, it's too late. I've got enough shit here,' he tapped on the pile of files, 'to throw you in the slammer for life. So stop wasting my time and yours. Why did you kill her?'

'I didn't do it.'

'She didn't want to fuck you, so you forced yourself on to her? Is that what happened? Well, I think it is. I mean, look at her.' He picked up the picture again. 'Nice, isn't she?'

Malcom nodded.

'And you didn't want to fuck her?'

'It's not like that.'

'I mean, I look at this picture, and, well, I'd fuck her. You did a good job with her pussy. Surely, this wasn't part of your photography course? Was it your teacher who told you to touch up little girls' pussies?'

Malcom raised his voice, 'Hey, you've got no right to talk to me like that. I didn't do anything. I'm not going to talk to you.'

Frank stood from his chair, sending it flying across the room. 'You're not going to talk to me? You don't have to talk to me. I don't need your version of why you killed her. Right now I'm so pissed, I don't know what I'm going to do.'

I couldn't tell if Frank was putting on an act. He looked damn angry, more angry than I had ever seen him be.

Without warning, he grabbed Malcom by his shirt and pulled him to his feet. 'I'm so pissed right now,' he said, 'I think I'm just going to do you here and now. What the hell, it's not like anyone's going to give a damn. I'll probably get a medal if I manage to turn you into mash potato.'

He threw Malcom away from the table.

Malcom lost balance and fell on his back. 'Jesus Christ,' he whimpered.

Frank approached him, his face beaming like a beacon. 'You don't want to tell me what happened? Fine, I'll get it out of you one way or another.'

Frank was about to kick him, but Malcom protested, 'All right, all right. I'll talk.' He managed to get back on his feet, rubbing his lower back with his right hand.

'Okay, let's talk,' Frank said as he took his seat back. 'Now, let me ask you again. Did you kill Tracy Noland?'

Malcom took his time.

'Did you kill Tracy Noland?' Frank repeated, raising his tone by a notch.

'Yes.'

'Louder. I can't hear you.'

'Yes.'

'Yes, what?'

'Yes, I killed Tracy Noland.'

'And did you kill Tracy Noland because she didn't want to have sex with you?'

'Yes.'

Frank had calmed down. 'You see, I told you it was easier to tell the truth. You don't have to stay in this room longer than necessary.' He gathered the pictures from the table and placed them back in one of the manilla folders. 'I'll see you in court, asshole.' Frank left the room with the files under his arms.

The video tape continued rolling for a while longer, the time it took Frank to get back to the monitor room and turn the video recorder off.

Malcom stood there motionless when the screen went blank.

I didn't know what to make of it. Frank had done exactly what I hoped he wouldn't do, but by the same token he gotten something out of Malcom. Still, I was damn angry he got Malcom to admit to the murder under threat. If a defence solicitor got hold of the tape, he would have a field day in court, explaining to the jury that this confession was useless because the suspect was forced to admit his guilt. And in a way, that's how it felt to me. Battering of the witness was illegal, and Frank knew it.

Or maybe Frank was right. Maybe Malcom had to be pushed for the truth to come out.

I swallowed the rest of my Chenin Blanc, feeling a headache coming on. No matter what the outcome, I was angry with the way Frank took over the interrogation when he knew how I was going to react. He knew I would have never done that to him. Where was this lack of respect coming from? After all the years we'd been working together, it was hard to believe he had the nerve to cross me the way he did.

I stood from the couch and made my way to the bathroom, dizziness taking over me. I couldn't tell if I was sick from the white wine or from what had happened at the police complex.

I lifted the lid from the toilet bowl and emptied the contents of my stomach.

# CHAPTER THIRTEEN

I spent the next three days at home, not wanting to see anyone, which wasn't easy since the third day happened to be the 25th of December, and I was expected to invest quality time with family and loved ones during the festive season.

On Christmas morning, after Michael unwrapped his presents, a non-violent Playstation game and a new pair of Nike running shoes, he asked me what was wrong. I told him nothing, but he knew I wasn't myself.

'You don't have to tell me if you don't want to,' he said while I was dicing up some capsicums to make a French ratatouille for lunch. 'But then there's no point hoping our relationship is going to improve if you keep secrets from me all the time.'

His comment took me by surprise. It seemed to be such a mature thing to say for someone who was only thirteen years old. I wondered if he meant it, or whether he heard the comment on television, or maybe overheard two adults talking to one another.

'I'm sorry,' I said, looking at him straight in the eyes. 'I don't mean to shut you out. It's work. I've had a hard time. Got into a fight with Frank, and I'm tired of all the lies and competition.'

'Quit.'

'Quit?'

'Yeah, if you don't like something, you don't have to put up with it. You've only got one life.'

All right, I thought, what pop star has he been listening to? 'It's not that easy, Michael. I've got to pay the mortgage and support the two of us.'

'Yeah, but you're an intelligent woman. You could make money some other way.'

So I was an intelligent woman now, not just his mother. I shook my head. 'And besides, I never said I hated my job. It's just people around me can be a pain at times.'

'Sure, but we already discussed this last year, and every year we go through the same thing over and over. I think you need a change of career.'

Michael began Secondary College this year, and obviously it had affected his thinking. He was advising me on a career change. Not that I thought his advice was invalid, but hearing it from my own blood didn't feel right.

'Michael, I don't want a change of career. I like investigative work, and I'm here at this point of my life because I choose to be.'

'You don't know that. You're too close to see what's happening. I'm outside you, so I can see things in better perspective. You're not seeing the whole picture. You know, like the brick-wall thing.'

'The brick-wall thing?'

'Yeah, like if you stand really close to a wall, then all you see is bricks. And then if you take a few steps back, then you realise it's not only bricks, but a wall. And then if you step a little further back, then you realise it's not really a wall, but a house. See, and right now you're looking at bricks.'

'Really?' I couldn't believe what he was telling me. It was like the last thirty-nine years of my life never existed. For someone who was supposed to be an intelligent woman, all I was able to see were bricks. God help me if that was the truth. 'You know, Michael, I think you've made some really good points, but I'm telling you that everything is under control, and I don't hate my job.'

'So why did you get drunk three days ago?'

I stopped chopping my capsicum. 'What?'

'You finished the entire bottle of wine that was in the fridge.'

'That was half a bottle. And what are you doing? Spying on me now?'

'I just noticed, that's all.'

'Okay, well, go and notice your homework. I wasn't born last summer. Give me a break, will you?'

'It's the holidays, mum. I don't have any homework.'

'Fine. Just go and do whatever it is you do these days.'

'Cool.' He was about to leave the room, but added, 'Hey, do you think we could go and see Jason again this weekend? There's this really cool trick he's gonna show me. You know, the one with the coin he did last week at the market?'

'We'll see.'

He disappeared into the lounge room. A minute later, I could hear gun shots and groaning. No doubt he was playing Doom on the Playstation again, a mindless violent game which Phillip bought him for his birthday. I can clearly admit I was unimpressed. I didn't even know they made such violent video games. But apparently, I was out of it. Every kid played Doom, and none of them turned into criminals. I couldn't wait to see the result of that in ten years time.


Now that the Tracy Noland investigation was coming to an end, I decided it was time for me to get back into shape. Michael's accusation of drunkenness made me wonder about my health, and, as a result, the following day I returned to Terry Bennetts' Gym on High Street.

Terry Bennetts' was on the first floor of an old building, above an automotive garage. The equipment was old but in working order, and the atmosphere was very industrial. I loved it. It was so cold in winter that you had no choice but to work out.

While at the gym the previous year, I befriended a man who worked at the State Library. Ken was a short guy with long hair and a grey beard. He was capable of lifting a one-hundred-and-twenty-pound barbell while carrying on a conversation. He had little to do outside work, so he spent four hours working out. Strangely enough, his muscle mass never increased. When I queried him about this observation, he confirmed he was eating little, therefore his muscles were starved of essential proteins and amino acids needed for tissue growth and repair.

Getting back into working with weights was hell, especially when you've stopped for a while. After my stretches, I soldiered on with bench presses and arms curls. The weights I used were considerably moderate since I hadn't worked out for a while, and I didn't want to injure myself.

I told Ken about the incident with Frank during Malcom's interrogation, and he responded by telling me I shouldn't have hit Frank.

'I was angry,' I argued, while dropping a ten-pound dumbbell to the floor. My biceps were killing me. 'It's not like I planned it.'

'I know, but you've given him something to fight back with. Filing an official complaint against him is a bad idea, especially when you slapped him. Why don't you give it a rest for a week or so and see how you feel?'

Ken was right, of course. Making hasty decisions out of revenge was never a good idea, not from my experience, anyway. I wasn't the kind of person who would go out of my way to get even with someone. To begin, I had little time to play these type of games. And then, I didn't have the heart. Deep down, I liked Frank despite the fact that some people thought he was vastly unattractive and not very impressive as a cop. His policing methods were questionable at times, and I wondered how he had lasted so long without getting his fingers burned. But many times he pulled through when I was feeling weak. He'd been like a big brother to me. During my first year at the VFSC, he showed me all the ropes and office politics, and was patient as hell. And although his kindness might have been the result of him wanting to get into my pants, the point is he treated me right when others wanted me to sink. But from the moment I informed him I wasn't interested in having a relationship with him, our lives had turned into a tug-of-war. I had no idea how I was going to win him back. All I wanted was our friendship to remain honest and respectful, but incidents like the one which took place at the St Kilda Road police complex did not facilitate the process.

While struggling with my leg extensions, I wondered if Malcom was really the killer. It was obvious from the video recording that he'd been pushed into a corner. The point was that the recording of the interrogation would never be shown as evidence of his admission to the killing of Tracy Noland. The only way Malcom would get convicted was if we charged him with something concrete, or if he signed a full confession, which I wasn't aware he had done to date. There was enough circumstantial evidence to place him under arrest, but little to convict him.

I eased into some stretches before farewelling Ken and leaving the gym.

When I got home at 5.32 p.m., I threw my gym bag in the hallway, letting it slide on the polished wooden floor, and headed straight to the kitchen for a glass of water. Automatically, I glanced towards the answering machine and noticed it was flashing. One message. The glass of water in one hand, I circled the kitchen bench and walked to the lounge room. I punched the PLAY button on the answering machine, next to the floral couch. It was Goosh asking me to call him back on his home number at my convenience.

I dialled the number he left on the answering machine immediately, reluctant to have him occupying my thoughts for longer than necessary.

He answered on the first ring.

'Well,' he said, 'I'll admit to being relieved you've found the killer. Frank Moore told me what a wonderful job you've performed and wants you commended.'

'Just doing what I'm being paid for,' I said, wondering if Frank was sucking up to me so that I wouldn't file a complaint about his interrogation techniques. 'There's still a lot of work to be done. We need to arrange a meeting with the prosecutor and supply the relevant evidence for a court hearing. I don't know if we've got enough to prosecute. I have to look into it.'

'And I'm sure you'll handle it just fine, like everything else. You're extremely fortunate to have someone like Frank working with you.'

'I know,' I answered for lack of knowing any better.

When he hung up, I felt a tightness in my throat. The bastard lacked diplomacy so much, he couldn't give me full credit when it was due. Maybe I was taking all this too much to heart. It was time to swallow my pride and move on. This whole investigation was now almost behind me, and I wanted to make the most of what life had to offer instead of dwelling in my own self-dramatised purgatory.

On Friday evening I rang up Jason Harvey and asked him if it was okay to come and see him on the weekend.

'Michael is fascinated by your magic tricks. He said you promised to show him how you did them.' I was calling from my home office, feet propped up on the desk, overlooking the traffic on Chapel Street, feeling myself again after having done nothing other than shopping for clothes at Prahran Central and catching a two-o'clock movie to kill the afternoon.

Jason's voice sounded cheerful. 'I'm glad he's interested. The only things kids want to hear about these days are computers.' Then he changed subject without warning. 'Did you arrest him? Has he been charged with murder?'

It took me a few seconds to realise he was talking about Malcom Sternwood. I explained to him how Malcom made a full confession on tape.

'Really?' He sounded genuinely surprised. 'Well, I'll be damned.'

'Why is that?'

'I never thought he'd just go ahead and admit to it. Especially when he denied everything to begin with. Jeez, well, it shows you can never tell.'

I'd also been surprised by Malcom's confession, but I never told Jason how Malcom came to admit he killed Tracy Noland under pressure from Frank.

He went on, 'I'm just glad you've arrested him at last. People like him don't deserve to live.'

I didn't feel like getting into a capital punishment debate with Jason, who seemed to have strong viewpoints on every topic in the universe. I told him I wasn't at liberty to discuss anything about the case while the investigation was still being carried out.

He sounded disappointed.

I farewelled him and told him we were looking forward to seeing him on the weekend.

I spent the rest of the evening doing some paper work and billing the VFSC for my services.

Sunday, Michael and I had lunch at Jason's. His cuisine hadn't improved since the last time I'd been there. He treated us to freshly cut tomato-and-cheese sandwiches, which I found hard to swallow.

During lunch, Jason Harvey made it quite clear he was delighted Malcom got caught. 'Just to think he was living in this street. It makes my skin crawl.'

We were eating in the backyard, around a white, round plastic garden table with matching injection-moulded chairs. The sun was high in the sky, making it one of the nicest days we'd had so far in December. My guess was that the temperature had stabilised at around twenty-five degrees Celsius, pleasant weather to be indoors or outdoors just the same.

After lunch, Jason was showing Michael some magic tricks while I was making coffee for two. Michael was too young to drink coffee, I felt, because of all the caffeine it contained. Of course, I was aware my fears were being ridiculed by the amount of Coke and other caffeine-enriched soda drinks he consumed during the day.

I could hear them chatting next door.

Jason: 'No, no. You do the knot clockwise, not anti-clockwise. See, you pass it around your wrist. '

Michael: 'Like this.'

'Hold on. I'll show you again.'

Pause.

Michael again: 'Wow, that's so cool.'

Jason: 'Wait until I show you the trick with the coin.'

'The one you did at the market?'

'You remember?'

'Sure I do. It's my favourite.'

It was great to hear them getting on so well with one another. I always felt guilty that Michael didn't have a father, although there was little I could do to remedy the situation. Phillip tried hard to be friendly with Michael, but to date I hadn't seen Michael taking to him too well. The problem was that they had absolutely nothing in common other than me and the fact they were male. But with Jason Harvey, Michael acted differently. Jason was young at heart, taking time to play and enjoy the few years he had left in front of him. He

147

possessed a zest for life, a rare quality in this day and age.

I walked into the living room with two mugs of coffee, one in each hand, just when Jason was showing Michael an act where he made his lucky coin vanish by rubbing it on the back of his forearm. He dropped the coin a few times, but on the third go, he did it perfectly, and when he unclenched his hand slowly, the coin had vanished.

'Wow,' Michael said, his eyes gleaming with excitement.

'It's that lucky coin again,' I commented.

Jason turned to me and smiled. 'Yes, the one everybody should have.'

The rest of the afternoon was spent quietly, discussing each other's life stories.

Jason told us he was married once, but she left him without warning.

'Our opinions differed too much,' he told us, a sad look in his eyes. 'She was conservative, always wanted to stay indoors and never see people. Me, I love people. Friends used to come over on the weekend, and she'd get really cross with me because I never told her when someone was coming over. One morning, she just left. Never heard from her again.'

'Did she leave a note or something?' I asked.

'Nothing. Didn't even take her stuff with her.'

I looked at him for a few seconds and said, 'So, how do you know she left? Maybe she got abducted or had an accident.'

He puzzled over my question, searching for something which he had buried somewhere deep in the past. 'Got a call from her sister two weeks later. She told me Elizabeth was okay, and that there was no need to track her down. She'd just had enough, full stop.'

'Mmm...'

The whole incident didn't surprise me. People had strange ways of coping with situations they hated and, all of a sudden, gave up on everything. Tens of thousands of people went missing every year, and nobody knew where they were. It was always difficult for family and friends, not knowing what had happened to their loved one. At least Jason had been lucky that his wife passed on some form of message to let him know she had disappeared by choice. I'd met people whose sons or daughters, or even parents, vanished without a trace and were never to be seen or heard of again. For years, the ones left behind held on to the hope of seeing their loved ones again. But time never solved the mystery, only concealed deep wounds of betrayal or frustration. Did the person run away? Was she abducted? Had he died in a accident, and no one had been able to identify the body?

Those with money hired private detectives who charged a hundred dollars an hour, sometimes to do nothing but type a report that the person had vanished and can't be found. Some private eyes were sincere to their customers, but others lied and told them their loved one would be found soon, but a little more money was needed. And within a few years, sometimes less, the family home would be sold and all savings drained with no resolution in sight.

Jason Harvey never bothered tracking down his wife. 'She left of her own accord,' he explained. 'Never gave me the chance to talk things over. I don't see why I was going to waste my time running around chasing after her when she knew exactly where I was.'

And who could blame him, especially if the flame of their marital vows had burned out years before she vanished.

The weekend had been such wonderful bliss that on Monday the 29th December, I found it difficult to get out of bed and get things moving. Outside my bedroom window, the sky was clear, and I could hear the heavy beginning-of-the-week traffic building up near the intersection fifty metres from my apartment. Many people were on holidays, but somehow there seemed to be more cars on the roads.

I hadn't heard from Phillip since the last time he stayed over. In fact, I was surprised he hadn't called or visited during Christmas. As I propped myself up to check the time on the alarm clock on the side table, I wondered if he was angry at me. I felt a certain coldness towards him, but I wasn't sure whether it was because I wanted more time for myself, or whether deep down I felt his commitment to me was less than genuine. Was it freedom I wanted, or being loved to death?

The time on my clock radio read 7.32 a.m. Noise in the kitchen told me Michael was having breakfast. I told myself I should get up to greet him before he left for the day for one of his unknown destinations with his friend Chris, whom he had arranged to meet at eight o'clock.

Unwillingly, I stepped out of bed and on to the woven Indian rug I bought at IKEA two years ago. I slipped on a white bathrobe and, slowly, made my way to the kitchen, yawning, and scratching the back of my neck all at once.

Michael was at the kitchen table, rubbing the back of his forearm with a twenty-cent piece.

'Look, mum. I can do it.'

I wasn't that interested but hated to upset him, so I said, 'Show me.'

He rubbed and rubbed, and dropped the coin on the table.

'Hold on,' he said. 'It's kind of tricky.'

And he tried again, and dropped the coin on the table.

'Hold on, hold on. One more time.'

This time, he rubbed and rubbed and rubbed, and suddenly he lifted his hand and the coin had vanished.

'Very good,' I said, wondering where the hell the coin had gone to.

He was about to do it again when the telephone interrupted us. It was not even eight o'clock, making me wonder why people rang up so early.

Before I snatched the receiver, I said to Michael, 'You better get ready, or you're going to make Chris wait for you.'

He twisted his mouth and went on practising his trick anyway.

Dr Charles W. Main was at the end of the line. He kind of surprised me because I was expecting either Frank or Phillip.

He greeted me and said, 'Are you too busy to get over here?', referring to the mortuary.

'Something important?' I was hoping to have another few days to myself.

'Let's just say I'd like to talk to you in person.'

I agreed to meet him at 9.30 a.m.

# CHAPTER FOURTEEN

**I** parked my Lancer at the VIFM at 9.25 a.m., finger-brushed my hair and straightened up the collar of my white blouse. On the way to Southbank, I wondered what was so important that Dr Main wanted to see me in person. I sort of guessed it might have something to do with Tracy Noland, but the fact that he wanted to see me face to face told me it was more than just routine stuff.

I reported to the reception, where I was advised to go straight through to Dr Main's office. I knew exactly where that was since I'd been there twice already, once last year when I broke into his office, and the other day regarding the Tracy Noland autopsy. I walked down the corridor, my feet sinking into the blue carpet, feeling the coldness of the place in my bones.

Dr Main looked as if he was expecting me. His grey hair was stylishly brushed back, and he wore a white shirt with a red neck-tie and a gold tie-pin. Although I had noticed in the past, today he looked even more handsome, his chiselled face tanned as if he'd just spent a month in the Bahamas, and his nails were short and clean. He had lovely hands, with long, thin fingers which seemed to dance every time he shuffled something on his desk.

'Take a seat, Dr Melina.'

'Thank you.'

His tone was formal, forcing me to remain business-like.

'I've got some toxicological results, which I have no doubt you'd be interested in.' He opened a manilla folder and skimmed through the first couple of pages.

'Was she poisoned?' I asked, trying to read over the table and guessing he was talking about Tracy Noland. His citrus aftershave whisked past my nostrils, sending a shiver of delight down my spine.

'No, not as such. Certainly no traces of arsenic, cyanide or strychnine.'

'So what have you found?'

He locked his eyes into mine. 'Swabs and scrapings from the mouth and nasal areas came up with traces of zinc stearate.'

I creased my brows. 'What the hell is that?'

'A compound of zinc oxide.'

'From what?'

'To my knowledge, combined with stearate and palmitic acid, it can be used as a smooth, dusting powder.'

I puzzled over this fact for a few seconds. 'And why would anyone use it to smother another person?'

He raised both hands to the ceiling, like a priest giving a sermon at Sunday mass. 'Wouldn't have a clue. And that's why I thought you might be interested.'

It certainly did raise possibilities. Maybe zinc stearate was a chemical used in photography. I was a competent photographer in my field of work, but darkroom techniques were not my speciality. However, as ignorant as I might have been, I knew for a fact I'd never heard of zinc stearate being used to develop a film. On the other hand, the only way I was going to get a clear idea of what the chemical was used for was to ask an expert.

On my way out of the VIFM, a copy of Tracy Noland's toxicology report tucked under my arm, I retrieved my mobile phone from my handbag and punched some numbers.

Forty-five minutes later, I was on the third floor of B-block at the TAFE (Tertiary and Further Education) division of Swinburne University in Hawthorn, where I taught Introduction to Forensic Investigation on Wednesday afternoons.

The university offered a Certificate IV in Applied Science with a major in Forensic Science to anyone interested and preferably working in the field. With over three hundred and fifty applicants for forty full-time positions the previous year, it certainly was competitive. The second year of the course, which was accessible only to members of the police force working in investigation or fingerprinting, led to a Diploma in Forensic Science. It was the first and only course of its kind offered at TAFE-level anywhere in Australia, and drew people from overseas. Last year, I taught a student named Stacey, who travelled all the way from New Zealand to do the course.

The academic year had ended last November, and the new one wouldn't start until the second week of February, and, as a result, when I walked down the corridor to room 306, where Basic Photography and Forensic Photography was usually taught, not a soul was in sight.

I peaked through the window of room 306, but no one was there.

I made my way to the other end of the corridor where the staff canteen was located. Deborah Klarner, the Forensic Science course coordinator, was sipping from a mug while reading an article from *New Scientist*. No one else was in the room.

'Hi, Deb,' I said, bringing attention to myself.

She looked up and smiled. 'Oh, hi, Katrina.' She wore a Cleopatra cut and a dark-blue power suit with a yellow shirt. Her expression was always cheerful, no matter the level of stress she was under. She had an expression which radiated friendliness and enthusiasm and was the most people-oriented person I had ever met. It didn't matter what she was doing, she always stopped to help a person in need.

TAFE people were relaxed about formalities. We called each other by our first names, a contrast to when I was working for Interpol in Europe as part of my training with the FBI in Quantico. Academics in France and Germany liked to be called by their surnames. In fact, no one really knew what their colleagues first names were. Even students were called by their surnames. In my forensic classes, I only remembered people by their first names. There was Monique, John, Brandon, Shaun, Prue, Sam, Bianca, Chelsea, Michael, Tony, and a multitude of others, whose faces were only associated to first names. A fine bunch of students who always made me feel like one of them in spite of me being much older.

'Have you seen Samuel around?' I asked, referring to the Basic Photography lecturer, a medical photographer who had been working part-time with us for just under a year, and who spent most of his time at RMIT (Royal Melbourne Institute of Technology) University. Samuel was the finest person I knew when it came to photographic knowledge. His expertise extended over a period of twenty years, and he had won many national and international awards for his outstanding work. The faculty was extremely proud to have him lecturing in photography.

'I think he's in the lab next to 306.'

I'd called Samuel on his mobile while leaving the VIFM, and he agreed to meet me within the hour.

I gossiped with Deborah Klarner for five minutes about other staff members and students. Apparently, a staff member, conducting an experiment on biological decomposition, had left five chooks rotting in the ceiling above one of the labs. Everyone forgot about the experiment until a week later when it began raining maggots on top of the students performing laboratory work. The lab stunk so bad, it had to be quarantined for an entire week.

I was still laughing whole-heartedly when making my way to the darkroom. I could visualise the expression on the students' faces when it began raining maggots.

Samuel was topping up chemicals for developing films when I walked in on him. He was as handsome as they came, but married and uninterested. He stood tall at one-hundred-and-eighty centimetres, and wore his thick black hair brushed back, carefully cut to highlight a crisp, pleasant face with two emerald eyes. He wore the obligatory lab coat when working in the dark room.

'Made it here as soon as I could,' he said, without greetings. 'Things are a bit quiet at the moment. Wait until the academic year begins. Back to high-octane coffee and sleepless nights.'

I nodded and asked, 'Ever heard of zinc stearate?'

'Should I?' He didn't turn around but continued to fill a ten-litre plastic container with developer.

'I don't know. Does it have anything to do with

154

photography?'

He paused for a few seconds. 'What did you say the stuff's called?'

'Zinc stearate. I thought it might be something used in photography.'

Another pause. 'Nope. Never heard of the stuff. If it's used in photography, it must be something new. What gave you that idea?'

I explained without much detail how it was found on a body at the mortuary, and the coroner wondered where it came from.

'Sorry,' he said. 'Can't help you with that. Why don't you go and see Brian?'

Brian Turner was a science lecturer in the building, whose eccentricity made him unpopular with the rest of the faculty. He had a philosophical approach to life and other people that bordered on personality disorder. For some unknown reason, he believed himself to be a wise soul whose opinion on a variety of subjects was a gift from God to share with the rest of humanity. Little did he realise that other people had existed before his time and had written philosophical discourses on topics he had never thought of to date and probably never would in his lifetime. What disturbed me the most was his cynical approach to other people, always assuming they were idiots unless they could prove otherwise. Other than that, he was a fine scientist.

Brian was in his office, his tall body hunched over his computer. I never got used to his gold, nose-ring and peroxide hair, and obviously other academics never did either, the reason why he never managed a university job in spite of his doctorate. He was an odd-looking man with goggling eyeballs, who was often seen walking proudly down the corridors, laughing and pointing at students who'd failed Introduction to Chemistry the previous year and had to repeat it the following year.

His desk was clutter-free, showing a need to control his environment. From the window of his office, one could observe half the campus, where only a few souls travelled to the library and back to their offices.

Brian Wood turned around, glanced at me, and returned to his keyboard.

'Someone's going to arrest you with a jacket like that,' he said bluntly.

I looked behind me, wondering if he was talking to someone else. When I realised he was referring to me, I chose to ignore his comment.

'Ever heard of zinc stearate?' I asked.

He didn't answer, but continued typing on his keyboard. Some people were designed to cause disharmony. I wanted to pull the ring from his nose.

'Hello, anybody home?' I said, irritation creeping into my tone.

He continued to ignore me for another thirty seconds or so before he answered, 'Not something I'm familiar with, but I can look it up for you.'

'I would appreciate it if you did.'

Silence.

'When would that be?' I asked.

'I'll call you when I've looked it up.'

I approached his desk and placed my business card next to his keyboard. 'Well, if you do get around to it, here's my number.'

He grunted in response.

I went on, 'Whatever you're working on, it must be damn interesting if you don't even take the time to acknowledge people's presence.'

I must have hit a nerve, because he shot darts with his eyes. 'Have you ever heard of time management? Those who achieve things in life are those who master the art of time management. Time management is the ability to focus on one's important goals for the day without letting oneself be disturbed by minor events. Of course, being a cop, you wouldn't know anything about time management. You have nothing better to do all day than harass people for information you could look up at a public library if you possessed the intellect to do so. Have you ever been on one of those guided tours at the library?'

'You can also reach me on my mobile number,' I said and left the room.

I was half way down the corridor when he slammed his office door, causing my heart to skip a beat.

Bastard truly lived up to his reputation.

The next time I saw Frank was on Wednesday the 31st December, at the VFSC, in the comfort of his office. It was 2.32 p.m., and he had just told me Malcom had signed a full confession carefully crafted and typed by Frank himself. The imprint of my hand was still etched on his face from the slap I gave him the other day.

'This is all the evidence we need to send him to jail where he belongs,' Frank said, brandishing a copy of the signed confession in front of my face. 'This case is now truly over.'

I explained about the zinc stearate.

'So what?' he said. 'It's not going to make any difference, and since no one knows what the hell this zinc stuff is used for, who gives a damn.'

I couldn't believe how indifferent Frank was to what I believed was important forensic evidence, and how hurried he was in getting Malcom in the slammer.

'I want to know under what condition you got Malcom to sign this confession. But most of all, I don't remember telling you to get him to sign anything. Wasn't I in charge of this investigation when it all began?'

'I got full authorisation from Goosh to proceed with the confession.'

'Eh?'

'Knowing you were going to disapprove, and knowing I was right, I did what I had to do.'

'You went behind my back *again* and got Goosh to authorise this?'

'Yep. And now if you don't mind, I've got some work to do.'

I stood from my chair, heat creeping up my face. 'Why are you doing this? Why aren't you letting me investigate this case properly? What's wrong with you?'

He laughed.

'I don't think this is funny,' I continued.

'Oh, I think it is. You're the one who told me the other day you didn't want to work with me any more, and somehow I have to cooperate with you. I'm not going to wait until you file your *official* complaint and get my arse kicked. I'm doing everything in my power to make sure this sonofabitch goes to jail, and you don't jeopardise this investigation.'

I was absolutely stunned. I couldn't believe what I was hearing. Listening to him, I began to wonder if he wasn't on drugs. Why had he suddenly turned his back on me and decided I was no longer worthy as a partner?

'You're really something, you know,' I said. 'I thought we were friends. I thought you and me were a team in all this.'

He shook his head vigorously. 'Oh, no, no, no. We're no longer a team, Katrina. You know as well as I do that you can't stand working with me, and I'm tired of seeing your face.'

'Is that so?'

'I'm afraid it is. You're just so up yourself with these justification theories, you can't see where you're going wrong. For Christ's sake, Tracy Noland is dead. Malcom Sternwood did it. You know it, and I know it. I don't have time to play little games because you think you have to do everything by the book. Fact is everyone wants an end to this investigation, and since we've got the killer, why waste another minute? You want to end the friendship? I don't have a problem with that. I've got a job to do, justice needs to be served, and I don't have time for all your goddamn irrationality.'

I was about to walk out and let him have the last word, but I slowly turned back and faced him. 'You know, Frank, you're the last person on earth I thought would turn on me. I'm going to continue with this investigation whether you like it or not. And if I find you did anything to mislead me or anyone else, you can kiss your career goodbye.' If I'd been a man, I'd probably have jumped over the desk and given him a square one on the jaw.

'*Dr* Kristina Melina, I don't give a shit. You can go and file your complaints to whomever you wish. Fact is you're only sub-contracted, and I'm not. Fact two is I'm going to make sure you never work for the VFSC again. You can expect your contract to be terminated by the end of the month. You don't want to make me your enemy. You're making a mistake.'

'We'll see about that. I'll sue you, Goosh and all the other arseholes in this place.'

I stormed out of his office.

'Way to go, Katrina,' I heard him say as I vanished down the hallway, 'Way to go.'

# CHAPTER FIFTEEN

**I** got home so annoyed, I wanted to immediately type my contract termination and send it via courier to Goosh. What was the point in anything any more? My partner considered me an impairment to Tracy Noland's investigation. Goosh couldn't wait for the day I left the VFSC. And I wasn't sure if I had the strength to fight a system which was constantly turning itself against me. But I knew if I quit now, they'd win.

And justice still had to be served.

I took a shower to let the anger dissipate. Tears came streaming down my face as I decided to go and talk to Malcom Sternwood. I wanted to know the details of why and how he'd signed the confession. I didn't believe for a minute he did it of his own free will. Sure, I wasn't completely convinced he was innocent, in fact all evidence showed otherwise, but I still believed he had the right to a proper investigation, and I had the right to know the truth. The only reason I chose this field of work was because I believed in justice, not quick fixes. I believed in looking deep into an investigation until all the evidence was extracted, not just bits of the puzzle solved so I could move on to the next case.

As much as I was angry, I could more or less understand Frank's irrationality. I had seen from the beginning of this investigation how angry he had been when we found out a young girl had been killed. And I knew in his mind all he wanted was revenge, so much it was blinding his reasoning. I'd been afraid to take on this case from the beginning, believing I wouldn't be able to cope. But it seemed to me he was the one who wasn't coping well. The way he spoke to me in his office had cut deep into my soul, making me doubt I would ever be able to forgive him.

I stepped out of the shower, my eyes red from crying, and dried my hair with a clean towel I pulled from under the hand-sink. I had this urge to ring Phillip and tell him I was sorry for being so cold, for not appreciating his company whenever he came around. Now that I was alone, standing naked in a bathroom, looking at my own reflection, I realised how fragile relationships were. I'd never felt so alone in my life and wondered how in the world I ever got myself into such a situation in the first place. Didn't we all deserve to be loved during our lifetime? Why did it seem so easy for some and so hard for others?

And then I laughed at my reflection, which laughed back at me. This whole thing was so absurd, it was almost funny. I knew I had to gather my strength and keep level-headed. The last thing I needed was to let my anger cloud my sense of duty and to throw it all away when I knew there was still so much to be done.

I stepped out of the bathroom and headed for the bedroom.

I slipped on a red cotton dress from Sportsgirl, tied my hair back, slipped on flat, black leather shoes, grabbed my keys, and left the apartment.


An hour later Malcom Sternwood and I were alone in the interrogation room of a newly-built correctional facility in Laverton North, fifteen minutes West of Melbourne. When he first entered the room, I wasn't all that surprised about the bruising around his right eye. I sort of figured out Frank had kicked the truth out of him, but I needed to see the evidence and wanted to hear it from Malcom's lips.

We were sitting on red plastic chairs, the type we had in high school, face to face, arms leaning over a shell-coloured table, looking at each other eye to eye.

'Did you kill the girl?' I asked.

'You know I didn't.'

I remained firm. 'No, I don't know you didn't. You signed a confession stating you killed her because she wouldn't have sex with you. That's serious stuff. You're going to be jailed for life.'

'They forced me to sign it.'

'Who's they?'

'That cop friend of yours.'

'Senior Sergeant Frank Moore?'

'That's him.'

'Who else was there?'

'Never seen them before. Two other cops.'

'How did they force you to sign the confession?'

'They said they knew I did it. They said they had enough forensic evidence to prove it. And then when I told them they were wasting their time, your friend grabbed me by the shirt, punched me twice in the stomach and once in the face. He sat me on the chair, twisted my left arm and forced me to sign a typed page.'

'Are you sure about this?'

'Jesus Christ! What do you think this is?' he pointed to the bruising in his eye.

I tried hard to feel sympathy for Malcom, but it wasn't easy. When I looked at him, I was reminded of Tracy Noland. And although I wasn't sure he killed Tracy, he certainly had an unbalanced obsession for seeing her naked. I'd studied the human mind long enough, and I knew there was a need for men to look at women because of their so-called high hormone levels and strong response to visual stimulation, but Malcom's sexual appetite for Tracy Noland was not considered normal behaviour. At his age he should have had a girlfriend, and if not, at least be interested in a relationship with a grown-up, not a child. But the way he transformed those pictures of Tracy Noland on his computer implied he wanted a relationship with a grown-up, making his case an intriguing one. As a result, I wasn't able to identify exactly what was going on in his head.

As I stood there, face to face with a person who could have killed the young girl, I forced myself to be considerate, not yell at him like he'd been yelled at before.

'I want to do the right thing,' I said, my eyes staring deep into his. 'I don't know what your story is, and I don't care.

What I want to do is catch the bastard who killed Tracy Noland. If you didn't do it, I don't want you to go to jail for it. But if you did it, and you're stuffing me around, there'll be hell to pay.'

I'd been trained to recognise nothing was black and white. No matter how many times Malcom told me he didn't do it, no matter how sincere he seemed, he could have been using me because he knew I wouldn't beat the truth out of him, because I was easier to lie to. Psychopaths could tell a thousand lies and still sound like they were telling the truth. I knew. I'd seen them and worked with them. I'd seen high-ranking detectives being fooled during an interrogation, only to find out later they'd been lied to all along. And in a way that was what Frank was trying to avoid. But I wasn't so cynical. As long as I kept my mind open to any possibilities, I believed I had the situation more or less under control.

'I didn't do it,' he said sheepishly.

'I think you need a solicitor. Have you got one?'

'No.'

'Get a solicitor as soon as you can. Tell him everything you told me.'

'I don't know anyone. I can't afford one.'

'Do you want me to get you one?'

'That'd be good.'

'I'll see what I can do.'

Due to the high profile of this case, I knew Malcom would have no problem securing a solicitor, even if he couldn't pay. This was good publicity for the defence, especially if the jury came up with a not-guilty sentence. It meant wealth was going to roll in faster than ever for the hot-shot solicitor who would make a fortune on other people's misery.

I told Malcom to wait for me.

I left the interrogation room for the car park. From the Lancer, I removed my photographic equipment and loaded the Minolta SLR with a brand new film.

When I walked back into the interrogation room with the camera, Malcom looked surprised. 'What's that for?' he asked, staring at the camera.

'Evidence.'

And he understood immediately.

163

I went on, 'If you're telling the truth, then I want to make sure you have enough evidence to prove what you're telling me. I don't believe in the bashing of witnesses or probable suspects.'

I made him take his shirt off. There was light bruising around the stomach area, confirming what he'd told me about Frank punching him just above the belt.

I shot from different angles with the help of a hand-held flash. I zoomed in on the wounds because I knew once they'd be blown-up, it would impress any jury. As much as I now was reluctant to take Frank to court, at least I had something to fight with if I felt I was dismissed unfairly. That and the video tape of the interrogation I kept at home.

I shot the entire thirty-six exposures.

I had the film developed at E.6 Plus, a professional photo lab in Bangs Street, Prahran, and the best shots blown to A4-size at Photo Production House at 245 High Street, just around the corner from the photo lab. The whole job was done in under three hours.

The A4-size shots of the bruising looked fantastic. I got home excited and filed them for future usage in my three-drawer filing cabinet. I felt it my duty to defend Malcom's rights, even though I didn't know if he was or wasn't the killer of Tracy Noland. What Frank had done was not only illegal, but down-right immoral.

Later in the evening, Frank agreed to meet me at my place. On the phone he seemed more relaxed and less certain of himself than when I saw him that morning.

'What do you mean you took photos?' His voice was edgy.

'That's right. I saw Malcom and took an entire film of your handy work.'

Pause.

'Katrina, there must be a way we can talk about this. We got on each other's nerves this morning. I'm sure we can straighten this thing out.'

'The only way we're going to straighten anything is by tearing up this fake confession you got out of Malcom and mounting a proper investigation.'

'You know I can't do that!'

'Oh, yes, you can.'

'But I already told Goosh we had the confession on paper.'

'That's not my problem. You're the one who lied.'

Another pause.

'Goddamnit, Katrina, you make everything so difficult. Why don't we get together and talk about his? I'm sure we can work something out.'

I didn't feel like seeing his face right now, but didn't want to be unreasonable like he'd been with me.

'Sure, you can come for dinner.'

'You don't have to make me dinner.'

'I want to. Just like old times. We'll pretend we're still friends.'

'Sure. I'll see you soon.' He hung up without adding anything.

Ten minutes later, Michael came home. At first I thought it was Frank, and I don't know why I thought it was him since he didn't have the keys to my apartment.

'Where have you been?' I asked, the photos of Malcom Sternwood's bruising, which I'd already retrieved from my filing cabinet, spread all over the coffee table in the lounge room. I glanced at my watch which read 7.43 p.m. and quickly gathered the pictures into one pile. But it was too late. Michael had already seen them. 'I was expecting you hours ago. Don't you live here any more?'

He gave me a look which implied I was getting on his nerves. 'Mum, why are you asking me all these questions? Where do you think I was? Don't you trust me?'

I felt kind of foolish, but it seemed that my questioning was not completely out of line. He was only thirteen and the only person I could call family.

'I was just worried, that's all. It has nothing to do with trust.'

'That's cool.' His smile meant my answer had been validated. 'I was with Chris. We went to Jason's. He showed us these other cool tricks. I can show you if you want.' He began to unzip his back pack.

'Don't bother. I've got Frank coming here any moment.'

'Okay.'

165

He went straight to the kitchen, opened the fridge and poured himself a Dr Pepper.

'Why don't you buy Coke like everyone else? I hate this stuff. It tastes like cough syrup.'

I wasn't focusing on what he was telling me. Instead, I wondered if it was a good idea that he'd spent so much time with Jason Harvey when the old man was still an important witness to the Tracy Noland murder. Having my son visiting one of the witnesses four or five times a week might give some ammunition to the defence. Could the witness be totally impartial in his opinion if he'd been a good buddy to the investigating officer's son? Someone would without doubt ask the question. I was certain everyone would see some conflict of interest when I knew there was none whatsoever.

I stood from the floral couch and said, 'You should spend less time at Jason Harvey's and more at home.'

'There's nothing to do here.'

I was about to reply, but there was a knock on the door.

'That'll be Frank,' Michael announced as if I didn't know. It gave him the perfect excuse to grab his back pack, his much-hated Dr Pepper, and disappear to his room where he would remain until tomorrow morning.

When I opened the front door, Frank stood there, looking awkward and uncertain. He wore jeans and a dorky-looking blue-and-white striped shirt.

We stared at each other for a few seconds, but neither of us said a word.

And then something strange happened. Without warning, we both stepped forward and hugged.

'I'm sorry,' he said. 'I don't know what's happening to me.'

'It's okay. We're all getting stressed by this investigation.'

The hug was short and sharp but showed us how badly we wanted to remain friends. Maybe if we managed to push our dignity aside, our friendship would come out intact.

I walked him to the kitchen and poured him a glass of water.

'Why did you hit him?' I asked, avoiding eye contact.

'I don't know. I'm just so sure he did it. You know how sometimes you know something, and it just annoys the hell out of you when it takes so long to prove. it. I guess it's a gut instinct.'

'But you didn't have to hit him.'

'That's just the way men are.'

The hormonal excuse was too pathetic for my liking. 'Frank, you're not a psychopath who can't control his temper. You're a cop. And you should know better than bashing suspects in a crime investigation.'

'You're right. It won't happen again.'

We circled the kitchen bench and walked to the lounge room where Malcom Sternwood's photos were still stacked up on the coffee table.

'So, they're the photos?' Frank asked.

'Yep.'

'Why did you take them?'

'Just in case there'd be a need to use them.'

He twisted his mouth and sat on the couch. 'You're not going to use those?'

'Not unless I have to.'

His voice lost its momentum. 'Okay, look, we'll retract the signed confession and start from scratch. Goosh is not going to like that.'

'Have you told him about the written confession yet?'

'Yes.'

'And what are you going to tell him now?'

'Wouldn't have a damn clue. I guess I'll have to take it as it comes.'

Frank must have concluded that the outcome of me filing an official complaint about his harassing a suspect would have been more damaging than putting up with Goosh and his attitude from hell.

'You know,' he added, 'I'm not just saying this, but I want us two to work together again. Like the old days. I'm tired of having to fight with you. What you said this morning made me think. We used to be a team once. And that made the job bearable. But now, everything is becoming an argument, an excuse to jump at each other's throat.'

I stood from the couch and said, 'I want nothing more than to solve this damn case and get on with our lives. You don't actually think I enjoy having arguments with you?'

'I know you don't. And the feeling is mutual.'

We said nothing after that, so I moved back to the kitchen and put some water on the boil for pasta. I promised him dinner, but I had nothing ready. He would have to eat what I could dish up in twenty minutes.

'So what's this thing about zinc...?' he asked across the room.

'Zinc stearate.'

'Yeah, that thing. Did you find what it was used for?'

'Not for photography, which makes me wonder where it comes from. If Malcom killed her, where did he get that stuff from?'

Frank didn't answer.

I emptied a can of peeled tomatoes in a pan with sliced capsicums and onions. I threw in a good measure of pepper and mixed herbs. I wasn't much of a cook and ate more pasta and sauce than a hot-blooded Italian.

'Okay,' Frank went on. 'If Malcom didn't do it, then who did?'

'Don't know. I'm looking for something solid. Maybe it's Mrs Noland.' I stirred the tomato sauce with a wooden spoon Michael bought me for mother's day when he was eight.

'I thought we'd covered that ground already.'

I walked back to the lounge room, licking the sauce off the spoon. 'I want to check her out thoroughly. I don't like the way she immediately took on a defensive attitude when I questioned her.'

He nodded without agreeing.

I continued, 'I'm going to look into her affairs tomorrow. Financial history, credit rating, debtors, creditors. Nobody has bothered with that so far.'

'You're wasting time. We're better off concentrating on Malcom.'

'Why don't you do that since you've gone a step ahead without me. Just make sure you don't cause too much bruising this time.'

He shook his head as if I was being unreasonable.

'I tell you what,' I went on, 'why don't you look into Mrs Noland, and I'll find out about the zinc stearate?'

He agreed with a non-committal expression.

We continued to make small talk about the case without expanding to anything new. I was actually enjoying talking to him. It had been a while since we'd sat facing each other without trying to discredit everything we shared. For the first time since we'd worked together on this case, I felt like he was my partner again, as if we had the same goal of solving this case and nothing else mattered.

Half an hour later, we were sitting at the kitchen table with a plate full of pasta and sauce.

Michael ran into the kitchen to grab a plate and flew back to his room.

'Is he always like that?' Frank asked with a mouthful of pasta.

'Like what?'

'Graciously sociable?' Sauce dripped from his fork to his striped shirt, but he didn't notice, and I wasn't in a critical enough mood to let him know.

'He's at *that* age.'

'Oh,' he said as if that explained everything.

When he left I felt a huge weight being lifted off my shoulders. Now that I knew I didn't have to fight Frank as well as having to figure out what the hell was going on with the Tracy Noland investigation, my mind was clear to work things out.

At 9.30 p.m., I went to Terry Bennetts' for a workout, but returned home within an hour because of lack of energy. And since Ken wasn't there, I missed out on the delight of one of his entertaining conversations, which gave me one more reason not to hang around the deserted gymnasium. The fact was that I needed some sleep, even though I had a thousand-and-one worries on my mind.

# CHAPTER SIXTEEN

On Friday the 2nd of January, sunlight filtered through the yellow drapes of my bedroom window and landed on my face. I tossed and turned a couple of times, trying hard to remain in the land of dreams. Finally, when all I saw was blood circulating behind my eyelids, I turned my head and checked the digital alarm clock on my side table. It read 6.22 a.m. in a red fluorescent display, and, in spite of it being early, I felt the weight of the day dragging me down. I decided to fight back.

Half an hour later I was showered, dressed in my usual skirt, blouse and jacket, and reading the *Herald-Sun* at the kitchen table, while washing down a multi-vitamin and an e-supplement with a mug of virgin black percolated coffee.

The Tracy Noland story was on the front page of the paper again, as it had been for the past two weeks. The middle spread of the newspaper featured a background story on Malcom Sternwood, the prime suspect in the investigation, so the feature writer kept on telling us. There was a small, dated black-and-white photo of myself in the right bottom corner. My hair was longer then, cut just below my shoulder blades, and I couldn't see bags under my eyes. A two-inch side-bar told how I was unwilling to talk to the media while the case remained unsolved. There was mention about my involvement in the Wilson murder the previous year, where a man had been found decapitated in his South Melbourne apartment. Goosh was quoted as saying, 'We've put the best team together to work on this investigation. Dr Kristina Melina is working around the clock on the case.' The kind journalist who covered the story must have purposely removed any nasty comments Goosh might have said about the unsuitability of an unsworn investigator leading the case.

I emptied my mug of coffee and flipped the pages to the comics to read Robotman and Monty, the only comic strip I bothered with.

Just then, Michael came out of his room, his hair out of place, rubbing his right eye with his fist. He wore blue-chequered pyjamas, continually pulling the bottom half up to his waist because the elastic had stretched. I made a mental note to get him a new pair at K mart on the weekend.

We greeted each other and made small talk about the forthcoming school year, while he prepared breakfast, which consisted of three times the recommended daily allowance of Coco Pops and half a litre of full-cream milk. Good for your taste buds, I thought, and the rest I closed one eye over. He was still young, and I could only hope one day he would become more sensible about his diet.

After breakfast, while Michael was getting ready for another day's outing with Chris, I switched on the laptop and modem in my home office, overlooking Chapel Street. I connected into the easily-accessible Medicare database. There was no such thing as *privacy*. This was a word used by the government to make us believe everything they kept on federal and state databases was inaccessible to the average computer hacker. Fact is anyone with a computer, a modem and half a brain has access to information kept in most government and privately-owned databases, be it medical records, electoral rolls, traffic infringements, outstanding warrants or credit ratings. Teaching yourself the techniques is as easy as tapping into the Internet.

However, accessing the Medicare central database proved next to useless since pharmaceutical prescriptions were not kept on record, only medical attendances.

I shifted in my chair, closed the database and looked up another telephone number in my address book. In less than thirty seconds, I was connected to the Department of Health and Family Services. I was hoping to find someone in the Albert Park area who might have bought zinc stearate from a chemist. To begin, I conveniently assumed the person who bought the chemical was entitled to a Health Care Card, issue by Centrelink for people who were on one form of welfare or another. I drew a blank. No one had ever sold the damn thing for as long as records had been kept.

I yawned and stretched my legs, overlooking the traffic from my second-floor apartment. A line of cars were banked up at the traffic light because of a tram, which was letting commuters in and out. The first driver in line was revving up the engine of his green Corolla, ready to stamp on the accelerator as soon as the last person stepped on the pedestrian walk or on the tram. One day someone was going to get killed, and everyone would play dumb and innocent.

The building adjacent to mine, which caught on fire the previous year, and as a result made the front page of the papers, was undergoing a major renovation. The constant beeping of a crane, which began its tune at around six-thirty in the morning, had become part of the cultural pot pourri of exotic city-living noises. Even when the beeping on the crane stopped, it was still ringing in the four corners of my skull for the next two hours.

The tiny units and bedsitters were being sold as 'exclusive St Kilda cosmopolitan lifestyle' apartments. Never mind that to date they'd been occupied with backpackers, drug addicts and small-time gangsters. That was all buried under freshly varnished floor boards and painted walls, with all the previous residents being evicted faster than I could blink an eyelid. I wondered if real estate agents had an obligation to tell prospective buyers that the previous occupants died crucified on a needle, or got butchered to death by a live-in-lover who snapped from crack frying his brain. Had they been told, maybe the buyers would have negotiated an additional ten-thousand-dollar discount. But in a world where money ruled and profits were the ultimate bargaining chips, we were only told what we needed to know.

I turned off my laptop and scratched the back of my neck. I was in awe as to what to do next about locating zinc stearate. Logic told me I should visit a local chemist and ask if he knew anything about the chemical compound.

The Amcal Chemist on High Street, just past Punt Road, was open twenty-four hours a day.

172

The pharmacist was a man in his late forties or early fifties with a grey crown and not much hair left on top.

'You wouldn't be able to get it unless you signed for it,' he explained when I mentioned zinc stearate.

'Do you need a prescription to obtain this stuff?'

'Absolutely, unless someone sold it under the counter, which is illegal. It's classified poisonous, so yes, you'd need authorisation, ID and a signature.'

I thanked the chemist and decided to try other chemists.

It took me a good part of the morning to visit chemists in the South Melbourne, Albert Park, St Kilda, Windsor and Prahran areas. The first fifteen informed me they'd never sold zinc stearate, and most had no idea what it was used for. Most of them preferred to refer to it as *zinci stereas*, for reasons I didn't bother to ask. Must have been the Latin or scientific name of your common household-grade zinc stearate.

Patience paid off, and at 12.54 p.m., I stepped into a small chemist shop at the corner of Chapel Street and Malvern Road in Prahran, not too far from where I resided. The pharmacist confirmed he'd sold zinc stearate less than a year ago.

The pharmacist, an Asian man in his mid-thirties going by the name Thuang Nugyen, was quite willing to answer my questions. I assumed he was Vietnamese in origin since I'd spotted more Vietnamese in Melbourne going by the surname of Nugyen than any other name. It must have been the equivalent of Smith in English.

'And who bought it?' I asked, relieved I was finally getting somewhere.

'Couldn't tell you that.'

'It's for a murder investigation. I have to know. Don't make me go through all the hassle of getting a search warrant.' My tone was dry and commanding. I felt short-tempered from having spent the entire morning in horrid traffic, bumper to bumper with trams and white delivery vans marked with dints in every conceivable corner.

'Oh, that's not it,' Mr Nugyen immediately retorted, his hands flying to his chest as if I was about to hit him. 'I help police. But six months ago, junkies broke into shop and destroyed lots of things, including book which contained name and signatures of prescribed poisonous materials.'

I gave him a look which implied I thought he was pulling my leg.

'Seriously,' he went on, 'all these junkies raid place during night, hoping finding something to get high on. But what they don't realise is we now lock scheduled drugs in metal cabinets with locks. No way to get them open. So junkies angry at us and trash place for revenge. We never recovered book. Junkies bad people. Thief. No good for business.'

His tone seemed sincere, and I couldn't see a reason why he would lie. I gave him my business card, inviting him to call me any time if he'd remembered anything.

When I left the chemist, I was annoyed that my search had amounted to little.


Later in the afternoon, while doing my shopping at Coles in Balaclava, my mobile phone went off. I placed a litre of milk in the trolley, and grabbed the cellular phone attached to my leather belt.

'Hi, it's me.'

I recognised Frank's voice. 'What's up?'

'I found something you'd be interested in.'

'What?'

'Mrs Noland has secrets. Maybe you were right after all. I think I found a probable motive as to why she'd want to have her daughter killed.'

'Okay, let's not discuss this on the mobile. Where are you now?'

'VFSC, but I can meet you at the St Kilda Road Police Complex in the next hour.'

'I'll see you there.'

I punched the end-button and wrapped up my shopping trip.


I parked in front of the St Kilda Road Police Complex at 5.34 p.m., my mind pre-occupied with what could have made Frank change his mind so suddenly about the killer of Tracy Noland.

After passing the security point and the metal detector, I made my way to the elevator.

When I arrived on the ninth floor, I straightened my navy jacket and adjusted my ID-card on my breast-pocket.

Frank was waiting by himself in a small conference room, which we often used to discuss police work in an unofficial manner. A bunch of papers and print-outs were spread in front of him on a mahogany table designed to accommodate up to ten people.

'So, what have you got?' I asked, while taking a seat at the table.

'Checked her back to front.'

'And?'

'No outstanding parking tickets or warrants. No particular debts of any kind, in fact nothing which looks particularly suspicious...' He shuffled some papers. 'She's practically owns the house she lives in. Worth about half a million dollars, and she's only got less than twenty-five grand to pay on it. She hasn't paid it off, why, I guess I'll never know. Her parents died in a car accident two years, leaving her a $150,000 inheritance She's kept it in the bank as cash flow.'

I was getting impatient. 'So? Get to the point.'

'Yeah, well, I began looking a bit deeper, rang up a few insurance companies, and bingo.' He pulled a sheet from the pile and passed it across the table. 'She took life insurance on her daughter nine months ago for an amount of $200,000!'

I stared at the pink-bordered TGB General Insurance document dated February the previous year, which confirmed a premium had been paid in full for a period of twelve months covering the life of Tracy Vicky Noland, be it death or serious injuries, such as blindness, loss of limb or other serious medical conditions. The amount to be paid in case of death was as Frank told me, $200,000.

I puzzled over the document for at least thirty seconds.

'Has she been paid?' I finally asked when the shock had settled in. As much as I had anticipated Mrs Noland was hiding something from us, I'd never thought it'd be so obvious.

'Don't know. I haven't found out yet. I can make a call, and you'll have an answer in two minutes.'

'Not now.' Then: 'And you say she had no debts whatsoever?'

'Nothing recorded anyway. Maybe she had some secret personal debts, but we won't know that until we ask her. It would have to be a hell of a debt, especially when she still has over a hundred thousand dollars in the bank.'

I examined the insurance paper and realised it was an original copy. 'Where did you get that from?'

'The insurance company.'

'How did you manage?'

'Know someone on the inside.'

I nodded, happy to see at least one of us had made a breakthrough. Still the zinc stearate came back to mind as I wondered what association it had with Mrs Noland and the life insurance she took out on her daughter.

'Something bothers me,' I said, cornering the document between my thumb and forefinger. 'If she was debt-free, and lived comfortably, why would she kill her daughter to collect $200,000?'

'Greed? Maybe she couldn't afford that nice holiday on Hamilton Island for six months.'

'I'm sure with $150,000 in the bank she could afford a trip to any islands around the world.'

'To the moon and back, then.'

'What about her husband?'

'She's been a single mother since Tracy was born. Didn't want him. Apparently he was cheating on her.'

'How did you find that out?'

'Had a talk to the father. They got married when she was pregnant, but it never worked out. She decided to keep his name for reasons he can't explain.'

I nodded, really impressed. Frank was obviously showing me he had investigative skills beyond threat and physical violence.

'Okay, this is what we're going to do.' My mind was working at a hundred miles an hour. 'I need to interrogate her, but since she's got herself a solicitor, it's not going to be easy. Any suggestions?'

'Talk to her solicitor first. See what he says.'

'And you expect mutual cooperation?'

'No, but if I tell him what we know, it's better that she talks to us than being charged with murder.'

I placed the palms of my hands on the table. 'You know we don't have enough to charge her with murder. Plus, we don't want to repeat the Malcom Sternwood scenario. He might still be the killer, and the insurance money might have nothing to do with Tracy Noland's death.'

Frank passed one hand over his face. He checked his watch, which I did at the same time. It was just on six o'clock, and I knew he was getting tired. It had been a long day for the both of us, and there was no denying the only thing I wanted to do was to go home, enjoy a hot shower, grab something to eat and curl up in bed with a good book. At the back of my mind, I decided that's what I would do as soon as we'd finished our discussion.

'I tell you what,' I went on. 'I'm going down to Mrs Noland's place to talk to her, regardless of what her solicitor says. Maybe if I confront her with the evidence, she'll break down and give the game away.'

'It's a good way of getting sued. We've been instructed not to talk to her unless her solicitor was present.'

'Yes, but it could save us a lot of time, which frankly we don't have since Sternwood is in jail right now. I can grab her on her way out of the house.' I stared at him, waiting for approval.

'Don't look at me. You call the shots. Remember, you've told me enough times you're in charge of this investigation.'

'Okay. Let's leave it at that.' I raised the insurance paper. 'Can I keep this?'

'Sure.'

We talked some more on our way down to the car park, but nothing to do with the investigation.

'Are you seeing anyone?' I asked as we stepped out of the elevator on the ground floor.

'Why? Are you interested?'

'Frank, I'm only trying to be friendly.'

He gave me a look which seemed to be questioning my trustworthiness. 'No, I'm not. I'm too old, too bald and too busy. That's what I keep telling myself, anyway.'

'You'll find someone. I'm sure you will.'

He mumbled something incomprehensible, smiled and

walked off towards the men's room.

I watched him go, thought what the hell, and aimed for the metal detector.

# CHAPTER SEVENTEEN

When I got home, Michael wasn't there, but he left a note on the kitchen bench saying he was at Jason's with Chris, and if I needed anything I could reach him on *that* number. I checked the number with the one from the miniature address book I'd just retrieved from my handbag. The telephone number matched Jason Harvey's. Good, at least I knew he wasn't somewhere in the city with a bunch of kids causing havoc and being tempted to join in their reckless behaviour.

There was this re-occurring fear at the back of my mind that one day I would get a phone call from the police informing me that Michael had been arrested for something illegal and down-right stupid. I did plenty of shoplifting between my fifteenth and seventeenth birthday, just like most girls do at that age, but I was lucky enough never to get caught. Just as well this never showed up on my resume, otherwise I'd probably be cleaning toilets for a living. These days, with surveillance cameras, laser detection labels attached to goods, security staff who look liked bored housewives, and severe punishment for whomever got caught, the enterprise of shoplifting wasn't an attractive one.

I went straight to the bedroom, stripped off my clothes and stepped under the shower. I let the steaming water cascade down my body for a good fifteen minutes. While I was under the shower, the telephone rang, but I didn't bother. Let the answering machine take it, I thought. I shampooed my hair into a thick lather, enjoying the soothing sensation of my fingers massaging my scalp. For a moment I thought about Phillip and longed for him. Or for someone. I couldn't tell if I loved him or was just desperate. In these difficult moments, I dreamed of falling asleep in the arms of a strong man, someone who'd protect me from the big bad world out there. But no such luck. I stepped out of the shower and hugged myself with a white bathrobe instead.

On my way back to the kitchen, I pressed the play-button on the answering machine. Phillip's voice came on: 'Hi, how are you doing? Haven't heard from you for a while. Give us a call. I miss you.'

I smiled to myself at the thought that we'd both desired each other at the same moment. I wondered if I'd been too harsh on him the other day when he told me to stop worrying about work. And although I knew my job was difficult, in a way he was right. I had to try to leave my work behind when I got home, otherwise I wouldn't last another five years.

I moved on to the kitchen, where I ate a light snack of crisp bread layered with butter and strawberry jam, dipped into a large yellow bowl of coffee. The caffeine was going to keep me awake all night, but I had plans to read a Sue Grafton novel I'd begun weeks ago and never got a chance to finish.

It was just on 8.30 p.m. when I hit the sack with *L is for Lawless*. My bookmark, which reminded me I was a Virgo and described me as practical, industrious, scientific, methodical, perfectionist, discriminating, fact-finding, exacting, critical, petty, melancholic, self-centred and sloppy, was stuck at the beginning of chapter ten. The lead character, dressed in a maid's uniform, attempted some illegal search in a hotel somewhere in Texas. I couldn't remember any of the story so far and dreaded having to start back from the beginning. One day, I would retire and do nothing but read. Maybe I should have become a book reviewer instead. Getting paid to read books. What a dream.

Half way through chapter ten, Malcom Sternwood kept poking at the back of my mind, and, after much resistance, I finally tossed *L is for Lawless* aside and headed for my study. I pulled out the three photographic albums I took from his room and returned to the bedroom.

My head propped up against two pillows, I flicked through

the albums methodically. I recalled seeing some of the photos, while others I had paid little attention to the first time I went through the albums. I stopped at a page where a group of children played together at the upper end of Vincent Court. I recognised some of the children as those whom I spoke to when I first visited the street. In a couple of photos, which I hadn't noticed before, Tracy seemed to be talking to a girl in a wheelchair. I pulled the picture out of the album so that I could take a closer look. The expression on the girl's face told me she might have some form of mental retardation, but I knew facial features were not a clear indication of someone's thinking ability. She could have had some kind of motor-coordination handicap, in which case she might still be able to think and reason at a normal level.

As I continued to flip through the album, I now noticed the girl in the wheelchair in more than one picture. I'd never noticed her in the past because she blended with the other kids. Altogether, there were five pictures featuring the young girl. Out of those, three also featured Tracy Noland talking to her or standing beside her. This indicated to me that they must have been friends. I hated to come to any hasty conclusions, but if the girl was in fact of friend of Tracy Noland, she must have known things about Tracy which other children didn't. After all, apart from Malcom, there was no indication Tracy was friends with anyone else. And come to think of it, everyone I interviewed so far failed to mention the girl in the wheelchair.

After a good fifteen minutes of flipping through the photo albums, I piled them up on my side table, next to the clock radio, and stared at the white ceiling, wondering about the best way to find out about the girl in the wheelchair. It didn't take me long to figure out Malcom would be the person to seek. If he and Tracy had a lot in common, like he claimed they did, then he must have known about the girl in the wheelchair. I decided to pay him a visit tomorrow afternoon, straight after my unannounced visit at Mrs Noland's.

It was 10.22 p.m. when I heard the front door being opened. I had just finished chapter eleven of *L is for Lawless*. I knew it was Michael, and when I realised it was so late, I decided that it was time to put a curfew in place. At the age of thirteen, he shouldn't have been riding his bike from Albert

Park to St Kilda, where there were so many lunatics around. Tracy Noland was virtually the same age as him when she got killed.

I stepped out of bed, slipped on my bathrobe, and headed for the kitchen, where I heard the fridge door creak, announcing Michael's presence.

'Is this a time to come home?' I asked, forgetting my manners.

He turned around, a stunned look on his face. 'God, you gave me a fright, sneaking up on me like that. And me who was trying to be quiet so I wouldn't wake you up.'

'Look at the time. It's nearly ten thirty. Where have you been?'

'I left you a note. Didn't you get it?'

'Yeah, yeah, you said you were at Jason's. All that time?'

'It was really cool. You should have been there.'

He looked so excited, I hated to be the one spoiling his good mood. 'Did you have something to eat?' I asked, wondering what he was looking for in the fridge.

'Jason ordered pizzas with lots-a-cheese-and-peperoni.'

'Mmm... you have to stop eating junk food, or it's going to eat you alive one day.'

He poured himself a glass of Coke, which I'd bothered buying for him after he complained about the medicated taste of Dr Pepper.

Then I remembered. 'You ever heard of some stuff called zinc stearate?'

'A compound of zinc oxide.'

'How do you know?'

'Did it in Chemistry.'

'What's it used for?'

'Can't remember. I know it's toxic if you breath it in. I might be able to get you some information on it from the Internet.'

'Really?'

'Yeah, there's these really cool data safety sheets, which are put out by chemical manufacturers. They have to provide instructions for handling and disposal of chemicals, otherwise they can be sued for negligence if one of the end-users injures himself from using the chemicals in question.'

Wow, I was impressed. And he'd only been doing chemistry for a year.

'And you learned all that at school?' I asked.

'Yes and no. They gave us an assignment to do where we had to locate safety data sheets on the Internet. It's really cool research.' He drank half his glass of Coke and added, 'It'll only take a minute. I can look it up for you now if you want.'

I checked the clock on the kitchen wall, which read 10.32 p.m. 'You better go to bed now. You can look it up tomorrow if you've got time.'

'Okay, cool.'

He gave me a peck on the cheek and left for his room.

Ten minutes later, I was back in bed, the light turned off, my weary head resting comfortably on my pillows. My five senses were ready to shut down for the day when the damn phone woke me up.

I stretched my hand, grabbed the handset and made a grunting noise which was meant to be 'hello'.

'Is that you, Katrina?'

'Phillip?'

'Sorry to call so late. But you haven't returned my call. I was worried something might have happened.'

*Oh, shit!* I'd completely forgot to call him back. Fully alert, I turned the light on. 'Everything's okay, Phillip. I just got home late and didn't get around to calling you. I was going to, I swear.' I didn't know why I was grovelling.

'I'm not bothering you, am I?'

'Well, no, not really. I just turned the light off, so I wasn't completely asleep yet.'

'No, I mean generally. You still want to see me, don't you? I mean I wouldn't want to hang around if you'd rather me not be there.'

'Don't be silly. If I didn't want you around, I'd let you know.'

'Okay, just want to make sure we're on the same track. I'd hate to be pushy. I need to know you want this too.'

God, it was too late at night to make any serious decisions. All I knew was that at this time of my life I didn't want to be by myself again. Not that Phillip was with me all the time, but

183

after I'd seen the look on Frank's face today when I asked him if he was seeing someone, it must have dawned on me that being single wasn't much fun after all. As much as I wasn't ready for a full on relationship, it was nice to know Phillip was around when I needed him. Was I being selfish? Who cared. My life was being led by these swinging moods. One day I wanted to dump him and regain my independence. The other I almost wanted to marry him.

'Listen, darling,' I said in my warmest voice, 'why don't you come over tomorrow night, and we can spend some time together?'

'That'd be great.'

'Okay, I'll see you tomorrow for dinner.'

We agreed to make it at around seven.

I hung up, wondering if this day was ever going to end.

I turned the light off and slept for eight hours straight.

By the time I crawled out of bed the next morning, Michael had already left the house. I knew because I heard him slam the front door, which was what woke me up in the first place. I glanced at the clock radio, which read 7.16 a.m., and wondered where the hell he'd gone to so early in the morning.

The night sleep had done some wonders, and when I stepped under the shower, I felt amazingly refreshed and alert. All my senses were switched on, and my mind was clear, as if it had just gone through the spin cycle of a heavily soiled wash.

While having breakfast, the usual coffee and vitamins, I decided to make it bright and early to Mrs Noland's, hoping to catch her so early in the morning, she wouldn't know if I was a friend or a foe.

It wasn't until I rinsed my empty mug in the sink that I noticed some ink-jet-printed pages Michael had left on the kitchen bench. There was a hand-written note attached to them.

*Mum, I looked up this zinc stearate you asked me about. Couldn't find it. The closest I found was zinc oxide. I assume the properties are closely related. I hope this is useful. Michael.*

I read the sheets top to bottom.

There was a section which briefly described the product:

184

```
Common Name:  Zinc Oxide
CAS Number:   1314-13-2
DOT Number:   None
Date:                    November 3, 1986
```

HAZARD SUMMARY
 *    Zinc Oxide can effect you when breathed in and may enter the body
through the skin.
 *    Exposure to Zinc Oxide can cause a flu-like illness called metal fume
fever, with
       symptoms of metallic taste in the mouth, headaches, cough,
shortness of breath,
       aches and chills, upset stomach and chest pain.
 *    Repeated high exposures may cause ulcer symptoms and affect liver
function.

IDENTIFICATION
Zinc Oxide is a yellowish powder. It is used as a fungicide and pigment in
rubber products, paints, lacquers, varnishes, ceramics and cosmetics.

REASON FOR CITATION
 *    Zinc Oxide is on the Hazardous Substance List because it is cited by
NIOSH and ACGIH.

This was followed by a several other sections: HOW TO DETERMINE IF YOU ARE BEING EXPOSED; WORKPLACE EXPOSURE LIMITS; WAYS OF REDUCING EXPOSURE; HEALTH HAZARD INFORMATION; WORKPLACE CONTROLS AND PRACTICES; PERSONAL PROTECTIVE EQUIPMENT; FIRE HAZARDS; SPILLS AND EMERGENCIES; HANDLING AND STORAGE; FIRST AID; OTHER COMMONLY USED NAMES; and ECOLOGICAL INFORMATION. Nothing of much interest to me.

I'd read enough to know that this stuff wasn't meant to be poured on breakfast cereals. Still, nothing I'd read explained why a compound of this product had been found around Tracy Noland's mouth. And there was no reference to the actual zinc stearate I'd been searching for.

I took the three sheets of inkjet-printed paper to my study and threw them in my in-tray.

I grabbed my handbag from the floral couch in the living room, locked the front door of the apartment and made my way to the building's car park.

Outside the sky was clear, and it looked as if it would remain the same for the rest of the day. An odour of cooking fish whisked down the hallway and out the main entrance. There were Asians on the ground floor, and every second day, they seemed to be having fried fish, leaving the door of their apartment open and, as a result, infesting the hallway right up to the second floor.

When I parked my car in front Mrs Noland's home at 8.27 a.m., the street was deserted. Being a Saturday, everyone was probably sleeping in or gone shopping.

I stepped out of the car, feeling awkward and intruding. But if this was the only way I was going to get some answers, then be it.

I crossed the front yard, looking over my shoulder, paranoid someone was watching me. I stood in front of the fly screen, a knot the size of a fist sitting in my stomach. I took a deep breath and pressed the door bell.

While waiting for someone to answer the door, I retrieved my ID-card and clipped it on the breast pocket of my navy jacket. With a flick of a hand, I cleared a strand of hair in front of my face. Oh, boy, I loved morning intrusions. I'd hate to be the one answering the door, facing some official-looking person, catching me in my T-shirt and underpants while having breakfast.

I heard footsteps coming down the hallway and automatically checked my watch. It was just on eight thirty, early enough to make my invasion of privacy barely legal. Quickly I removed the copy of the TGB General Insurance papers under Mrs Noland's name. Hopefully throwing the evidence in front of her face would give me some leverage.

The door opened fully. I could hardly make out the person on the other side of the fly screen, but I did recognise the voice.

'What are you doing here?' Mrs Noland asked.

Well, good-morning to you too. 'I just needed to ask you a couple of questions.' I felt really awkward talking to a fly screen with a human voice.

'You know as well as I do,' she snapped, 'that you have no business coming here. Unless you have a warrant of some sort, you've got to deal with my solicitor.'

'The idea had occurred to me Mrs Noland, but I thought it would be best to talk to you first, just to give you the chance to consider... well, I've got some information here that you might like to see before your solicitor gets his hands on it.'

Instead of answering me, she unlocked the fly screen and pushed the door open. I glanced at her grey tracksuit outfit with Boy George printed on her front, something I hadn't seen since the mid-eighties. She glared at me as if I was the one who'd killed her daughter.

Without saying a word, I handed over the TGB General Insurance papers.

'What's this?'

'I believe it's a life insurance policy you took out on Tracy about nine months ago.'

Her face turned beetroot red. 'Where did you get this from?' Anger rather than shock infested her tone. 'These are personal documents. Who gave you this?' I could see the muscles on her neck tensing up.

I remained calm, an attitude I deemed appropriate for a debt collector since the reaction I got from Mrs Noland made me feel like one.

'That's not really important,' I said with authority. 'What's important is that your daughter is dead, and I find it slightly coincidental that her life was insured for $200,000 nine months prior to her murder. Care to share some opinion on this?' I made sure I spoke loud enough for the whole neighbourhood to hear me.

'Get in here,' she ordered. 'And keep your voice down.'

Yes, ma'am, otherwise I might end up by the banks of Albert Park Lake with a mouthful of mud.

I moved inside the hallway while she shut the door behind me. I glanced over my shoulder every three seconds, just in case she decided to end it all here and now.

But instead, she walked right pass me and said, 'This way.' And then: 'You know, you shouldn't be doing this. I'm going to talk to my solicitor regarding these documents, and there's going to be hell to pay. You guys have no ethics. Coming here in my own home and throwing wild accusations.'

'I didn't say anything. I just felt it appropriate to inform you of what I'd uncovered.'

Not another word was said until we reached the kitchen. Breakfast dishes were soaking in the sink, and I could smell cigarette smoke in the air.

She glared at the piece of paper in her hands, shaking her head. 'I can't believe you guys are wasting your time digging dirt on me. I thought Malcom Sternwood confessed?'

I didn't recall informing her. 'We've got to cover every angle. And my interpretation is that the amount on this life insurance is a damn good motive for wanting someone dead.'

Her eyes locked into mine. 'Are you accusing me of murder?'

'I'm not accusing anyone of anything. I'd just like you to explain to me why you took life insurance on your daughter nine months ago.'

'Because I cared about her.'

'But I don't see how that can be beneficial to her. If she was to die, you'd get the money. How does that show you cared about her?'

'And? What about injuries? I wasn't thinking about death when I took the insurance out. In case something happened to her, there'd be enough money to help with medical expenses and on-going treatment.'

I decided to ignore her perfectly valid reply and to push on with the finger-pointing. She probably had worked out a-thousand-and-one answers in her head just in case someone happened to find out what she'd been up to.

'As far as I know Tracy wasn't a bread earner,' I continued, 'so unless this amount is supposed to replace child allowance, which you're not entitled to in the first place, then I can't find a reasonable explanation to your action. No one does something for no reason, and you don't have to be a genius to figure that out.'

She threw the insurance papers at my face. 'You're so full of shit! These documents don't show anything. I would have never killed Tracy, and even if I did, you'd need more than that to prove it.'

Charming. Her attitude certainly didn't radiate innocence, but I probably would have been more worried if she just stared at me and smiled instead. As much as I hated to admit it, her reaction was that of an innocent person. If someone had accused me of a murder I hadn't committed, I would have gone off my head as well.

Not wanting to give in just yet, I rattled my throat and said, 'You understand that with this evidence, I can get a search warrant for your home?'

She slammed her fist on the kitchen table so hard, my heart almost came out through my chest. 'You get the hell out of my home. You understand me?'

And then, just as I turned around, ready to take a sprint down the hallway before the next thing she hit would be my face, I noticed a box of Turkish Delight near the kitchen window, the top flap half open. The brown box and the gold lettering looked familiar, but I couldn't recall where I'd seen them, so I moved on.

'You get your sorry arse out of my home,' she shrieked, 'before I call for help.'

I didn't have to be asked twice. I opened the front door myself, pushed the fly screen open and walked steadily down the pathway towards my car.

'And don't you come back here,' she screamed at the top of her lungs.

I tried to make myself the size of a lab mouse as I slid behind the wheel of my car. She slammed the door of her home in great fury, sending a shock-wave through my body.

I revved up the engine, cracked the gears and did a u-turn, causing the tyres to scream.

In ten minutes I was home.

I climbed the stairs to my apartment, still looking behind as if I'd been followed. The woman was mad. I swear to God, I thought she was going to hit me square in the face.

I fumbled with my set of keys and dropped them on the floor. My hands were shaking. When I entered the apartment, I realised I'd forgotten the insurance papers at her place. Great, that meant Frank would have to get another printed copy from the insurance company because there was no way I was going back there without back-up.

I filled myself a glass of water from the kitchen tap and drank it in one go. This was followed by another glass.

I opened the doors to the balcony in the lounge room,

letting some fresh air through the rooms. I played Saint-Saens'
Symphony No. 3 in C Minor with its slow and hesitant *Adagio*.
My elbows up against the metal railing, I studied the traffic
below, trying to come up with some type of conclusion.
Because I was still shaken by the whole incident, I found it
difficult to listen to my inner voice.

Was Mrs Noland the killer or not?

What about Malcom Sternwood?

Great, now I had two prime suspects, making this job feel
more like Rubic's Cube than a murder investigation.

Three hours later I was face to face with Malcom Sternwood
in a prison cell, selected photographs from his photo albums
in a large yellow envelope. He looked beaten, as if he'd been
deprived of sleep for a whole week. He wore a five o'clock
shadow and heavy bags under his eyes. And who could blame
him. If he was in fact innocent, one wondered what was going
through his mind.

The cell was three by five at the most and could have
almost passed for a motel room if not for the security screen
on the windows. The walls were painted white, matching a
hand-sink and shower of the same colour.

'How are you coping?' I asked.

'How am I coping? Jesus Christ! What does it look like?'

He didn't seem as shy as when I first met him. In fact he
seemed quite angry.

'You don't look too good.'

'You've got to get me out of here. I hate this place.'

I didn't want to state the obvious, but prisons were not
designed for enjoyment, although with colour televisions,
gymnasiums and basketball courts, many would argue
otherwise.

'Just hang in there a little longer,' I said. 'You're safer on the
inside, anyway.'

'Yeah, well, I didn't do shit, so I shouldn't be here in the
first place.'

I didn't like the way this whole conversation was going.
Malcom was being aggressive, and I didn't expect him to be
too cooperative. But hell, I came to see him for a particular
reason.

'Have you ever seen this girl before?' I slipped the two black-and-white pictures of the girl in the wheelchair out of the yellow envelope and pushed them in front of him.

'Well, of course, I took those pictures.'

Silly me. I re-phrased my question. 'No, I mean do you know her? Has she got a name?'

'Yeah, she's got a name. Everyone's got a name.'

'Are you making fun of me?'

He considered my question for a few seconds, shrugged and said, 'Her name is Lucia. She's got cerebral palsy. She can only move one arm.'

'And she was a friend of Tracy?'

'Yeah, in a way she was. I'd seen them together often. I don't know if they had much in common, but they met on regular basis.'

I flipped to the other photos, the ones with Lucia and Tracy in them. 'And when did you take those?'

'God, I don't remember. In the past year. Anyway, they met at least once a week. Lucia used to watch the other children play in the street because she couldn't participate.'

'Mmm...and do you know where Lucia lives?'

'Not sure, but some of the neighbours would know. Ask Tracy's mum. I'm sure she'd be able to help.'

I knew Mrs Noland was one avenue I wouldn't bother with.

'How long had they been friends for?' I asked.

'As long as I can recall.' His eyes rolled to the ceiling and back to me. 'Let me see. I've been in the street for five years, yeah, so that'd be no less than five years, I guess.'

'Did they go to school together?

'I don't think Lucia was capable of going to a normal school. If she did any schooling at all, my guess is that she had a tutor coming over to her place.'

'Did Tracy ever mention what they were talking about?'

'Who?'

'Her and Lucia.'

'How would I know? I don't know everything about Tracy.'

'You said you had a lot in common with her.'

'True, but I didn't know everything about her, like she didn't know everything about me.'

I bet she didn't.

Then Malcom shifted in his chair and changed the topic. 'Do you think someone else killed Tracy?'

'I'm working on it,' I said non-committally.

'Because you know I didn't do it.'

'I don't know anything at this stage. I'm still working on it.'

'What about my solicitor?'

'I'm working on that too.'

'Jeez, I'm tired of being locked in here. When can I go home?'

'Very shortly. Maybe in a couple of days.' I stood from my chair, but he grabbed me by the arm.

'I'm tired of being locked up. I want to get out of here. It's not nice in here. I'd like to go outside, but all they do is keep me locked in here all day.'

'Let go of my arm, Malcom,' I said, staring at his grip.

'Oh, I'm sorry, it's just that... I just want to go home.'

'I understand that. But at the moment we're still investigating the case, and you're still a prime suspect. If we find you had nothing to do with Tracy's death, you'll go home on the double.'

He gave me a defeated look, and I thought he was going to cry.

I grabbed the photos, slipped them in the envelope and headed for the door.

When I got home, I remembered Phillip was coming for dinner. As much as I anticipated his arrival with some excitement, with everything happening at once, suddenly, it felt like the worst time in the world to have him over.

In my study, feet propped up on my desk, I dialled his number at work.

'Hi, darling. It's me,' I said when he picked up the phone.

'Good to hear from you. So, what time did you want me over tonight?'

'Well, actually, I rang to cancel. Something came up with work, and I won't be able to fit you in.'

Silence.

'Phillip?'

'I'm here.'

'I'm sorry. I don't mean to hurt you. It's just that I'm closing in on this Tracy Noland investigation, and I don't have much time for anything else.'

'I gathered that.' His voice was dry, lacking emotion.

'Don't be like that, Phillip. You know what it's like when work catches up with you.'

'Sure, I do. Except that in your case, work always seems to catch up with you.'

Oh, God, I didn't want to get into one of these work-relationship debates again. 'Phillip, I'm trying my best here. You know I like your company. Why would I have rang you back last night if I didn't want you around?'

'You didn't call me back, I called you again.'

I looked at him and I realised he was right.

'Listen to me, Katrina. Relationships are not about wanting to see someone. They're about *seeing* someone. And the little amount of time I'm spending with you, I don't know if we can call that a relationship.'

'What about the weekends? I always spend time with you on Sunday.'

'But Michael's there.'

I felt a lump in my throat. 'So what?'

'So what is that I want to spend time with you, not Michael. This is not a threesome, Katrina.'

'Is that how it is?'

'Looks like it.'

'Okay, in that case, I guess we're not meant for each other.'

Before he had time to reply, I slammed the handset back in the receiver.

Ten seconds later the phone rang.

I pulled the plug from the wall.

# CHAPTER SEVENTEEN

Her full name was Lucia Melinda Ruxton, and she'd just turned eleven the previous week, exactly ten days after Tracy Noland's body was found in Albert Park.

I spoke to her parents on the phone, and they felt obliged to help after what happened to Tracy, but told me I might be wasting my time. I decided to take a chance.

At 5.23 p.m. on Wednesday the 7th January, I parked my car two houses from the intersection from where Tracy Noland used to live. This was the second time in a week I had come knocking on some stranger's door. I cared little for disturbing any family life by now. My nerves were highly strung, and I wanted to get to the bottom of this case. The investigation had just cost me my relationship, although at the back of my mind I knew Phillip and I would never have made an item for life. I became increasingly aware that the incident I had with him on the telephone that afternoon might not have been an incident after all.

I saw Lucia in the backyard of the Victorian home she shared with her family. It was still daylight and mild enough to be sitting on a patio over a drink. We were surrounded by bushes, while a smell of cooking swept past us from the kitchen.

Lucia was a surprise. I knew she'd be handicapped, but when I saw her, I realised why her parents told me I might be wasting my time. Like Malcom mentioned, only her right arm was moving freely. The rest of her body seemed hopelessly unstrung. Everything she did was random, as if every limb in her body had a life of its own. Even her speech was garbled. It took me about five minutes to realise she was actually saying something and to get used to her extended vowels and shortened consonants. But her eyes sparkled with life, as if she was a person trapped in a body she had little control over. And when we began our conversation , I realised that's what it was.

In the past I found it difficult to communicate with severely handicapped people, and as a result found it awkward to relate to them. The little time I spent with Lucia taught me people were people, no matter what shape they were in. And although I'd known that for a long time, putting it into practice was a totally new experience.

Lucia had dark hair down to her back, clear blue eyes and was slightly overweight for her age. She wore blue tracksuit pants with a matching top.

'How well did you know Tracy?' I asked.

Lucia's head tilted sideways, a stream of saliva dripping down the side of her mouth and onto her chest as she answered my question. 'We were good friends. She treated me like a normal person, better than a normal person.'

I wanted to tell her she was normal but refrained myself. We both knew she wasn't, and I would have only ended up looking like a fool by trying to please her.

I went on, 'Did Tracy have any enemies you knew about?'

She thought about that for a little while. 'She didn't like the other kids. She said they were too childish.'

I was still having problems understanding every word she said. 'What about another person? Did she hate anyone in particular?'

Lucia puzzled some more.

'What about Malcom? You know, the kid who lives at twenty-two Vincent Court?'

Her eyes met mine. 'She liked Malcom. She never said anything bad about him.' More saliva running down the side of her mouth. 'She said he was into photography, and they'd spend all this time taking pictures of her.'

'Did you see Malcom's pictures?'

'Some I did. She wouldn't show them to anyone else

because she was embarrassed.'

'How's that?'

'In some of the pictures she was only wearing her underwear.'

I was surprised Lucia knew about that. 'Did Malcom tell her to undress?'

'I don't think so. She was more mature than the other kids. When you talked to her, she talked like an adult. Like you. When she showed me the pictures, she seemed excited, as if it was something she wanted to do.'

'And Malcom never touched her or did anything to her?'

'She never told me, but I doubt it. She told me everything else. If Malcom had done anything to her, I would have been the first person to know.'

Her comments made me wonder if we'd made a mistake about Malcom after all.

'Is it possible that she asked Malcom to take those pictures?' I asked.

'Yes, absolutely. She liked models. She said she wanted to become a model when she grew up. Her favourite model was Kate Moss. She said she looked thin, just like her.' Suddenly her body jerked as if it had been subjected to an electrical current. But then it stopped. More saliva down her top.

Kate Moss looked like a fourteen-year old to my eyes, so it was no wonder young people looked up to her rather than the other supermodels.

'Okay, so she liked Malcom?'

'Yes, she did.'

'Was there anyone she didn't like?'

'She didn't get on that well with her mum, but I think she still loved her.'

'Did she say anything about her mother?'

'Not really. They were always fighting about one thing or another.'

'Did her mother hit her?'

'No, they just screamed.'

I shifted on my chair and sipped from a glass of lemonade. Lucia did the same with the help of a straw, but not all the liquid entered her mouth.

'Do you need a hand with that?' I asked, feeling embarrassed for her.

'I'm okay.'

I continued, trying to hide my discomfort, 'Was there anyone Tracy hated in particular?'

'The only person I can think of is Paranor.'

'Who?'

'Paranor.'

'Who's Paranor?'

'I don't know.'

'What exactly did Tracy say?'

'She brought the name up a few times. Sometimes she would say she had enough of school, enough of living in this street, enough of Paranor. She wanted to go somewhere else, somewhere where she would be happy.'

Was that the reason Tracy was a difficult child? Because this Paranor person made life hell for her? Was it a person she was referring to or maybe a place or a thing?

'And you're sure you don't know who Paranor is?'

'No idea. I don't know why, but I never asked her. I might have once, but I think she didn't tell me, so I didn't ask again. Maybe it was someone at school. Maybe one of her teachers.'

I began to notice that Lucia seemed tired, and she could have done with a box of tissues. She probably wasn't used to having to make conversation with someone for so long. I decided to wrap up the questioning.

'Is there anything else you'd like to tell me about Tracy?' I asked.

Her eyes met mine, and she said, 'I miss her. She was the best friend I had.'

Lucia insisted on walking me to the car, so I pushed the wheelchair to the front of the house. Her mother promised to come and get her as soon as I took off.

'Do you think you're going to find who killed Tracy?' Lucia asked when we were standing next to my car.

'I'll do the best I can.'

I was about to unlock the car door when she asked, 'Do you have a gun?'

I wasn't sure I'd heard properly, especially with the way she pronounced her words. I thought she asked me if I had a *gum*.

'What was that?'

'You work for the police?'

'Yes.'

'So, you have a gun?'

'Yes, I do.'

'Can I see it?' I hesitated for a few seconds, so she added, 'I've never seen a real gun before. I want to see what it looks like.'

She locked her eyes into mine, and I thought, what the hell.

I opened the door of my car and retrieved from my glove box the .380 semi-automatic Frank bought me last Easter, wondering if I was doing the right thing. But then I reasoned Lucia would probably never get to see a real gun for the rest of her life. I'm sure she could have done without the experience, but what was I supposed to do? She'd already experienced little in comparison to other children, and I didn't want to contribute unnecessarily to her inability to enjoy life to the full.

'Here,' I said, while holding the gun in front of her face.

Without warning she grabbed it with her right hand.

I was going to take it back, but restrained myself.

'What is it?' she asked.

'A Mustang Plus .380 semi-auto,' I said while she handled the stainless frame handgun featuring a blue slide and adjustable sight.

'Have you ever killed anyone with it?'

'No, and I don't wish to.'

'So why do you carry it?'

'For self-defence. In case someone like Tracy's killer attacks me.'

'Would you shoot Tracy's killer?'

'Only in self-defence.'

She nodded approvingly.

'Guns are not a nice thing,' I said. 'If there weren't dangerous people out there, I wouldn't be carrying one.'

She continued to handle the gun, aiming it towards the car. The safety lock was on, making it impossible for her to shoot by accident.

'So, how do you use this thing?'

'Well, first you have to unlock the safety lock, there.' I pointed at the locking mechanism. 'But you're not going to do that here.'

'Of course, I'm not.'

'Then you aim and shoot. And repeat every time you want another bullet to fire.'

Suddenly Lucia's mother opened the front door of the house.

I snatched the gun from Lucia's hand. 'I've got to go now.' I tossed the gun on the passenger side of the car and slammed the door.

'I'll see you later, Lucia,' I said, waved to her mother, circled the vehicle, unlocked the driver's door, and slid behind the wheel.

'You're going to come back and visit again?'

'I will. I promise.'

Lucia waved with the only limb she could move.

When I made a left turn at the corner of Vincent Court, I felt a hot tear rolling down my left cheek.

I spent the rest of the evening in my study with the Tracy Noland file opened and its contents spread all over my desk, jazz music in the background.

One at a time, I looked over the crime-scene photos, hoping to find something I might have missed when I was there. What did the word *Paranor* stand for? I checked my Encyclopaedia of Dictionaries by my desk, but there were no entries under *Paranor* in French, Italian, Spanish, German or Greek. Maybe it wasn't a foreign language.

At the back of my mind, I felt some sense of relief Phillip and I had broken up. As much as I missed him at times, I guessed he had been right when he suggested that what we had together was not in fact a relationship. I found myself caught between a need to exercise my freedom and wanting the comfort and security of being in a relationship. But Phillip wasn't ready for someone whose career stretched beyond office hours. I refused to play the docile woman in someone else's life. My faith in the opposite sex was weak as a result of my marriage break-down at around the time when Michael was born. I'd had on-and-off flirtations with other men over the years, but found no one whom I really trusted or wanted to spend the rest of my life with. Maybe one day the right person would come along. After all, it seemed everyone around me was getting matched up at some stage down the line, and some were far more busy than I was. But for the time being, the only thing which mattered was my job and Michael.

Thinking about Michael made me look at the time. When I realised it was 9.27 p.m., and he was home late for the third night in a row, I knew I would have to have a serious talk to him. I looked up Jason Harvey's telephone number because my guess was that he was still there. The phone rang twice and Jason picked it up. I asked him if Michael was there.

'Yes, he is,' Jason said, his voice filled with excitement.

'Well, could you tell him to come home right away?'

'Oh, but we're having such a good time. Chris is here too. Why don't they stay here overnight?'

Alarm bells began to ring in my head. 'Mr Harvey,' I snapped unexpectedly, 'my son is not your son. I want him home now on the double. Have I made myself clear?'

There was a pause, and then he said, 'You don't have to get nasty with me.' His tone was dry, and I could feel his hurt.

'I don't mean to be rude. It's just that Michael hasn't been home for the last few nights. We spend very little time together as it is, and I would like to see him.'

'All right. I'll send him home right away.'

'Actually, put him on the line.'

'Sure.'

I didn't know what came over me. Suddenly, with all crime-scene pictures spread on my desk, the realisation that Tracy had been about Michael's age, and that it all happened in that neighbourhood, something inside me snapped.

'Mum?'

'Michael, why aren't you home?'

'I'm here with Chris. We're learning all this magic stuff.'

'Are you okay?'

'Of course I'm okay. What's wrong?'

'Nothing. I just want you to come home now.'

'Sure.' He didn't resist. He must have known from the tone

of my voice that I was upset. 'I'm on my way now.'

I changed my mind. 'Actually, stay where you are. I'm coming to pick you up.'

'Okay.'

I hung up, grabbed my keys from the kitchen bench and raced down the hallway.     God dammit! I wasn't sure why I'd suddenly become so afraid of losing Michael.

I was sick and tired of spending half my life on Vincent Court. At night time, there was a creepiness about the area, but I reassured myself that it was merely my distorted viewpoint which caused the illusion. A young girl had been killed in that street. Her mother was defensive and obnoxious. A young man collected soft-pornography of the young girl. Traces of zinc stearate had been found around the young girl's mouth. So far, I hadn't been able to locate where the chemical compound came from. And my son was spending a great deal of time with an old man at the end of the street. Everyone who had seen and experienced what I had in the past weeks would have thought the area to be creepy as well, I reassured myself.

As I stepped out of my car, I suddenly realised how involved I was with the residents of Vincent Court. I was a part of their lives, for better or worse.

I climbed the steps up to Jason's home. The light outside hadn't been turned on, and I couldn't find the door bell button, so I knocked twice on the door.

Michael opened the door.

'You're ready?' I asked before he had time to say a word.

'Yeah...you don't mind dropping Chris home?'

'Where does he live?'

'Elwood.'

'It's not really on our way. Why doesn't he call his parents?'

'Come on. Just this once.'

'Okay, fine. Just hurry up.'

'Cool.'

I waited by the door, not wanting to come in.

Then Jason Harvey appeared. 'How are you?' he said, a broad smile on his face.

'I'm fine. I just want to go home.'

He moved closer and said, 'I'm sorry if I've upset you. I didn't think I'd done anything wrong by letting Michael come to my place.'

'You didn't do anything wrong. Michael should spend more time at home, that's all.'

'Sure, you're his mother.'

No doubt about that, I thought, not wanting to get into a debate.

'You wanna come in?' he offered.

'No, no. I'm fine.' I screamed over his shoulder: 'Michael, hurry up.'

'Coming!'

'You're all right?' Jason asked.

'I'm fine, Mr Harvey. Just tired that's all.'

Michael appeared behind Jason with his friend Chris, whom I'd never met before. The boy was one head taller than Michael and wore dark-framed spectacles. He looked like the intellectual type and seemed somehow mismatched with Michael. Not that I thought Michael had a low I.Q., but I'd imagined Chris to be someone wearing loose-fitted jeans and oversized T-shirts like Michael, not slacks and a chequered shirt with a mobile phone clipped to his Pierre Cardin leather belt.

No one said much on the way back.

I dropped Chris at his place in Elwood and headed back to Chapel Street.

When Michael and I were alone in the car, he said, 'What was all that about?'

'What was what?'

'You seem upset or something.'

'I'm just tired.'

'No, you're angry at me.'

'All right,' I said, pulling the car into the driveway. 'I'd thought you'd want to spend more time with me, that's all.'

'But Jason is showing me all these cool magic tricks.'

'And what? You're going to become a magician?'

'Ha, ha,' he laughed sarcastically.

When we got upstairs, there was a message on the

answering machine. I pressed the play button while Michael was in the kitchen, going through the contents in the fridge.

'Hi, Katrina. It's John Darcy from the lab. I got some results from Tracy Noland's stomach contents. I meant to call you this afternoon, but I got tied up with other things. You know what it's like. You can call me at home tonight, even if it's late.'

I checked my watch, which read 10.35 p.m. Although I hated to call John at home after hours because he was married, and I hated to be thought of as the other woman, but since he had invited me to call so openly, I didn't hesitate.

He answered the call on the third ring.

'It's Kristina Melina.'

'Oh, hi, Katrina. How're you doing?'

'Fine.'

We made small talk for a couple of minutes before he got on to the subject.

'Remember the smell of rose water from Tracy's stomach contents, which Dr Main had on his autopsy report?'

I did remember something vague, especially since I had read over the report less than two hours ago. 'What about it?' I asked.

'Well, we've done some comparison tests in the lab and came up with a probable match of what the smell is from.'

'What?'

'It's from Turkish Delight, an expensive imported brand.'

'Turkish Delight?'

'Yep, which means one of the last things she ate was Turkish Delight.'

'How did you work that out?'

'Long story. Lucy at the lab recognised the smell. She received a box as an Easter present and still hasn't gone through the entire box. Doesn't like the stuff. Says it makes her want to puke. She took the box to the lab. I did tests on a sample and Tracy's stomach contents, and came up with a match.'

I puzzled for a few seconds, remembering the box I saw at Mrs Noland's place. 'What did the box look like?'

'Why?'

'It might be important.'

'I'm not sure.'

'Was it brown with gold lettering?'

'It might be. I really don't know. I'll have to call you back tomorrow from the lab, or maybe you can give Lucy a call. Or if you're in the area, come and visit. The box is still in the lab.'

I thanked him for his help and decided to wait until the following day. There was no urgency in calling Lucy, especially since I didn't know what the contents of the box I saw at Mrs Noland was. Even if it was the Turkish Delight Tracy ate, what exactly was it going to prove? That Tracy had Turkish Delight at home? Not exactly a surprise. On the other hand, since rose water was still in her stomach when she died, it meant she'd consumed the sweets shortly before she was killed. So, if Mrs Noland did in fact have Turkish Delight at home, then this put her even closer to the time of death, although that conclusion in itself wasn't very satisfying. Tracy could have taken some Turkish Delight with her when she left home.

After I hung up, I turned to Michael, who was helping himself to a glass of Coke.

'It's way past your bedtime. From now on, I want you home by nine o'clock.'

'Nine o'clock?'

'Nine o'clock, no ifs or buts.'

'You know that—'

I interrupted him, 'Listen to me. This is not a debate. You're thirteen years old, I'm your mother, and I want you home by nine o'clock every day. End of conversation.'

'Fine,' he snapped, grabbed his glass of Coke and left for his room.

'Shit,' I muttered to myself, not knowing if I was angry at him or at myself for being such a meanie.

I returned to my study and flipped through the Tracy Noland file once more. Still there was nothing which jolted my mind or connected the Turkish Delight with the events of her murder. I wondered if I was just grasping at straws with all these clues and hypotheses.

At 11.20 p.m., my head heavy from a long day, I decided to call it quits and hit the sack.

I took a quick shower, dressed in pyjamas and slid between

the sheets of my double-bed.

The lights out, thoughts were parading before me, keeping me awake longer than I wanted to be. The minutes on the digital clock on my side-table passed slowly. Everything I knew about the Tracy Noland murder was turning in my head. Something was wrong about the way this investigation was going, but I wasn't sure what. I'd tried hard to follow logical leads, but now I wondered if I was looking in the right direction.

Maybe I had to step back a little.

Maybe I was looking at bricks and not the entire wall.

# CHAPTER EIGTEEN

At 10.32 a.m. on Thursday, I met with Frank Moore at the VFSC to review what we had so far. I also made the drive to Macleod because I wanted to see the box which contained the Turkish Delight John Darcy mentioned. Looking at it with my own eyes, I'd be able to compare it with the box I'd seen at Mrs Noland's place, which was better than if someone described it to me over the phone like John Darcy had done the previous day.

I was sitting in Frank's office, sipping from a mug of coffee. I just finished explaining what John told me about the rose water smell from Tracy's stomach contents.

Frank listened without interrupting. His eyes were heavy, an indication he still wasn't getting the sleep he needed. I could have sworn he was losing more hair by the week. Had I been in his shoes, I would have taken the whole lot off. Shaved heads were in fashion, anyway, and certainly looked better than a few strands combed over the top, trying to conceal a bald spot wider than Ayers Rock.

'And you're sure it was a box of Turkish Delight you saw at her place?' Frank asked, flicking through a lab report John had just given me.

'No, I'm not. But I just came from the lab, and the box Lucy brought from home is a dead ringer for the one I saw in Mrs Noland's kitchen. I can't be one hundred percent certain, but I say we get a warrant to search her place.'

He looked thoughtful and said, 'I'm not sure we have enough evidence to be granted a search warrant.'

'What about the insurance money? Isn't that plausible motive?'

'Sure, but...'

'And the Turkish Delight? And the fact that she refuses to cooperate with us?'

He inserted one finger in his ear to remove whatever amount of wax he had forgotten to get rid of that morning with a cotton bud. He wiped his finger under his desk and said, 'I'm going to make a few phone calls and see if we can get a search warrant. You understand Mrs Noland's solicitor will threaten us with a lawsuit if nothing comes out of this? Plus he has to be told about it. Chances are he will call his client, and she'll probably get rid of the evidence at her place, if she is in fact the person who killed Tracy Noland. You're aware of the risks we're taking? This might amount to nothing.'

'How else are we supposed to prove anything?'

'Okay, okay. Like you said the last time, you're in charge of the investigation, and I'll let you call the shots.' He made it sound like he had a choice.

'How soon can we get the warrant served?'

'This afternoon.'

'Let's do it.'

At 2.32 p.m., I was in my study, doing some billing for the VFSC, when Frank called me to announce he had the search warrant for Mrs Noland's home in his hand.

'Her solicitor's been advised,' he said, 'and he's fuming. He said he wants to be present during the search.'

'Fine with me. I'll pick you up on the way.'

At 3.14 p.m., I parked in front of the Noland's. While we were unpacking the PERK and photography equipment from the boot of my Lancer, a grey Lexus parked behind us.

'Must be the goddamn solicitor,' Frank muttered.

I glanced sideways from behind the car and saw a distinguished man in a dark suit stepping out of the Lexus. He looked in my direction, and I diverted my interest back to the contents of the boot of my car.

Too late.

I knew he'd seen me.

'Dr Melina?' I heard him call as he approached us.

I stepped from behind the boot and tried my best to look surprised. 'Yes?'

'I'm Jonathan Blacker, Mrs Noland's solicitor. I believe you're serving a search warrant.'

So much for greetings. I glanced towards Frank, who rolled his eyes.

'Dr Melina?' Mr Blacker insisted.

'I heard you. What is it that you want from us?'

'A copy of the search warrant to make sure you're operating under legal procedures.'

As he got closer, I noticed his dark suit was the expensive four-figure type, which only solicitors, politicians and underworld figures could afford. Mr Blacker looked in his early fifties, hair cut short and brushed back in a style which vanished two decades ago. He bore a straight nose, clear complexion, and seemed to have managed more sleep than I had for the past two weeks. His voice was that of a young man, lacking authority.

'You can have the search warrant as soon as I've served it on Mrs Noland,' I said matter-of-factly. 'As far as legal procedures are concerned, you can rest assured that our work consists of upholding the law, not breaking it.' I made my way past him. 'Now, if you'll excuse us, we've got work to do.'

He paused for a few seconds and said, 'You understand this is all wrong. If you find nothing in my client's home, I intend to sue you personally, and the VFSC. My client is already under enough stress as it is, and she doesn't need the type of harassment you feel so obliged to provide her with.'

'I've already been informed of your good intentions, Mr Blacker.' I turned around and glared into his eyes. 'What you don't seem to understand is that we're not the criminals here. Our job is to find who killed Tracy Noland, that's all. But then, I suppose, if I was being paid $150 an hour, I probably would have to justify my existence by showing up at Mrs Noland's doorstep and threatening law-enforcement officials with lawsuits.'

He opened his mouth but failed to find a reply.

I could see Frank smiling from the corner of my eye. I bet he was glad he didn't have to do any talking.

We walked up the pathway to the door steps. I was leading, and therefore knocked on the front door.

Mr Blacker stood behind Frank without a word.

We waited in silence for thirty seconds, after which I knocked again and pushed the doorbell button.

Nothing.

I turned around, looked at Frank, who shrugged, and then looked at Mr Blacker.

'Did you inform Mrs Noland we were coming?' I asked Mr Blacker.

'I certainly did.'

I nodded and pushed the doorbell button again. I knocked louder.

Thirty seconds passed.

Nothing.

'There doesn't seem to be anybody home,' I said.

'That's strange,' Mr Blacker said. 'I had her on the phone less than half an hour ago, and she assured me she would be home.'

Frank's eyes met mine, a worried expression on his face.

I knocked and rang, yelling across the door, 'Mrs Noland, this is the police. We have a warrant to search your premises. Could you please open the door.'

The three of us stood frozen, listening for any sign of life inside the house.

Nothing.

'All right,' I said. 'We're going to have to break in.'

Mr Blacker stepped forward onto the patio. 'Absolutely not.'

'I beg your pardon?'

'There is no way you're going to enter these premises without my client being present.'

I shifted from one foot to the other, feeling heat on my face. 'Mr Blacker, I don't know when you graduated from law school, but this thing's called a warrant,' I held the document in front of his face, 'which gives us authorisation to search the premises with or without Mrs Noland's presence.'

'You do that and I'll sue you for breaking and entering.'

Suddenly, Frank stepped in front of Mr Blacker. 'Buzz off, buddy. We've got better things to do than listen to your whining.'

'I'm not letting you enter these premises without Mrs Noland's presence,' Mr Blacker retorted as he circled Frank and placed himself in front of the door.

'If you don't get out of the way,' Frank said, 'I'm going to handcuff you and arrest you for obstruction of justice.'

'I'd love to see that.'

'Fine.'

Without hesitating, Frank slipped out a pair of handcuffs he had attached to his belt, hidden under his jacket.

When Mr Blacker realised Frank was serious, he stepped aside and said, 'Go ahead. But I can assure you this will not go down quietly.'

Frank smiled to himself, while I pulled the fly screen door open. As expected, the front door was locked.

'I've got to get the lock-picking kit from the car,' I said, addressing myself to Frank. 'Wait here.'

I pushed my way past Mr Blacker, who seemed to be having an internal argument with himself.

I kept a lock picking kit in my glove box, a toy I bought during my eighteen-months training at the FBI in Quantico.

My lock picking kit consisted of a pick and a tension tool made from spring steel.

I returned to the front door, observing that Mr Blacker and Frank were not saying a word to one another.

I used the tension tool to control the pressure on the lock. I inserted the pick in the keyhole. After a few seconds of manipulation, I raised the pins to their opening point. The tension tool, placed directly under the pick, kept pressure on the pins while rotating. The pins were held in their open position by the pressure applied from the tension tool. With my fingers, I could feel the vibration of the pins. I listened patiently for a distinctive click, and then pushed the door open.

'Mrs Noland?' I shouted down the hallway.

Nothing.

'Maybe she's gone shopping,' Frank joked.

Suddenly an uneasiness took over me. I knew something

was wrong and dreaded the worst.

Mr Blacker was following Frank, like someone's pet.

'Mrs Noland?' I repeated.

Nothing.

'Okay,' Frank said, 'She's not home.' He tried to go past me.

'Hold on a sec,' I said, stopping him with the palm of my hand against his chest. He didn't protest.

There was a strong smell of alcohol coming from the kitchen ahead of us. I stood and breathed in. 'Whisky or bourbon?' I said without an explanation.

Frank remained behind.

I slowly crept down the hallway.

'Mrs Noland?' I almost whispered.

Don't let it be, I thought, but somehow I knew even before I found her.

The first thing I noticed when I walked in the kitchen was the empty bottle of Johnny Walker Red Label on the floor. To my right, slouched over the kitchen table, was Mrs Noland. All I could see of her head was a crop of grey hair. She was still dressed in her nightgown.

'Oh, shit!' I said as I circled the table. I felt a pain in my chest.

Three small plastic prescription containers lay next to her. At first glance, all seemed empty.

'Damn!' Frank said behind me.

'Shit,' I said. 'I think she's overdosed.' I placed my hand at the back of her neck. She was still warm, but I couldn't feel her pulse. I turned to Frank. 'Call an ambulance,' I ordered.

Without protest, he ran back down the hallway.

'What's going on?' I heard Mr Blacker say from down the hallway. He appeared at the door of the kitchen. 'Jesus Christ! What the hell happened?' The blood drained from his face. 'Oh, my God! Is she dead?'

'Yes, she's dead, Mr Blacker. Could you please get out of this room. This is a crime-scene area. I'm containing the crime scene, and I'm ordering you out of the house.'

'A crime scene? She killed herself.' He pointed a finger at me. 'And she killed herself because of you.'

I snapped. 'Mr Blacker, get the hell out of this kitchen

before I kick your arse out!'

He looked at me, stunned, unable to figure out whether to take me seriously or not.

'Now!' I shouted to his face.

He mumbled something about suing me and the entire police force before vanishing down the hallway.

I hated to do this, but I knew I had to try to resuscitate Mrs Noland. I slid her off the chair and lay her down on the floor.

Frank walked back in the room. 'What the hell did she take?'

'Why? Call an ambulance.'

'They want to know what she took.'

'It's on the table. Whatever she took, she washed it down with alcohol.'

He grabbed the three plastic containers from the kitchen table and disappeared down the hallway.

I began mouth-to-mouth resuscitation immediately. Her lips tasted like alcohol. I knew it was too late, but I had to try. Something inside me refused to accept she was dead. I began external cardiac massage. One, two, three. Back to mouth-to-mouth. Nothing. Cardiac massage. One, two, three. Nothing. I could feel tears in my eyes. *Come on, God dammit! Wake up!* I tried mouth-to-mouth again. Nothing. My hands were shaking, and my back was bathed in perspiration.

'Forget it, Katrina. She's dead,' Frank said.

I didn't even hear him coming back in the kitchen.

I knew he was right, but I refused to give up.

Mouth-to-mouth.

Someone grabbed my arm. 'Forget it, Katrina,' Frank said, pulling me away. 'It's over. The ambulance is coming.'

I looked at him and then back at Mrs Noland. 'She's dead, Frank. I killed her.'

'You didn't kill her. She killed herself.' He pulled my arm, forcing me to get up on my feet. 'Get yourself together. The paramedics are going to be here any minute.'

I nodded, wiping tears from my eyes. 'All right, all right. I'm okay now.' But I wasn't. My mind was filled with self-hatred. 'Why did she do it, Frank?'

'Don't know.' He was holding on to my arm.

'Do you think she killed herself because we pushed her?'

'No one knows, Katrina.'

'Do you think she did it because she felt guilty? Maybe she killed Tracy, and she couldn't live with herself.'

'We'll never find out.'

'But I need to know. I need to know what happened.'

He wrapped his arms around my body.

I was sobbing.

'It's okay, Katrina. Everything is going to be fine.'

'It's not going to be fine, Frank. She's dead. What are we going to do?'

'There's nothing to do. You just take it easy.'

I rested my head against his chest, drowning in the comfort of his familiar smell of Paco Rabanne and cigarettes. 'I didn't want her to die, Frank. You know I didn't want her to die.'

'Of course, I know. Nobody wanted her to die.'

And then I heard sirens screaming down the street.

# CHAPTER NINETEEN

Mrs Noland died from a cocktail of prescribed medication mixed with alcohol. Orphenadrine, mebendazole and flucysine to be exact. All hazardous if combined with alcohol. Flucytosine was used for the treatment of generalised candidiasis, mebendazole for treatment of intestinal worms and other parasitic infestations, and orphanadrine for relief of painful muscle spasm or symptoms of Parkinson's disease, all which had been prescribed under her name at one time or another. With the amount of tablets she took, combined with alcohol, she had little or no chance of surviving.

Mrs Noland's burial was scheduled for Friday afternoon, two days after she died. I felt obligated to turn up since I couldn't shake off the fact that I felt, if not fully, at least partly responsible for her death.

I did recover the box of chocolates from her kitchen bench, and, yes indeed, it was a perfect match with the one I'd seen at the lab. All I could be certain of now was that Tracy ate high-priced Turkish Delight before she died. Was the Turkish Delight she ate from her home? More likely than not, I thought.

Wednesday morning I slept in, unable to face the day. From the beginning of this investigation, I'd known better than to get involved. Now I knew I'd been right. So much for trusting one's instinct.

I got up at 10.53 a.m., my head heavy from oversleeping and my stomach grumbling from hunger. For the first time in years, I managed a breakfast of Michael's Coco Pops and a glass of orange juice. I hadn't eaten the previous night, and as a result my body's biological equilibrium was out of whack, sending pulsing signals to my blood-sugar-deprived brain, which would soon suffer from a massive headache.

After rinsing my dishes in the sink, I crossed to the lounge room and opened the balcony doors. I stepped outside, feeling a warm wind from the ocean slapping my face.

A green tram rolled up Chapel street, sending traffic into chaos, when my mobile phone went off. I raced back inside and snatched it from the kitchen bench.

'Is this Dr Melina?' asked a person with an Asian accent.

'Speaking.'

'This is Mr Nugyen from the pharmacy on Chapel Street.'

My mind did a somersault before it connected who it was.

'Mr Nugyen...how are you?'

'Good, yourself?'

We went on about each other's health for another thirty seconds.

'Dr Melina, my son he goes to university, study pharmacology.'

'Yes?'

'He look up zinc stearate for you. He think he also remembers person buying zinc stearate a few months back. You want talk to him?'

I puzzled over this for a few seconds. 'Why don't I come over and see him instead? I'm just down the street.'

'Oh, really?'

'I think that'd be much better.'

He hesitated. 'Sure, but please hurry because he got class this afternoon.'

'Give me half an hour.'

We said goodbye and I punched the end button.

I parked in a no-standing zone, just near the corner of Malvern Road and Chapel Street in Prahran. At 11.45 a.m. mid-week, I had no chance of getting a parking space, unless I parked in a suburban street or the university car park, which I didn't want to bother with. Prahran was sandwiched between

Windsor and Toorak, along Chapel Street, making it one of the most congested suburbs in Melbourne, other than the City centre. But then any suburb attached to Chapel Street was hell to park in.

Thuang Nugyen saw me coming into the chemist shop. He waved with his hand to come forward. He called someone, and within seconds a young Asian man stepped from somewhere behind the counter.

'This is my son, Lee,' Mr Nugyen announced as I approached the counter. 'He'll show you information on zinc stearate.'

Lee greeted me with 'Hi' and indicated towards one side of the counter. He wore sand-coloured chinos and a pale blue shirt, no tie. His look was warm and inviting. His black hair was fashionably brushed back and his skin free from acne or pimples, which was uncommon amongst people of his age. He wore round, rimless spectacles, giving him the advantage of looking intelligent even before he opened his mouth.

'I'm Kristina Melina.'

'I know,' he said. 'My dad told me.' His tone was warm but authoritative, and, unlike his father, he had no trace of an accent. He flipped through some hand-written notes he had laid on the counter. 'I looked up this stuff for you, and this is what I found.' He read from the notes: 'Zinc stearate is a compound of zinc oxide with variable proportions of stearic acid and palmatic acid. It tends to be used as a smooth dusting powder. Zinc oxide by itself is a mild astringent agent used primarily to treat skin disorders, such as nappy rash and eczema. It's readily available in many compounds other than zinc stearate, such as a cream with arachis oil, oleic acid and wool fat, or with ichthammol and wool fat. It's also combined with castor oil to form an ointment, or with starch and talc to form a dusting powder.'

'So,' I said, impressed by his research so far, 'Zinc stearate is basically some form of talc?'

'Not chemically. Talc is a monoclinic hydrated magnesium silicate while zinc stearate is zinc oxide combined with stearic acid, a monobasic fatty acid obtained from mutton suet or by reducing oleic acid. But in physical properties, they're both pretty similar. The thing is zinc stearate is toxic, so no one uses it these days.'

I shifted from one foot to the other, trying to digest the mumbo jumbo he'd just thrown at me. 'And you told your father you remembered who bought zinc stearate a few months back?'

Lee looked up over his rimless spectacles. 'Well, yes I do. It's an unusual prescription, and since I'd never heard of it myself at the time, I do recall who bought it.'

'Who?'

'Unfortunately I can't give you a name. As my father told you, vandals broke into the shop not long ago, and they destroyed the register which held the names and signatures of people who bought poisonous goods. I can tell you what she looks like, though.'

Our eyes locked. 'Go on.'

'Kind of a large woman, short dark hair, spiky on top, and dressed in tracksuit pants.'

I had Mrs Noland in mind, but she didn't have short hair. 'And that's it?'

'Yeah, basically. She was kind of average looking, but butch, if you know what I mean.'

I wrote all this down. 'You don't mind if I take these notes with me,' I said, pointing at the hand-written pages he'd been reading from.

'Sure.'

I folded the pages in half and stored them in my handbag.

'Well, thanks a lot for your help. And if you remember anything else, make sure you give me a call.' I handed him a business card.

'Will do.'

We shook hands, and I did a one-eighty degree turn to leave the chemist.

Half way down the shop, between the vitamins and facial creams, Lee called out, 'Oh, Dr Melina?'

I turned around. 'Yes?'

'Something else I remember.'

'What?'

'She had a tattoo with some flowers on her left arm.'

The second time I met Linda Coleman was at Mrs Noland's

funeral on Friday the 9th of January. Jason and Lucia were there as well, and so was half the neighbourhood. She fitted the description I was given by Mr Nugyen's son. Short, spiky hair, butch look and tattoo, which was currently concealed by a black cardigan. This was also how I remembered her when I visited her at the beginning of this investigation. It had dawned on me that this was a woman of great physical strength who could have been capable of anything a man was capable of, that is, in the physical sense.

The day turned out to be nice, weather-wise, anyway. The sky was clear as far as the eye could see, and there was no sign of it getting worse. The funeral was arranged by Better Funeral Services.

Frank came with me to the funeral, not really to mourn the loss of Mrs Noland, but to observe who turned up. He thought that the killer of Tracy Noland, if not Mrs Noland, might have decided to come to the service. I hadn't told him yet how I knew Linda Coleman bought zinc stearate some time ago. I thought I'd leave it until after the funeral for no other reason than the fear of botching the investigation. I'd hate to see him snap and say something to Linda Coleman, revealing what we knew so far.

After two days at home, I began to surface and realise that there might have been more to Mrs Noland's death than me *harassing* her. People didn't commit suicide for so little. One could argue she was depressed because of the death of her child, but nothing so far showed me she truly loved Tracy. Maybe she was part of a grand scheme with someone else. The more I thought about it, the more I wondered why we'd assumed only one person was involved.

At the end of the burial, we were invited to the funeral home for refreshments and sandwiches. I took the opportunity to talk to as many people as I could, since everyone more or less lived on Vincent Court or its adjoining streets.

Jason came to me while I was helping myself to a glass of orange juice.

'How are you coping?' he whispered, as if we were the only two who knew Mrs Noland had died.

'I'm fine. Not the kind of place someone looks forward to visiting.'

He circled the room with his eyes. 'Where's Michael?'

'Not here.'

'Didn't he want to come to the funeral?'

I turned around, my glass of orange juice in one hand, and spoke straight to his face, 'Michael's out with his friends. That's what thirteen-year old kids do in case you didn't know.'

He moved back one step as if I'd just spat on him. 'All right. You don't have to be so nasty, Katrina. I was just asking, that's all. Gee, when did I start becoming the bad guy all of a sudden?'

His eyes were those of a man who'd been betrayed. 'I'm sorry,' I said. 'It's best if you don't stay around me today. I'm saying things without thinking.'

His look softened. 'It's okay, Katrina.' He patted my shoulder. 'We're all in this together.' And then he moved to talk to someone else, but I caught him by the arm.

'Jason, how well do you know your neighbours?'

His brow crossed and he said, 'As well as you do by now, I assume.'

'Okay, I'll get to the point. Do you know if Mrs Noland and Linda Coleman were good friends?'

He seemed to struggle with an answer. 'Gee, I don't know. I wouldn't want to say the wrong thing. But, yes, I've seen them together. To say they were good friends might be stretching the truth. That they knew each other, that I can confirm.'

'But it's possible they were really good friends?'

'It's possible. Anything is possible. I mean, god, what we thought once impossible has happened in Vincent Court.'

I couldn't disagree with him. Life was full of surprises, and I knew the Tracy Noland case was still filled with them.

'Okay, that's all,' I said and let go of his arm.

From the corner of my eye, I caught Lucia all by herself. Her mother was busy talking to a man I'd never seen before. Obviously, no one wanted to embarrass themselves talking to a person in a wheelchair.

When she saw me, she smiled. 'I'm glad you came,' she managed to say. I was amazed that I understood her speech immediately, unlike when she first spoke to me.

'Do you want to go outside?' I asked. 'It's stuffy in here.' What I really meant was did she want to talk in private.

'Okay.'

I pushed the wheelchair past the entrance door, crossed the foyer, struggled on the thick burgundy carpet, and stepped outside where the sun blinded us.

'How have you been?' I said, kneeling next to Lucia.

There was a sadness in her eyes, which broke my heart. 'Good. Any news on Tracy's killer?'

'Not at this stage. Say, did Tracy ever offer you Turkish Delight?'

She puzzled over my question and said, 'Never.'

'Are you sure?'

'Of course I'm sure. She couldn't stand the stuff, so why would she offer it to me?'

I wondered if I'd heard properly. 'Tracy didn't like Turkish Delight?'

'She hated the stuff. She told me many times.'

'Well, that's interesting because I found a box at her place.'

'Oh, yeah, her mother liked them.'

I didn't want to tell Lucia we found Turkish Delight in Tracy's stomach. I wasn't sure if she'd ever heard of autopsies and thought I might upset her. 'Do you know where she got the Turkish Delight from?'

'One of the neighbours sells them down the street now and then. She works for some charity of some sort.'

'Who?'

'Woman down the street. Don't know her name.' She paused for a few seconds. 'Actually, she was at the funeral this morning. She's probably still in there.' She pointed at the funeral home.

'Can you show me who she is if we go back inside?'

'Okay.'

I stood straight, stretched my legs and wheeled Lucia back inside the building.

People were in small groups, chit-chatting in low voices.

'Where is she?' I asked Lucia.

She circled the room with her eyes, and suddenly stretched her only moving arm in one direction. 'There.'

Lucia was pointing at Linda Coleman, who happened to be having a conversation with Jason. Well, I couldn't really say

220

that I was surprised. Her name had come up twice in a matter of days. I made a mental note to make her a priority in my investigation.

I thanked Lucia for the information and quickly crossed the room to where Frank was standing. He was talking to one of the funeral director's assistants.

I closed in on Frank and whispered in his ear. 'We need to get together as soon as you're done. I think I've got a breakthrough.'

He nodded and went on with his conversation.

I glanced towards Linda Coleman, who was sweet-talking another one of Mrs Noland's neighbours. I thought I was being discreet, but suddenly, she tilted her head and glared into my eyes. Her lips were tight and her look daring.

I shifted uncomfortably and began making my way towards the exit.

But the pain at the back of my skull told me it was too late.

She knew I knew.

# CHAPTER TWENTY

Frank and I met on the ninth floor of the St Kilda Road Police Complex immediately after the funeral. We were alone in a private room, two mugs of coffee barely touched. My empty stomach was filled with orange juice, causing a heartburn. I was dying for something to eat, but I wanted to get a hold of Frank before he disappeared.

I detailed what I'd found out about Linda Coleman.

'Are you sure?' he asked, obviously not wanting to make another mistake.

'I'm telling you. This guy at the chemist described her to the letter. I mean, how many women do you know who wear short hair and have a large tattoo stamped on one arm?'

'Not many, thank God.' He puzzled for a few seconds, sipping from his coffee mug. 'So where does that leave Malcom Sternwood?

'As much as I'd hate to admit it, I think we've got the wrong guy. Other evidence, like the zinc stearate and the Turkish Delight, points away from him.'

'Damn... I don't know what to tell you. What are we going to do now?'

'We can go and confront her on the basis of the zinc stearate she bought a few months back.'

'You realise this is only circumstantial evidence. You won't be able to mount a case with that little information.'

'You're probably right, but if we can search her home, maybe we'll find other evidence. What we need to do is move in fast, take her by surprise.'

He shook his head. 'I don't know, Katrina. That's what we did with Mrs Noland, and look what happened.'

'We don't know that she wasn't involved. Maybe the two of them worked together. Maybe Mrs Noland killed herself because she was remorseful. It was her daughter after all.'

'Probably. But what about a motive? You know we'll never convince a jury unless we can show the killer had a motive.'

'We'll find one if we keep digging. Maybe Mrs Noland owed a lot of money to Linda Coleman, and they made a deal where Tracy would be killed to repay Coleman with the insurance claim. Who knows, greed brings out the worst in people.'

Frank shifted uncomfortably on his chair and said, 'Okay, look, in the meantime we're going to have to let Malcom Sternwood go. His solicitor wants bail, says we've got nothing concrete to tie his client to the murder. I kind of still think he could have done it. He certainly fits the profile better than Linda Coleman.'

'Then let him go.'

Frank let out a sigh and emptied his mug. 'I'm going to get a warrant authorised for this evening. Just make sure you've got your mobile phone on so I can reach you when the paper work is done.'

I nodded and stood from my chair. 'I'm going back home anyway. Some things I need to check on.'


I spent the entire afternoon going through my files on the Tracy Noland murder. Something was on the verge of being disclosed, something locked at the back of my mind, a detail I hadn't paid attention to. And it's funny how the mind works because it seemed to know more than I did. It was only a matter of time before I would be able to link everything up.

I spread the crime scene photos all over the floor, a cup of coffee on the carpet at risk of being knocked at any time. My focus was one hundred percent on the task. No jazz or classical music to distract my thoughts. I was in a cocoon, ignorant of what was happening outside my window. Typed reports of my interviews with the neighbours were piled up on my right and left. There was something in there which led to the truth. It was a matter of opening my eyes and ciphering through the contents thoroughly.

I re-read the reports I'd written about my initial interviews with Tracy's neighbours. There had to be something, a connection which would lead me in the right direction.

And then, all of a sudden, it hit me like lighting. The truth was staring at me, but I'd been too busy to see it. I stared at my pages again and re-read the section I'd found over and over. There was no doubt. This couldn't have been a coincidence.

I sprang to my feet, knocking the coffee cup all over my paper work.

*Damn!*

I stared at it, as if the dark stain on the salmon carpet was a time bomb, ready to go off in my face. Then I shrugged and raced to Michael's room, my heart pounding.

I pushed the door open, knowing he wasn't home. The room was a mess like I expected it to be. Clothes spread all over the floor, school books, games, empty packets of chips and half emptied soft-drink canisters. My eyes scanned the room, but I couldn't find what I was looking for.

Fear crept at the back of my mind.

*Could it be possible?*

I went down on my hands and knees, sniffing around the rubbish, my head down on the carpet. Exactly what I was looking for, I wasn't sure.

And then I found it.

It was there, right under his bed, next to a pile of Sport Illustrated and Smash Hits magazines.

My pulse quickened at the sight of it. I had to re-adjust my focus to make sure I wasn't dreaming. But the damn thing was as real as the five fingers on my right hand.

I flicked it over with a push.

The box was empty.

Michael had eaten all the Turkish Delight.


Within half an hour, I was in Albert Park, my heart drilling out of my chest.

*Oh, God, don't let anything happen to Michael!*

Horrid images of Tracy Noland appeared in my mind's eyes, but then Tracy became Michael, and I nearly smashed my car into a semi-trailer, which stopped suddenly at red traffic lights. I wanted to go faster, but six-o'clock traffic was as bad as this morning's peak-hour. I felt foolish not noticing something so obvious. Sometimes, caught in all the forensic complication of an investigation, it seemed too damn easy to overlook simple things. If anything ever happened to Michael, I knew I'd never have the strength to carry on.

Turning the corner to where Tracy lived, I could have sworn I saw Lucia in her front yard with her wheelchair. I looked in the rear mirror to double-check, but no one was there.

I parked the car in Jason's driveway.

His Mazda 626 wasn't there.

Nervous, I checked for my .380 semi-automatic in the glove box, but after struggling with my conscience, I decided to leave it behind. It was bright daylight, and nothing much could happen. Instead I took the lock picking kit with me.

I slipped out of the car and slammed the car door, not bothering to lock it.

Checking my surroundings, I climbed the steps to the front door. I wondered if anyone could see me across the large bay window of the lounge room. But his car wasn't there, so why would he be home?

I turned the front door knob, but not surprisingly it was locked. Anxious, I pressed the buzzer and knocked on the door. My mind was racing at a hundred miles an hour, imagining the worst could have happened.

Nothing.

I glanced around one more time.

Vincent Court was deserted. Just a quiet street in the middle of suburbia. At first glance, no one appeared to be watching me.

I removed the lock picking kit from my bag, and in less than thirty seconds, I heard the distinctive click made by the pins. The thirty seconds had taken forever. A single thought kept running in my head like the tune of a scratched record.

*I'm too late. I'm too late. I'm too late.*

I pushed the door open.

'Jason? Michael?'

Not a sound.

I closed the door behind me and stood still for about a minute, listening for any noise.

But all I could hear were birds chirping outside.

When I was convinced no one was in the house, I made my way down the hallway, hugging the wall with my back. I wasn't sure what I was looking for. Initially, I came looking for Michael because I feared for his life. And I had every reason to after the connection I'd just made while going through the Tracy Noland file in my apartment.

I eased past the lounge room and the kitchen. Everything was as I remembered, clean and in its place.

The sink was free of dishes and clutter.

Dish rags were carefully folded over the handle of the oven.

The kitchen table had been wiped to a polish.

Mr Harvey had an obsession for tidiness. That's something else I should have paid more attention to.

Fear creeping down the back of my neck, I stepped back down the hallway. There were two doors to my right, both of them shut. I hesitated for a few seconds and decided to go for the one on the right.

One hand on the door handle, I glanced over my shoulder, feeling I was being watched.

But no one was there.

Perspiration dripped down my back.

My hands were trembling.

I hunched my shoulders, turned the knob and hesitantly pushed the door open.

What if I was wrong?

What if I'd just broken into someone's home unjustly?

I stepped inside.

The room was bare of furniture, other than a table covered in a black, velvet cloth. To my right were two cardboard boxes with Turkish Delight printed on the side and the name of the importer. Make-up, two pair of wings and assorted clips and combs. Above the table was a large mirror where the old man could see himself change into a clown or a magician. I scanned the top of the table and noticed a large jar, which I first believed to be cold cream. But inside was a white powder. Automatically, I though of zinc stearate. But what was it for? Something to do with magic?

Before I had time to come up with an answer, I saw the printed name in gold letters on the black, velvet cloth. I stared at the word for thirty seconds, trying to accept what I was faced with.

I thought about Michael.

This had to be a nightmare.

The word *Paranor* stitched in Gothic, gold-lettering stood like a diamond in the front of the cloth.

The conversation I had with Lucia was playing back my mind.

*'Was there anyone Tracy hated in particular?'*

*'The only person I can think of is Paranor.'*

*'Who?'*

*'Paranor.'*

*'Who's Paranor?'*

*'I don't know.'*

Paranor.

Paranor.

Paranormal.

The damn word was probably a stage name.

'Michael!' I screamed, surprised by the loudness of my voice.

Then I heard the door creak behind my back.

I did a half-circle, felt the impact of god-knows-what on my forehead, and everything turned to black.

For a spilt second, before I lost consciousness, I thought I was about to die.

# CHAPTER TWENTY-ONE

**W**hen I woke up, my head was on fire. Whatever had hit me caught me off-guard and did a good job of disorientating me. At first, I wasn't sure if I was sitting, standing or lying down. Then, as I became increasingly aware of my surroundings, I realised that the white surface in front of me was not a ceiling, but a wall. I think it might have been a window on my left which helped me assess my surroundings.

I tried to breath-in through my nose, but it was blocked, and all I could taste was blood in my mouth. I tried to reach for my face to sooth the bruising on my forehead, but I couldn't move my hands. Horrified, I realised I was tied to a chair and stripped to my underwear. It took me another thirty seconds to understand what was happening.

Yes, I remembered being at Jason Harvey's home, searching for Michael. Then I found a room and a table and a cloth with the word *Paranor* written on it. I felt like a fool letting myself become a friend to the man who killed Tracy Noland. At least, I was now certain he did. What was he going to do to me? What happened to Michael?

I tried to stand from the chair, but it was useless.

Why in the world had I been stripped to my underwear?

During my time at Quantico, I'd learned about psychotic behaviour, and knowing what I'd learned, I realised the situation I found myself in was alarming. What were my chances of getting out of here alive? Based on statistical information I had lodged somewhere at the back of my cranium, virtually none.

'Somebody help!' I heard a voice scream.

Silence.

And I realised it was my own voice.

The fear of not knowing what had happened to Michael gave me the strength to fight back.

I tried to pull my hands forward, but whatever was tying them together was cutting at my wrists. There's nothing quite like pain to bring you back to the reality of life. I would have given anything right at this moment to be in the comfort of my lounge room, overlooking Chapel Street, listening to neighbours argue, putting up with Michael's disrespectful behaviour and losing myself in a good book. But the fact was that I was near-naked in someone's torture room, my head drowning in confusion and pain, my body shivering from cold and fear.

And then I heard voices coming from somewhere distant.

Two voices.

A man and a woman.

That's when I realised I'd been right.

Back in my study, I'd gone through the interview reports, and something jolted me as unusual. There was a pattern which I hadn't notice at the beginning of the investigation, a coincidence which would have triggered my mind into another direction had I been more attentive to details.

After the look Linda Coleman gave me when I left Mrs Noland's funeral, I rushed back home and went through my reports. And only when I re-read all of them, I realised Jason Harvey and she had pointed the finger at Malcom Sternwood. They were the only two who brought up Malcom as a probable suspect. In fact, Jason was the only person who defended Tracy, telling me people had no idea what they were talking about.

The voices were getting louder. It almost sounded like an argument.

I wanted to scream, but refrained myself.

The voices turned into whispers, and then a door opened behind my back.

'She's awake,' the female voice said.

Whoever was with her didn't bother answering.

The woman circled the room.

Unstartled, I recognised Linda.

Jason was beside her. 'Hi, Katrina,' he said, as if everything that was happening was perfectly normal. He looked at my breasts, and then his eyes met mine. 'I wish things could have been different.'

My tongue felt like cardboard inside my mouth. I didn't know what to reply to such an obvious statement. I racked my throat and said, 'Where's Michael?'

He gave Linda a look and said, 'I don't know. He's not out with his friends like boys of his age are supposed to be?'

'You bastard!' I shouted. 'If you've done anything to him, I'm going to get you.'

He laughed.

Linda was staring at me coldly, and I felt as if she was going to eat me right here, alive.

'What do you want from me?' I asked, horrified.

'Katrina,' Jason went on, 'it's not what I want from you, it's what you want from me. I tried hard to steer you the other way. But you just had to persist.' He removed his lucky coin from the right pocket of his chinos and rotated it between his fingers. 'I like you, and you know that.'

'Why did you kill Tracy?'

His brow creased. 'Hey, hold on. It's wasn't like that. You're trying to make it sound like she was murdered. It was an accident. It truly was.'

Linda wasn't saying a word, and it kind of frightened me. They'd obviously planned something, but were not telling. The fact that I was only wearing my underwear explained my fear.

'What was it then?' I asked, not only because I was curious enough to find out what truly happened to Tracy Noland, but also because I knew that if I kept a conversation going for long enough, I might be able to convince them to release me.

'I was teaching her some magic tricks, just like Michael.'

'You didn't touch Michael? Did you?'

'Now why would I do that? What do you take me for?'

I was losing patience. 'Just get me out of this chair. This has nothing to do with me.'

'On the contrary, you made it your choice and made it

something to do with you. And now, we've got a problem that needs to be solved.'

I didn't know what was coming, but I knew I wouldn't like it. 'What exactly are you talking about?' Then I turned to Linda. 'And tell her to stop looking at me like that. She's giving me the creeps.'

They both laughed whole-heartedly as if we were sharing a joke.

'Well,' Jason said, 'You don't have to worry about Linda for much longer. The two of you are going to get to know each other in ways you've never experienced. At least I don't think you have.'

I kind of guessed what he was suggesting, and when I looked at Linda, my worst fear had been confirmed. She smiled at me, and all that did was get me even more confused.

What had actually happened to Tracy Noland?

Who killed her?

Jason or Linda?

Or both?

And why?

'You're going to tell me what happened?' I asked.

Jason moved forward and said, 'I told you it was an accident. We were playing a game, and —'

'What kind of game?'

'The kind of game we're playing with you now.' He moved back. 'Look, thing was she started to scream, and all I did was put my hand over her mouth, and the next thing you know, she wasn't moving.' He turned to Linda. 'Isn't that right, dear?'

She nodded without a word.

*Well, I guess that made it all right then. If it was an accident, everything is under control. Now that you've explained yourself, the investigation is over. We won't go ahead with any criminal charges, and life can go on as usual.*

'You guys are really sick,' I said as an afterthought to my internal dialogue. 'And what did you use the zinc stearate for?'

They looked at each other puzzled.

I went on, 'We found traces of zinc stearate all over her mouth. Linda bought the stuff from a chemist. No point denying it, it's on record.' A lie, but in the position I found myself, it didn't really matter any more. Fact was that Lee

Nugyen had only described Linda Coleman to me, and the record of her buying zinc stearate had been destroyed.

'Oh, that!' Jason said, mildly surprised. 'It's a dusting powder I use when doing card tricks. It makes the cards more slippery, easier to handle.'

So much for the mystery of the zinc stearate, I thought.

He moved to the side and said, 'Well, if you don't have any other questions, we'd better get moving. Getting rid of a body is not that easy. But you must know that, since it's your field of work.'

I jerked on my chair, trying to throw myself forward.

Without warning, Linda hit me on the side of the face, sending me flying sideways.

I crushed against the wood-panel floor, bones crashing, pain jolting throughout my skull. I couldn't believe what was happening.

'How did you get Mrs Noland to agree with this?' I asked, blood spilling from the side of my mouth.

'Eh? She had nothing to do with it,' Jason said. 'Perfect timing she killed herself when she did. Made it easier on all of us.'

'And what about Michael? You could at least tell me what's happened to Michael.'

He shrugged. 'Nothing has happened to Michael. I haven't seen him today.'

'Liar!'

He smiled, obviously enjoying my torture. 'I'm going next door for a while, leave the two of you alone.' He bent over towards my face. 'Well, I guess we won't be seeing each other again. Damn shame. I kind of liked you in that cute underwear. You remind me of Tracy. Innocent, naive little thing that she was.'

'You bastard!'

'Goodbye, dear.'

He slipped out the room.

I was left alone with Linda.

Without warning, she cranked the chair back up on its feet. I could feel burning on both sides of my face, where she hit me and where I hit the ground.

She moved to one corner of the room, which was partly obliterated from my view because of the angle I was sitting in.

'What are you doing?' I said, despair coming over me.

No answer.

'Why don't you say something? Is that how you did it with Tracy?'

'Shut up.'

I did.

I sat for what seemed an eternity, wondering what she was doing behind my back. Was this going to be some kind of rape-thrill kill? In the state I was in, blood dripping down my chin and onto my breasts, I wondered what kick she would get out of using my body for her own gratification.

Finally, when I was too busy wondering how bad my face looked, she appeared in front of me, a syringe in her hand. I'd almost forgotten she worked as a nurse at St Patrick's Hospital.

'What's this stuff?'

'It'll put you to sleep.'

I was getting desperate. 'Don't do this, Linda. It's not the right thing. You know it's not the right thing.'

"I'm way past doing what's right.'

'Everyone knows I'm here. I've already spoken to Senior Sergeant Frank Moore. Anything happens to me, and he'll come straight to you.'

I jerked on my chair, trying hard to free my hands from behind my back.

Linda took her time, savouring every second of my despair.

'Let me go, Linda. If you let me go, I'll make sure you'll get the best defence lawyer.'

She sniggered without bothering to answer. Instead she checked the contents of needle to the light.

'Is this going to kill me?'

'It's not Prozac, if that's what you're asking.'

She flicked the needle a couple of times, and with her right hand, felt her way around my neck.

'You don't have to do this, Linda. You know you don't have to do this. We can work something out. Just let me go. I won't tell anyone anything.' I was losing it, making promises I knew I wouldn't keep.

'Just relax,' she said in a nursing manner. 'It's less painful if you relax.'

'Oh, God!'

I closed my eyes, images of Michael and me spending time together. I was going to miss him.

I clenched my teeth when the needle pierced the side of my neck.

Death was only seconds away.

But none of the contents of the needle entered my left jugular.

Instead, a fire-cracker-like noise exploded in the room.

The needle slid back from my neck.

I could smell gunpowder.

I was alive.

*Oh, God, I'm alive*

I opened my eyes.

Linda had fallen backwards, her brain splattered all over the white wall.

# CHAPTER TWENTY-TWO

Lucia managed to untie me from the chair. With only one hand working, it wasn't easy, especially when she'd dragged herself all the way up the stairs to Jason's house without her wheelchair.

She shot Linda with my gun, which she had tucked in the elastic of her tracksuit pants.

'How did you get the gun?' I asked, avoiding the sight of blood and flesh in front of me.

'You left it in the car.'

Sure I did, and I was even stupid enough not to lock the door. On the other hand, stupidity saved my life.

'How did you know I was here?'

'I saw you go in.'

And then I recalled thinking I had seen Lucia when I first entered Vincent Court.

'What about Jason and Linda?'

'They pulled over in his car after you broke into the house.'

'Why did you decide to go in with the gun?'

'I saw you go inside his home. When I saw his car pull into the driveway, I knew he didn't invite you in. And then it occurred to me that maybe Jason was the killer, only because you broke into his home.'

My hands free, I wiped the blood from my face.

'Have you seen Jason,' I asked.

'No.'

I grabbed the .380 semi-automatic which Lucia had dropped on the floor.

'You stay in here,' I ordered, not that she would want to go out there again and face another lunatic. 'He's still somewhere in the house.'

I didn't know what to do with my lack of clothes. Jumping around someone's home in my underwear with a gun seemed an odd thing to do. But then, the whole afternoon had been pretty strange so far, so why worry now.

'Don't you go anywhere,' I insisted. 'I need to find out where he is.'

I peeked out of the room, but no one was there. I checked the chamber of the handgun. Five bullets, and all was in order.

*I'm coming after you, asshole, so you better be ready.*

I eased myself into the hallway and closed the door behind me. I was breathing through my mouth because coagulated blood had blocked my nostrils, making it impossible for me to breathe normally.

My back against the wall, I moved down to the kitchen while keeping my eyes and ears open. My hand was tightly gripped around the handgun, finger on the trigger,

I knew someone was going to get hurt badly. Unless Jason took off in his car, which I doubt he did, then confrontation was inevitable.

I passed the kitchen, wondering where the hell he had vanished to.

Then, I noticed the laundry door, which lead to the backyard, had been left ajar.

I crept through the back door.

Outside it was getting darker. I could still make out where I was going, but the sun would vanish within the next twenty minutes or so. Instinctively, I checked my arm to where my watch used to be. But they had taken the watch away from me as well. What was the idea behind all this? Were they going to kill me and donate my clothes to the Salvation Army? Such well-behaved and thoughtful citizens.

There was no trace of Jason.

Standing near-naked with a gun in my hand, I almost laughed at the ridiculousness of my situation. But when I heard a noise coming from the garage, the whole incident didn't seem that funny after all. For a few seconds I contemplated the thought of taking Lucia with me and getting the hell out of this place.

I walked on the damp grass, which had been watered only recently, and made my way towards the brick veneer garage. I noticed light on the inside from a small window. He was in there, probably stitching up my body bag.

I wondered if it'd be better to wait for him to come to me or to take him by surprise. But waiting made me feel nervous and out of control. My fear had turned to anger, and I couldn't wait to get my hands on him.

I closed in on the door.

Two choices.

Burst in or creep in.

I decided to burst in.

With a mighty thump, I kicked the door open and jumped into the room, the way I'd been trained to do. My arms extended, I circled the room with my eyes and the gun. It took me a few seconds to register what I was seeing. Towards the left side of the shutter door, Jason had his back on me. When he turned around, I had to look twice as hard.

Michael was tied to a chair, masking tape over his mouth, wearing nothing but his underwear.

'Get the hell away from him!' I ordered, the semi-automatic pointed in his direction.

He racked his throat and said, 'I wouldn't do that if I was you, Katrina. I've got a knife.'

'Move or I shoot.'

Swiftly, he circled the chair and placed himself behind Michael, giving me no chance to shoot without risking Michael's life.

I went on, 'If you don't throw the knife down and step forward, I'm going to blow your fuckin' head off.'

'Oh, no, you won't.'

He placed the blade under Michael's chin.

Michael's eyes were filled with panic.

I froze, the gun tightly gripped in my hand, assessing the situation. If I shot and missed, he could kill Michael in less than a second.

And there was no point wondering whether he was capable

of doing it or not. We both knew he was.

'All right, all right,' I said reluctantly. 'I'm putting the gun down, but you move away from him.'

'Not until the gun is on the floor.'

'I'm doing it. Just take it easy.'

His grip loosened, but he still held the knife under Michael's throat.

Slowly, I kneeled down and placed the gun on the concrete floor.

'It's down. You can let him go now,' I said.

'No way. Kick it over here.'

'Move away from him, goddamnit!'

'Kick the gun.'

Shit, there was obviously not much room for negotiation.

'I'm kicking it,' I said. With my right foot I pushed the gun in Jason's direction. It came landing halfway between him and me.

'You did that on purpose.'

'I swear to God I didn't.'

And that was the truth. All I wanted was for him to release Michael. I didn't care about anything else. Not even about myself.

'I kicked the gun,' I said. 'Now, let him go.'

'You're not making this easy, Katrina.' With one hand he gripped the back of the chair, the knife still under Michael chin. He dragged the chair and himself towards the gun. 'You make one move and I cut his fuckin throat.'

*Oh, God, don't let anything go wrong.*

'Why did you do it, Jason?' I asked, not knowing what else to say.

'You wouldn't understand.'

'I'd understand. If there's one person in the world who'd understand, that would be me.'

He continued dragging the chair to where the gun was.

I could see the fear in Michael's eyes.

Hopelessness was taking over me. If Jason got to the gun, he would kill the both of us. That much I understood.

'I like kids,' he said, 'but not the way you think. That's Linda.'

'What?'

'I just like kids, full stop. Linda likes to see them undress. She likes to play with them.'

Maybe that was why we found nothing on Tracy's body which indicated she'd been sexually assaulted. The usual forensic evidence wasn't there. No semen residue, no enlarging of the vaginal walls, no cuts or bruises in the anus.

'So what exactly did she do?'

'Nothing much. She got off looking and touching.'

'And that's what happened to Tracy?'

'That's what happened, I swear.'

Even if he had fifty bibles stacked on top of one another, with both his hands on it and a jury in front of him, I still wouldn't have taken his word for it.

He was now half way to where he started and where the gun was. Making him talk slowed him down a bit, which was partly the reason why I carried out a conversation with him.

'And why did you kill her?' I asked.

'Because she started to scream when Linda was touching her. I didn't mean to kill her. I told you before. It was an accident. I gave her Turkish delight so she would shut up, but she didn't. So I placed my hand over her mouth. And I didn't know. I didn't know she ran out of breath. I've never killed anyone before.'

'So, it was an accident.'

'It was an accident.'

'Okay, Jason, if it was an accident, then why are you doing this?'

He stopped two metres from the gun. 'What am I supposed to do? No one would believe me anyway?'

'You don't know that until you try.'

'Maybe it's not a chance I want to take. I'm retired, Katrina. I've spent my life working. I don't want to be behind bars.'

'You told me it was an accident. It was more Linda's fault than yours.'

He looked at me puzzled. 'You know that no matter what happens, I'm going to jail anyway. No one's going to release me on a good behaviour bond.'

He was right about that, but I didn't have the heart to tell him.

'Okay, but doing what you're doing now is not going to improve anything. Frank Moore knows I've come to see you. If I disappear, he'll be looking for you. What are you going to gain from this? Nothing. Give up now before it gets worse.'

He was half a metre from the gun.

I stood five metres from him.

Too far to attempt anything.

I had to think fast.

'Jason,' I continued, 'tell me why you helped Linda. You must have known what she did was wrong. Why help her?'

'It's complicated. I don't know where to start. We became friends when she moved in the area five years ago. And I've never had a friend like that before. She cooked for me. It was not long after my wife left. Linda was good to me. I guess one thing lead to another. I never really thought about it. It was just a progression.'

'And you never thought it abnormal what she was doing?'

'I knew it wrong, but what was I supposed to do? I liked her. She came as a whole package. It wasn't like I could choose one part and leave the other. It's like living with a drunk. You can love the person and not like the drunkenness, but you put up with it.'

Oh, so, now Jason Harvey thought himself a philosopher, and child molesting was nothing more than having a regular scotch.

He stood just above the gun.

'Okay, Jason, why don't we work something out?'

'You know I can't do that.'

He let go of the knife, bent down and grabbed the gun.

Just then, I looked at Michael, who looked back at me.

I blinked and he knew.

Just as Jason stood back on his feet, Michael titled forward and head-butted Jason in the lower back, sending him flying across the concrete floor. The gun came sliding towards me.

Before he had time to realise what was happening, I had already grabbed the semi-automatic and aimed it at his head.

'It's over, Jason. It's all over,' I yelled, blood spitting from my mouth.

# EPILOGUE

Summer is over, and the Grand Prix is back at Albert Park. Moomba, Melbourne's own celebration of itself, is at full swing in the city. March is the one month of the year where Melbourne really comes alive. The *Herald-Sun* decorates its front page with car racing fever, leaving the important news to the third or fourth page. The Tracy Noland story, which came in with a big bang, dies quietly in the midst of all the festivities.

The Monday paper devotes only a small column to a follow-up of the Tracy Noland murder, which had been front page news since January.

Jason Harvey is dead.

After searching his home, skeletal remains of his vanished wife Elizabeth were found in his backyard. Forensic tests showed she died from head fracture. We never got a chance to ask Jason about her death, but he was obviously not as innocent as he tried to make me believe when I had him face to face in the garage the day he was going to kill me and Michael.

I'm sitting in the lounge room, the balcony door open, letting some fresh air into the apartment. It's quite a nice day, and autumn doesn't come to mind when faced with a clear blue sky. Vivaldi's Spring Concerto in E, the first part of The Four Seasons, fills the house with a joyous atmosphere.

I read the column for the hundredth time, my face now only slightly bruised from the blow Linda Coleman gave me.

I'm quoted as refusing to comment on the case as I leave the detention centre where Jason Harvey was being held. One would think journalists would have given up on me by now.

I learned of his death the previous day via Frank. When I asked Frank over the phone how Jason died, he told me no one knew.

'What do you mean?' I asked. 'Did he hang himself?'

'No.'

'Is he bleeding?'

'There's nothing. They found him in his bed dead. Just as if he died in his sleep.'

I rushed to the prison.

When I arrived, Jason was in bed, looking peaceful. The tension I had seen on his face over the past week had vanished.

I stood above the bed, but couldn't see anything suspicious.

Then I noticed his right hand was made into a fist.

I kneeled down and undid his fingers one at the time.

Tucked in the palm of his hand was his lucky coin.

I took the coin, and it came apart in my hand. Inside the coin was a small chamber, which I guessed had once been filled with something.

Frank stood behind me.

'So?' he said.

'He poisoned himself.'

'With what?'

'Don't' know yet. We'll find out at the autopsy.'

Within twenty-four hours, Dr Charles W. Main announced Jason Harvey had died from absorbing approximately one gram of potassium cyanide, which would have killed him within four hours. Jason must have known one day something would go wrong, and he'd prepared himself. His lucky coin had saved him from the humiliation of facing a jury.

I fold the newspaper and sip from a glass of Dr Pepper filled with ice. My brain is confused from everything which has happened in the past few weeks, but in time I know I will recover.

I think about Malcom Sternwood for a little while, wondering how his life is going to turn out now his name has been linked to the murder. Last time I heard, he moved to the Northern Territory, where few people had heard of him. At least I tried to defend him the best I could. I don't know how Frank sleeps at night.

I invited Lucia and her parents for dinner last week to thank her for saving my life. She made it sound like it was no big deal, but I knew it was, and I'll be forever indebted to her.

Michael is in his room where he spends more time than ever before. He refuses to talk to anyone, and I worry he is never going to get over this.

Phillip and I have broken up for good. He was right. I was only using him without having any intention of committing to a serious relationship.

Last night I invited Frank over for dinner. It was good to see a familiar face, someone I could still call a friend in a world where I never knew who my enemies were.

I haven't heard from Goosh and don't expect to, unless he has something to complain about.

I finish my Dr Pepper and ponder over the idea of setting up my own private practice, working on missing people, white collar crime and other second-priority felonies.

I stand from the couch, walk up to the balcony and overlook the traffic on Chapel Street.

I feel lucky to be alive.